REDEMPTOR

THE VALDUCAN — BOOK 4

BY SETH SKORKOWSKY

"There are cameras all over us," Matt said, keeping his voice confident and steady. "So we're going to behave ourselves, right?"

The little nun stared at him for five full seconds, her dark eyes large and calculating. Finally, she gave a single nod. "Agreed."

"Hands away from the radio, Gast," Matt said to the suit whose posture showed he'd been considering it.

"Do as he says," Sister Gaze ordered, her plump lips completely expressionless.

The two women in the room had ceased their perusing and now watched the little standoff with increasing attention. Matt relaxed his grip on Dämoren, but didn't remove his hand from the satchel. "Fancy meeting you here," he said in friendly Italian.

Picking up on the cue, Sister Gaze smiled warmly, revealing white teeth, a small gap between the front two. "Indeed it is. May we step inside? No need for us to block the entrance, is there? We are friends, after all." Despite the pleasant smile, her eyes were anything but warm.

Gast wasn't even trying to act.

"Of course." Matt took a single step back, maintaining his position between them and Ozkareen's display. The phone in his pocket began buzzing. Probably Uwe freaking out. Matt ignored it. Uwe was too smart to come charging inside. He'd notify the Order, wait, and worry.

Placing her hand on Gast's arm, she led him into the room, stopping only a few feet from Matt. "So what brings you to Uruguay, Mister...?"

"Davis," Matt said.

"No." Her brows drew together. "That's not it. Hollis, correct?"

Matt nodded. If the nun wanted to shake him up, she'd have to try harder than simply knowing his name. "I don't believe we've met. Sister...?"

"Paladin," she corrected. "Paladin Felisa Gaspari. And you haven't answered my question. Why are you here?"

*For Clay Sanger, who patiently reads
every First Draft no matter how rough it is.
Thanks, Brother.*

I have arrived in this new world broken, battered, but alive. God and the Holy Church have forsaken me.

Why should I live while so many perished? Redemptor is gone.

CHAPTER 1

Azuay Province, Ecuador

Thunder rumbled low in the distance, its echo lingering through the mountains like a mournful spirit. Bernardo glanced up, noting the thick, tarnished-pewter clouds. This year's *invierno* had been particularly strong. While the rainy season was drawing to its end, one good storm would bury all his work. *No.* Bernardo banished it from his mind. They were too close now.

Clenching his teeth, he plunged his arm into the cold, muddy water and looped the chain as far behind the great stone box as he could reach. Keeping it taut, he sloshed up the incline and affixed the hook to the rear of Juan's tractor. He hurried back behind the half-flooded trench and drove a cut pole into water behind the sarcophagus. "Go!"

The tractor growled. The chains tightened, dripping water as they lifted from the muddy pool. Straining, Bernardo heaved the pole, levering the massive coffin from the opposite side. Beads of sweat welled across his brow. The pole bent, threatening to break.

Come on. Come on. Wood cracked, but he continued to pull, using his entire weight. Black diesel smoke belched from the tractor's exhaust. The box shifted. "It's coming!"

A coarse sucking noise came from the trench and the sarcophagus inched forward. Brown water poured around it, filling the vacated space. The box slowly slid up the earthen ramp a hand's length before jolting to a stop.

The chains groaned, but the giant box refused to move. *Come on, damn you!*

The wooden lever cracked and splintered. Leaving the broken pole there, Bernardo seized a thicker one, practically a tree trunk, and rammed it behind the giant stone block.

Something popped. The box jolted up and surged forward, riding along one cornered edge for two meters before tipping and landing on its side.

Juan dragged it up the rest of the muddy grade before shutting off the tractor. "That it?"

"You got it," Bernardo laughed, unable to hold his excitement. Discarding the pole, he hurried around and set his hand on the worn stone side, its surface smeared with dark mud.

Six days ago, part of the fence along his property had come down, sending him scouring the area for a pair of lost heifers. There, in an old creek bed, he'd found the stone box peeking out of the mud like an old tombstone. Bernardo had found artifacts before, bits of pottery, a *boleadoras* stone—he'd even found a chunk of worked copper once, but couldn't begin to guess what it was for.

But the carved stone box was something entirely different. After days of careful digging, Bernardo realized the full scope of his discovery. Over two meters long, one high, and one wide—a sarcophagus. It wasn't Incan. The worn cross and skull engraved on its lid attested to that. But whose was it? What riches might it contain?

Not owning a tractor had forced his hand. Juan agreed to help for a forty percent cut.

"I was worried it wouldn't work," Juan said, inspecting the chains now pinned beneath the tipped coffin.

Bernardo wondered if they'd even be able to get them out from under it, but depending on what they found inside, would they even care? A lot of gold could fit in there. Gold always sold. There were always buyers for antiques, no questions asked.

Depending on how much, he could buy more land, cattle, men to work it. He might never have to work again.

He inspected the rusted bands holding the lid on. The third one had torn free when they'd hauled it out. Bernardo scratched the iron medallion on the top, peeling off a rusty flake with his nail. Whatever symbols or image had decorated it had long since disintegrated.

Juan grunted. "Looks like this is what caused the trouble."

Stepping around to the other side of the sarcophagus, Bernardo now saw that what he'd mistaken to be a medallion or holy seal was in fact the head of a long spike piercing all the way through the box. The protruding point emerged from the back side and had been bent into a curl to keep it from sliding out.

Juan tore the tangle of roots clinging to the metal loop. "What is this?"

"Hell if I know," Bernardo said with a grin. "Keep thieves from opening it. The fact that it's still there means we're the first to find it."

Juan scratched his scruffy black beard as he surveyed the bent spike. "Shouldn't be too hard to cut."

Another rumble of thunder echoed through the Andes.

"Come on," Bernardo said, fetching his tool bag. "Let's get this open before the rain." He removed a pair of orange-handled chisels and a worn hammer. A dribbled collar of black-tarnished lead sealed the opening around the protruding spike. He chiseled along its edge and popped the seal free with a hard strike. Setting the wider blade against the spike itself, it only required five solid hits before the brittle metal broke. It was a blessing that the box had tipped. Otherwise they wouldn't have known about the spike and opening the box might have required sledgehammers, possibly breaking any valuables inside.

He set the narrower chisel straight against the bottom of the broken spike and gave it a solid whack. It didn't move. He struck it again and again, chewing the end up with each blow.

"We might need to break it at the other side," Juan suggested.

"We don't have time."

"Rain won't hurt it."

Bernardo shook his head and struck the chisel again. "Someone might find it."

Juan snorted. "No one's going to find it out here."

"No." Fueled by anger, Bernardo struck the chisel hard. The rusted spike plunged inside as a puff of mud and dust spewed from the hole, like puncturing an aerosol can. Coughing on the foul air, Bernardo stepped back, covering his mouth and nose with the back of his hand. He chuckled at his good fortune. Pressure meant that no water had gotten inside.

Metal grated on stone as Juan pulled the tapered rod out through the other side. "Got it." He held it up. Brown powder, probably rust, dusted the square iron pole.

The two remaining bands broke without much effort. The thick lid required pry bars. After much heaving, the lid fell open, hitting the ground with a solid thump.

"What the hell?" Bernardo said, kneeling before the open box.

"What were you expecting?" Juan asked with a snort. "You never seen a body?"

A mummified corpse lay on its side, withered and brown. White teeth grinned from behind dried, withdrawn lips and a black pointed beard. It wore an elaborate breastplate, framed in gold with deep reliefs. A square hole pierced the center of its chest.

"Not like this," Bernardo answered. The stump of a severed hand peeked from the crumbling right sleeve. The protruding bones told that the wound hadn't healed before he'd died. Maybe that was what had killed him. Jeweled rings and bracelets decorated his left hand, now withered into a skeletal claw.

"Conquistador." Juan laughed. "Rich one."

An uneasy dread tickled the nape of Bernardo's neck. He ran a hand down his moustache, his gaze meeting the hollow, oval pits of the mummy's eyes, still framed in black lashes. "Why bury him like this?"

"He was probably a vampire."

Bernardo looked at him, brows arched.

"Or maybe just an asshole." Juan chuckled. "A rich asshole."

He reached for the bundle of necklaces draped from the body's neck. They rattled as he clutched a fistful of gold, pearls, and cut stone.

The dead man's hand shot up with the speed of a striking snake, grabbing Juan by the hair. Juan screamed. The mummy yanked him closer, its legs wrapping around him, the rotted boots ripping free at the motion. It bit into Juan's throat.

Eyes wide in horror, Bernardo took an involuntary step backward. His heel snagged on a root and he fell into the mud.

Blood sprayed as the creature tore a mouthful from Juan's neck. Red froth welled from the gruesome hole. Gurgling, Juan's head fell back. Blood streamed from his mouth and across his face.

Finding his voice, Bernardo screamed. He scrambled backward on all fours, twigs and rocks digging into his palms. The dead thing lifted its head toward him, its teeth smeared in blood and then Bernardo was up and running.

Blind with terror, he plowed through the jungle, racing up the slope. He didn't know where he was going and he didn't care. Juan's blood-streaked face filled his vision. He saw it with each blink, frozen behind his eyelids. His best friend, his sister's husband—dead. Branches tore at his clothes, but he didn't slow. What was that thing? Was it behind him? Bernardo didn't look. He only ran.

Rain began to fall, slow at first, but gaining speed, the drops thumping off the large jungle leaves. Panting, Bernardo reached the edge of the sharp slope. He peered down the twelve-meter drop. Upthrust rocks lined the bottom like stone cacti. He looked behind him, seeing only jungle.

Careful not to fall on the slick rocks, Bernardo followed the edge as it worked its way down. Once he cleared that, he could follow the valley back to the village. Shit, what would he tell them? What would he tell his sister?

"Bernardo!" someone yelled, the hoarse voice distant through the trees.

He froze, breath caught in his throat. Bernardo looked behind him.

"Bernardo … where are you?" it called again.

He opened his mouth, struggling to find his voice. Finally, he called back. "Juan?"

"Yes ... yes," Juan shouted back. His voice sounded pained, wheezing, but definitely his. "Help me."

"Juan?" Bernardo repeated, his terror softening. Cautiously, he climbed back up the slippery hill toward the voice. *How?* The bloody face flashed across his mind.

"I got away ... but I'm hurt. I'm ... hurt bad."

Bernardo paused. What happened to that *thing*?

"You ... left me," Juan called. "Why? Why did you go?"

Shame welled in Bernardo's gut. "I'm coming!" he called, pushing his way through a tangle of leafy plants. He reached a small clearing and wiped the rain from his face. "Where are you?"

"Over here!"

Bernardo ran toward his friend's voice. Thunder boomed above, echoing through the mountains. "Juan?" he called.

"Over here ... hurry."

Bernardo's foot caught on a root, sending him staggering into the undergrowth. He looked around, seeing no one.

"Hurry," Juan wheezed again. It sounded close, just beyond a huge kapok tree.

"Hold on!" Bernardo rose to his feet and hurried toward the voice, his boots sloshing through the puddles. "I'm coming." He hopped over the tall ribbon-like roots and looked around, seeing no sign of his friend. "Juan?"

No reply.

"Juan?" He trudged past a moss-coated log and called again, "Juan?"

Leaves shuffled behind him. Metal clinked. Bernardo spun. The *thing* was right there, closing in. Necklaces rattled against its breastplate. Rain-streaked blood covered its face. But it wasn't the mummy's face. It was Juan's, his cheeks hollow and emaciated. It raised the pry bar above its head.

Bernardo screamed.

The metal bar smashed into his skull. Brilliant white pain flashed across his vision. He staggered, lifting his arms to shield himself, and fell onto his back.

The thing with Juan's face swung the pry bar again, striking Bernardo's extended hand. Bones popped. Bernardo howled. It swung again and again, smashing the pry bar into his knee and his ribs. Bernardo gasped, unable to breathe.

A hand grabbed his face and pressed it down. Bernardo thrashed. He swung his broken hand and hit the creature's armor. He screamed and clenched his eyes in pain as the Juan-faced monster dipped its head for his throat, mouth wide.

The terrible crunch rippled through his body. Blood sprayed across the leafy ground and Bernardo's screams faded into a choking wheeze. His hands, pounding against the creature's back and arms, slowed and fell to his sides.

The monster lapped at the rushing wound. The muscles in its arms and hand swelled with the fresh life rushing through its old veins. The beast slowed its licking and lifted its head.

Juan's scruffy beard was gone, replaced by a thick moustache. The creature's cheekbones widened. It croaked, blinking at the body of the dead man before it, the man whose face it now wore. It looked at its re-grown right hand, flexing its fingers. Standing, the creature lifted its chin skyward and let the rain wash away the blood. It smiled and ran its fingers through the black hair, wringing out centuries of muddy dust. Freedom.

Its smile vanished. It cocked its head as if hearing a distant noise. It turned its gaze eastward, and began to walk.

We have traveled through New Castile to Lima, although I can't fathom the reason. Without my master or Redemptor, I have as much purpose as a bridle without a horse.

CHAPTER 2

Buenos Aires, Argentina

Matt's breath fogged in the night air, adding to the gray haze. Pale coronas glowed from the few exposed bulbs in and above the dank slums. Villa 31, they called it. The word always conjured opulence—inlaid floors, carved wood, freshly cut flowers, spaciousness. The Valducans owned several villas around the world, and they all met, if not exceeded, that expectation.

However, Villa 31, the most notorious shantytown in the city, was nothing at all like those palatial estates. It was a *villa miseria*—local slang for such a miserable collection of hovels—and the name fit. A weird honeycomb of repurposed scrap and cinderblock rose on all sides. Bent and broken antennas and twisted spires of rebar jutted from the rooftops like rusting branches. A dizzying web of power cables, extension cords, strands of broken Christmas lights, and clotheslines seemed to encase the entire slum like a net holding in the poverty.

A plastic bottle crunched under Matt's steel-toed boot. Trash and filth were the only paving these streets had ever known. He was grateful for the cold air, knowing it suppressed the already terrible stink. There was no sewage for the 40,000 residents of Villa 31. The place was a demonic mecca of despair.

Matt pulled his jacket tighter as a gust blew down the street, trailing garbage. Dämoren, his sacred revolver, hung below his armpit, her weight more comforting than the Kevlar vest beneath his shirt or the Ingram machine pistol slung under his other arm.

"A flamethrower would do well here," Uwe mumbled beside him. A Frisbee-sized plastic disk covered the head of his spear, Tuerie, giving it the semblance of a boat paddle or priestly staff. Between that and his brown trench coat, the German looked like some junkyard wizard. The fact he was a dead ringer for Peter Lorre didn't help the image. "Burn it down and start over."

Matt grunted, not rising to the bait.

"Maybe a tsunami. Wash this shithole out to sea."

"Well," Matt said, checking the bottle of pale pink liquid in his hand. "I don't think fire or giant waves keep isolated like that. Part of what makes them disasters. Besides, what about the people?"

Now it was Uwe's turn to grunt. "Good point. Why not bulldoze one acre? Put up one of those micro-apartment complexes like in Tokyo? Solar panels, water filtration. Green, you know? Employ the residents to build it, gives them some money. Once done, you bulldoze another, then another. Have this place cleared out in no time." He smiled, obviously proud of his solution.

"I think if these people could afford an apartment they'd live there." Matt eyed a pair of dark figures watching them from a balcony, their faces hidden in shadow. He checked the bottle again. Still pink.

Uwe shrugged. "Maybe if you—"

"*Matt*," Luiza's voice buzzed in the ear bud. "*What's your position?*"

Matt thumbed the microphone at his shoulder. "Approaching the overpass. No contacts."

"*Nothing on our end, either,*" she replied.

"Just keep an eye on your compass. It's here somewhere." Matt glanced up at the concrete highway ahead, bisecting the sprawling slum. The glow of headlights zipped through the fog above.

"As Uwe was saying," Uwe continued. "Maybe if they built up a solar farm. Let the people live under it and pay them what it draws."

Matt half-listened to Uwe laying out his next great idea to clean up the villa. Uwe always had some plan he was droning on about. His ability to see things from different angles was what made him a good hacker, but it also made him a bit annoying. That, and his insistent referral to himself in the third person. Matt hadn't even noticed the quirk at first. One of Dämoren's gifts granted him the ability to understand spoken languages, sometimes without even realizing it. He'd always heard Uwe say *I* and *me* like a normal person until Allan had brought it to his attention. Now, he nearly always noticed it. Matt's tolerance for the quirk was why Luiza, Matt's wife, had assigned them together. She'd taken Luc as her partner on this job, and Matt, being the lowest-ranked knight on the team, got Uwe. He didn't mind. Uwe was a good guy.

Besides, the German seemed more than happy to let Matt take the lead.

They stepped beneath the towering bridge, passing the shacks clustered beneath its shelter. Huddled figures, lit by the glow of trash fires, fell silent as the two men strolled by. Shadows slid across shadows. Matt blinked, fighting tears from the stink of wood smoke and burning plastic. Far to his right, someone was frying fish. Raised voices echoed somewhere off to the left. Uneasy tingles skittered along the back of Matt's scalp. His hand itched for the Ingram. Last thing he needed was some fool mistaking them for easy marks.

Twenty feet past the bridge and the mumbled conversations resumed. His shoulders relaxed, the tension receding.

Uwe paused mid-monologue. "Relax. They're not going to try anything."

"Maybe." Matt glanced over his shoulder. A pair of men in ratty jackets watched them. "But maybe they're not human."

"Results would be the same."

The assurance didn't comfort him. Matt glanced back again. The two men had left the shelter of the overpass. One met his eyes. *Shit.* They were still a block back. "We might have company."

"Surprised it took this long. Human?"

Matt checked the blood compass. "Still pink."

"Then human." Uwe turned to face the two followers.

The men stopped. One grinned, revealing a pair of missing teeth. The other sniffed and straightened.

"Good evening," Uwe said, his German accent so obviously foreign that the toothless grinner's lips stretched into a predatory smile.

"What are you doing?" Matt whispered to his partner.

"Trust Uwe," Uwe replied. "Good night for a walk, eh?" he said to the men.

They started moving closer. One slid his fingers into a frayed pocket.

"Are you lost?" Uwe opened his coat a little, revealing the black butts of the HK pistols holstered under each arm. "Because Uwe thinks you should go the other way."

The men froze. One of them smoothly slipped the partially exposed knife back into his jeans.

"Go," Uwe said.

The men both took a step back, turned, and ran.

Uwe snorted. "See? No problem."

Matt shook his head. "They might tell someone."

"Who? There isn't a cop within two kilometers. Even if they called one, they wouldn't come in here at night."

"It's not the cops I'm worried about." Matt continued walking.

"Don't worry about them. Worry about the eel."

"Yeah, but if they warn it we're coming ..." His words trailed off as he glanced at the bottle. The pink fluid had cleared and now a large red bead of his blood pressed against the inner wall, pointing ahead and to the left. He thumbed the transmitter. "Got a hit."

Uwe was instantly at attention, his grip tightening on the paddle-topped spear. He drew a rectangular GPS unit from his coat.

"Where is it?" Luiza asked.

Matt peered at the LCD screen in Uwe's hand, their locations marked with blue dots. Luiza's and Luc's dots were almost due north, five hundred feet. "It's northwest of us, so continue west."

The dots pulsed to the left, following the streets' crazy course. Matt checked the bottle. The bead hadn't moved, though if the demon was moving either closer or away, he wouldn't know until the bead either dissipated or the monster was on top of them. He'd charged the compass with fresh blood in the last half hour, giving it a maximum range of a hundred yards.

"*Got it,*" Luiza said. A yellow dot appeared beside their blue markers. "*Let's zero in.*"

The two teams began walking the perimeter of the compasses' ranges, moving outward until the bead vanished, marking that spot on the GPS and continuing around in a rough ring. Matt searched the misty shadows for anyone paying them too much attention. Familiars might be all around them. If a single one alerted its master, then the demon could bolt.

Matt's life as a demon hunter began the night a pack of wendigos had eaten his family. He'd been twelve. The only reason he'd survived was because Clay Mercer, demon hunter and protector of Dämoren, had saved him. Clay had become his new father, and Matt's life changed to a single focus: kill monsters. He was good at it, too.

Now, twenty-nine, and a knight in the Order of Valducan, Matt's focus had changed. He had a wife, a child, the other knights and their own sacred weapons, and while each of those were important, the life of a weapon-bound meant that killing demons always came first.

Three years ago, a group of cultists had summoned Tiamat, the Goddess of Demons. Before the Valducans could kill her, Tiamat had birthed at least six flying eels, each with the face of Anya, the knight who had betrayed them, and nearly wiped out the Order. Those eels were something entirely different. Each one served as a nexus demon. Every person that an eel bit became possessed with a demonic spirit entirely unique to that eel. They were carriers of a new demonic plague. Patient Zero. And the one that had made its way to Argentina was especially nasty.

"Got it," Uwe radioed.

Matt studied the little screen, its light blinding in the gloom.

A jagged half-circle dominated the Villa, bordering the concrete wall separating the slum from a train yard. Somewhere in the heart of that yellow ring was the monster that had been eating the city's residents—the ones no one would miss.

"*Here we go,*" Luiza said, as they arranged their positions on either side of the ring so that their blood compasses pointed directly at one another. "*Do not engage until we've met in the middle.*"

"Got it," Matt replied. While Luiza would say that the reminder was intended for Uwe's benefit, Matt knew better. It wasn't his fault demons attacked him on sight. It was just the price for the sacred bullet lodged in his chest—fantastic power, monsters wanting to eat your face off. Give and take.

The blood compass before him, Matt headed into the perimeter, Uwe at his side. Two weeks they'd been in BA, and tonight this would end. He couldn't wait to get home to Gabi.

They followed the narrow streets past dilapidated hovels. Nervous excitement tingled through his veins. Music thumped in the distance ahead. The orange glow of a cigarette drew Matt's eye. A man and a woman huddled in a doorway, sharing a smoke beneath scrap metal eaves. Their curious eyes didn't shy away as Matt met their gaze.

As they rounded a bend, a large three-story building came into view. It dominated the entire block. Torn tarps and drying laundry draped its sides like banners from a medieval fortress. A few lights burned in the open windows. Blue plastic drums formed a line of makeshift water towers along the roof. Matt checked the compass. The bead pointed straight at it. *Of course it does.*

A group of people clustered around a fire burning within a blackened metal cage. Greasy smoke and embers drifted into the sky, adding to the smog. Music blared from a cheap boom box. Its buzzy, metallic undertone said that one of the speakers was blown.

Matt glanced at Uwe's GPS. Luiza and Luc were approaching the opposite side of the building. He thumbed the mic. "It's inside somewhere. Do you have an entrance on your end?"

"*Two,*" Luiza replied. "*People outside both of them.*"

"Cold night to be hanging outside," Uwe muttered, but didn't radio.

"We have one. Same deal. Crowd outside. What's the plan?"

It was quiet for several seconds. Luiza was probably conferring with Luc. Finally, she said, *"You two enter that side. Stick together. If this thing makes a run, we'll trap it between us."*

Matt bit his lip. This place looked like a Class A Deathtrap. "Roger that. Be careful."

"You too."

A pair of bearded men looked up from the group as Matt and Uwe drew near. Conversations slowed and soon all eyes were on the outsiders. The music continued blaring.

Matt clenched his right hand, pulsing his fist a few times, and then wiggled the fingers to get the feeling in them. He always knew when shit was about to go sideways and this was one of those times. He glanced behind him. Two figures approached up the street, their shoulder bent inward like stalking predators.

"Two behind us."

Uwe just nodded.

Matt checked the compass. Still only one bead. That was a good sign.

A balding man with a frayed brown jacket spat into the fire. "You police?"

"No," Matt answered.

"You look like police." The man stepped away from the fire. The others all rose to their feet. Six in total.

"I said we're not police. Just passing through."

"Passing through?" Baldy ran his tongue across his teeth. "No one passes through here."

"Uwe doesn't want trouble," Uwe said.

Matt groaned. *You were supposed to let me do the talking.*

Baldy exchanged a look with a short man beside him. "Who the fuck is Uwe?"

Uwe cocked his head. He thumped his chest. "Uwe."

The man snorted, then laughed. He slapped his friend on the arm. "That's Uwe."

The group joined in the laughter.

Matt glanced over his shoulder. The two behind them were

closer now, but along the side of the street, hanging back. What were they waiting on? He turned back to the laughing group.

A long-haired woman moved behind them, clutching something down against her side.

"Gun!" Matt yelled. His hand moved to Dämoren's ivory grip but not before she brought a battered AK47 up to her shoulder.

Uwe dropped to a crouch, Tuerie before him in both hands. The plastic disk peeled back from the leaf blade as if he'd thrust it into an unseen wall. A faint shimmer, like a heat mirage, blossomed from the spearhead, visible for only an instant. The machine gun roared, its muzzle flash blinding.

Dämoren out, Matt dropped to the trash-strewn ground and scrambled behind his partner. Bullets thumped and zinged, pelting the air before Uwe and bouncing every direction.

Baldy stiffened. His eyes bulged and with a wet crunch the top of his skull shattered open. The exposed, pink brain swelled and the folds unwound into a trio of glistening tentacles, two ending in finger-long bone sickles, and the third with a tooth-lined circular maw. The skulls of two other attackers also exploded, revealing the monsters within. Three demons, three familiars. Skin puppets always worked in pairs.

The girl fired another burst. Again, Tuerie's invisible shield deflected the shots. The other two familiars charged.

Matt twisted around to see the two followers running toward them, a boy and a girl. The male, maybe sixteen, held a slender knife. Glistening pink tentacles wiggled from the girl's open skull.

He raised Dämoren and fired. The round took her in the throat. Blood gushed from the wound, but she didn't fall. *Damn it.*

They were getting closer. Matt fired again, nailing the girl through the right eye. Blood and golden teal fire spewed out of the back of her head as she crumpled. The knife-wielding familiar fell, his master slain and soul freed.

"*I hear shots,*" Luiza shouted over the radio. "*Status?*"

Matt let go of the bottle and hit the transmitter button. "Little busy."

Crouching, Uwe held his ground as the attackers charged.

One swung a rusty rebar pole with a tape-wrapped grip. It rang as it hit the invisible shield.

"Uwe says, fuck you." He rammed Tuerie's point into the man's chest, twisted, and yanked. The attacker staggered and fell, wheezing. "Fuck you, too!" Uwe stabbed the next one, a short-haired woman clutching a serrated kitchen knife.

"We're heading in to intercept the eel before it escapes," Luiza said.

One of the demons crouched behind a rusted car body, tentacle writhing above it. The other two fled for the building. Matt leaned out for a shot on the demons, but a machine gun burst sent him back behind the shield's cover. He swung out again and fired, missing. He cocked the hammer and shot again. Gold-teal fire spewed from a fleeing demon's head.

Another burst of machine gun fire peppered the ground around him, sending up plumes of dirt. A round hit the top of his foot, shooting a white-hot shock of pain up his entire leg.

"Sonofabitch!" He rolled onto his side and drew the Ingram up in his off hand. He squeezed the trigger, and the machine pistol unloaded thirty .45 caliber slugs in a loud rip. They shredded the car, shattering windows and perforating the doors. Two rounds hit the demon but with no effect. The girl with the AK collapsed behind the car, but he couldn't tell how badly he'd hit her.

"You all right?" Uwe asked.

"Gah! Foot."

Uwe glanced at Matt's boot, blood streaming out the top and bottom. "You'll be fine. Cover me."

Blinking away tears of pain, Matt drew a fresh magazine and checked it. Silver jacket with yellow jade tips. Aluminum and quartz hadn't worked. Maybe these would. He loaded it into the smoking Ingram. "Go."

His spear out front, Uwe sidestepped and charged the vehicle. Gunfire erupted once he came around the side. Uwe hunkered down behind the force field.

Still on the ground, Matt fired a burst beneath the flat-tired car. The shooting stopped and Uwe rushed and pushed onward. The demon hopped back, its wormy tentacles lashing.

Matt fired the Ingram again. Bullet holes stitched up its

body, but the wounds instantly closed. *Scratch silver and yellow jade.* He lifted Dämoren, but Uwe was already on it.

The German rammed his spear into the monster's chest and shoved, driving the beast down onto its back. The demon's arms and tentacles flailed, striking the unseen shield behind Tuerie's head. Uwe ripped the spear free and plunged it into the center of the squirming mass. It shuddered and fell limp, demon fire igniting from the wound.

Matt looked around, seeing no one. The demons had either fled or were dead. Civilians were hiding. He checked the compass. Tiny red beads, like fish eggs, filled the side facing the building. Each bead pointed to a separate demon. The last, and only, time he'd seen that many was when they'd killed another eel beneath Paris.

Uwe raced toward him. "Good shot."

"Help me to that one," Matt said, motioning toward the girl he'd shot, her head engulfed in golden teal flames.

"Uwe has a better idea," he said running past.

Matt's vision swam. Blood loss was making him dizzy. He hit the transmitter. "Three down. Rest are inside."

"Roger," Luiza said. *"Are you hurt?"*

"I'll be fine," he said through gritted teeth. He sucked a breath, trying to push back the throbbing pain.

Uwe dragged the dead woman across the street, flaming blood trailing behind her. "Here." He dropped the body before Matt.

Matt slid his fingers into the open skull, plunging them into gooey mass. The fire wasn't hot. It was simply the demonic spirit burning away. A soothing wave coursed up his arm as he touched the monster's blood. It flowed down his leg and the flesh and bones of his foot reknitted.

"You need to stay behind Uwe," Uwe scolded. "Don't be sticking your foot out."

"It's not like I did it on purpose." Matt wiped his bloody fingers onto the dead woman's shirt and stood. The boot sole flapped from where the bullet had torn through.

Uwe pulled on a black face mask. "Yet you always get shot. Uwe thinks you like it."

Matt snorted and put on his own mask. Now that there was shooting, the last thing he wanted was some cell video showing up online. He replaced his half-spent mag with a fresh one. Maybe pewter or amber would hurt them. "Come on. Let's get this bastard."

They hurried past the burning corpses and into the building. The filthy floor was tiled in a crazy assortment of random colors and sizes. It complemented the doors along both walls, each a little different and all in varying shades of shit. A palace made of scraps. It was dark, cavern-like. A single broken bulb hung from the ceiling. Uwe turned on a bright flashlight and clamped it onto the spear's shaft. The passage extended fifteen feet before splitting to the left and right.

Matt popped the lid on a large spice shaker and spread a line of powder across the entrance. He checked the compass. Most of the red beads clustered to the left. A few moved along the top of the bottle, indicating demons on the upper floors. Two moved below.

Shots echoed somewhere ahead.

"Left," Matt said, and Uwe hurried, taking point. The uneven hall was narrow, jagging at odd intervals. It stank of sweat, overcooked vegetables, and smoke. Matt's floppy boot splashed in something cold and wet. He prayed it was only water.

A crusty aluminum ladder ran up one wall and through a square hole in the ceiling. Matt kept his eye on it as they moved past. A shadow slid across the hallway ahead.

Uwe hunkered low behind his spear. Sweat glistened along the back of the German's neck, below the short-cropped hair. While Tuerie's disk-like shield could extend out to five feet wide, it couldn't grow larger than the narrow hall allowed.

The figure leaned out. A pistol flashed. *Boom. Boom.*

The knights dropped lower. The bullets *zinged* off the shield.

A red bead in the compass moved around behind them. Matt turned in time to see a slender man in a yellowed tank top coming down the ladder. A tentacle-headed skin puppet dropped down behind him. The man lifted his hand. Light gleamed off the black-blue revolver clutched in his fist.

Matt fired Dämoren, the boom deafening in the cramped

hallway. The blessed slug blew a hole in the familiar's chest. The man's gun discharged once, pelting a cinderblock wall, and he fell. The demon's spiked tentacles shot up the hole and yanked the monster upward toward safety. Matt cocked the hammer and shot before the head disappeared through the opening. The beast fell and golden teal firelight filled the passage.

More shots came from behind. Two shooters pummeled Uwe's invisible shield. Ricochets blasted into the walls and ceiling, punching holes through shitty wood and drywall and raining puffs of dust from the red brick of the right wall.

"Can we move forward?" Matt asked, his head low as shots flew past.

"Shield is too big. Uwe'd have to drop it to move up."

Matt peered past the German. The hall stretched for about twenty feet. Two tentacle-headed forms stood behind the shooters. He checked the compass. The red beads on the right side were lessened now. Another one burst apart, the blood quickly absorbing into the other beads. Evidently Luc and Luiza were having better luck. Another bead vanished.

"Matt, what's your status?" Luiza panted through the radio.

"We're pinned down." He opened Dämoren's loading gate and pushed out the spent, engraved shells. He slipped them into a bag on his belt. "Where are you?"

"Western side. This place is a maze."

Matt loaded seven new rounds. Only thirty cartridges in the world would fit the blessed revolver. She only had twenty-three more to finish this fight before he'd need to take the hours to reload each of the bronze shells. Matt holstered Dämoren and drew the Ingram up, thrusting its giant suppressor above the shield's protection.

He squeezed the trigger. The two shooters ducked behind cover as the machine pistol sprayed the hall. A few rounds struck a skin puppet, but didn't seem to hurt it. Hot brass, ejected from the gun, bounced off the walls and rained around them.

Uwe lifted one of his HK pistols and fired twice, one striking the skin puppet in the head. Blood and brains splattered the back wall and the demon fell.

Matt checked the compass resting between his knees. A

bead vanished, but another one appeared directly beside it. The crunch of a bursting skull accompanied the appearances as the demonic spirit moved to its former familiar.

"What were those?" Matt asked.

"Chrome with brass tips," Uwe said.

Shit. He didn't have either of those. *Figures.* Matt thumbed the radio. "Chrome or brass works."

"Roger that," Luiza replied. *"We hear your shooting. You still pinned?"*

"Affirmative."

Something heavy thumped on the floor above. Matt checked the compass. No new beads. It thumped again, moving closer to the hole in the ceiling. He drew Dämoren.

"We'll try to come through. Watch your fire."

"Are you on the second floor?" Matt asked.

"Negative."

Matt trained the revolver on the opening.

A bare foot moved into view. It hesitated, then hurried away. Matt kept his aim.

"There's one down there," a woman yelled in Spanish. "This way." More feet ran past the opening, not even slowing.

Matt released a breath. Just innocents. Maybe even freed familiars trying to get out.

A pair of shotgun blasts boomed down the passage. Matt glanced back to see more shooters clustered ahead of them. If they managed to circle around there was no getting out of this. *Better get here fast, Luiza.*

The wall behind the shooters exploded in a spray of dust and shattered brick. A huge black-clad man stepped through, a flanged mace in one hand. He smashed it into a skin puppet and the demon flew back in a spray of igniting fluids. He spun, slamming the weapon into a familiar raising his gun. The familiar's head vaporized under the inhuman blow.

Luiza stepped through behind him, Akumanokira gripped in both hands. She slashed the katana through the air, the blade passing through a skin puppet's shadow cast by Uwe's brilliant light. The worming tentacles severed as if the blade had actually hit them, and gold-teal fire jetted from the stumps.

She lunged out of Matt's view and a man screamed.

Matt and Uwe were up and running. They reached the intersection as the giant man lifted the suppressed pistol in his off hand and dropped a charging familiar with three quick shots.

"Cavalry is here," Luiza said.

"Just in time." Matt stepped over a bullet-riddled corpse covered in brick dust. The smoky passage stank of gunpowder and hot blood. He nodded to Luc. Flaming gore flickered from the black mace's head. "One hell of an entrance."

"I'm just happy I didn't bring the whole place down on us." The Frenchman's deep voice was how a mountain might talk.

Luiza checked her compass. Six beads moved inside, all of them down and to the left. "Come on. Uwe, take point."

Matt held the rear, covering their backs with Dämoren as they followed the jagged passage. Muffled shouts echoed from all sides as the human tenants cried for help and fled the warzone. The silvery haze of gun smoke only added to the chaotic funhouse feel. A horrible stink emanated from ahead.

Two more familiars rushed from a doorway, armed with a hatchet and a club. Luiza dropped them both with her pistol before they even made it to Uwe's spear.

"They might be out of guns," she said as they continued past.

"Good," Uwe grunted. "Uwe's tired of getting shot at."

They rounded a corner to find a ladder extending down into blackness. Uwe positioned Tuerie's shield above the hole as they circled around it. Judging by the footprints, the mud floor below was deep. Judging by the putrid stink, it wasn't dirt.

Matt's head swooned from the stench.

A shadow moved below. A shot flashed and bounced off Tuerie's shield. A second one blasted up through the floor, spraying shards of broken tile.

"Fuckshit!" Uwe shouted as a third came up next to his foot.

A skin puppet ran past the opening, its body that of a fat man painted in bad tattoos.

Matt checked the compass. One of the beads rolled in a straight line away from the rest, very far. "They're getting away."

"No, they're not." Uwe stepped through the hole and dropped eight feet, mud and shit splatting beneath his boots. He lifted his spear in time to deflect a thrown hammer.

Luiza was down an instant later, pistol out.

Matt sucked a breath and dropped down behind his wife. Cold ooze squirted in through his open boot.

Luiza was already firing at a group of charging familiars. Tentacle-headed demons clustered against the wall at the back of the room. Something huge, glistening, and fish-belly pale moved behind them. A familiar woman's noseless face peeked out and then it was gone.

"Eel!" Matt yelled. He aimed Dämoren and fired, the round taking the fat one in the chest. Another glimpse of shiny pale and Matt fired again and again, blasting holes through the wall of bodies. A fourth shot took a skin puppet in the wriggling head, and demon fire ignited. The eel was gone.

One of the skin puppets dove into a rusty pipe near the floor, its head tentacles grabbing the inner walls and dragging it with incredible speed. Matt ran through the sticky filth. He shot, wounding an already bleeding puppet as it retreated into the pipe. Metal pinged as those bone sickles grabbed the walls to hurry it away.

Dropping to his knees, Matt fired down the pipe and was rewarded with golden teal flare fifteen feet ahead. The corpse nearly filled the two-foot tube. He fired once more, hoping to hit something past the demon's body, but there was no fire. Dämoren was empty.

The last of the familiars had dropped unconscious as its master had died, leaving the hunters alone in an Argentinean cesspool.

"Where does that lead?" Luiza asked.

"Train yard, I think," Luc said.

The last blood bead in the compass broke apart as the demon left its range, returning the water to pink. The eel had escaped.

With nothing else but my name, I have begun work as a smith.
I have traveled across the world only to accept the trade I sought to
escape.

CHAPTER 3

Vatican City State

Felisa hated tardiness. Or at least she hated it in others. For her, punctuality was an ever-elusive paragon. The only two people she truly avoided being tardy for were His Holiness and Paladin Kofi. Unfortunately, this was the latter case by ten minutes.

Clutching the slender case at her side, she hurried along the grounds, her shoes clacking on the ancient stone. Birds twittered in the gardens around her. It smelled of flowers and cut grass, the serenity a stark contrast to her mood. Felisa quickened her pace, trying not to *appear* as if she were running.

A sudden pang snapped the back of her scalp, as if someone had plucked out a single hair. She wheeled to face the attacker, but there was no one there. A gawking crowd shuffled along the dome of Saint Peter's Basilica high above. Felisa narrowed her eyes, spying a single man among them, the wide barrel of his telephoto lens aimed directly at her.

He looked up from his camera, seeming surprised that his subject had suddenly turned toward him, and waved.

Tourists, she grumbled, turning away. For many she was invisible, easily confused for a simple nun or sister. But inevitably, one always seemed to single her out for a photograph. She felt it every time. For that, Felisa hated coming home.

She rounded the bend before the Palace of the Governate, a wide four-story building converted to offices. Kofi Aggrey stood beside the door, dressed in black, white collar, his own square calf-leather case at his side. Tall, slender, with chiseled cheekbones, he looked more akin to one of the many models gracing the billboards around Rome than to a holy warrior. Eyes hidden beneath square mirrored glasses, he smiled as she drew near, his teeth ivory white against his ebon skin.

"Good morning, Paladin," he said as she ascended the wide steps. His Ghanaian accent always made him sound overly formal.

"You as well," she replied. "You didn't need to wait for me."

Kofi shrugged. "I have no interest in waiting with Father Soldati. He can wait for the both of us. Besides, you would have done the same for me."

Felisa grinned. "One day we'll find out."

Kofi nodded. It wasn't his nature to point out that even on those rare occasions when she'd arrived early, she'd never had to wait on him. He was her opposite in every way, God bless him for it. No one could ever ask for a better partner. He opened the door and together they entered the palace.

Unhurried, they passed beneath the grand ceiling murals, up the intricately inlaid stairs, past galleries of portraits and busts and stopped at a non-descript door on the third floor. The sliding brass plate read, "Georgio Soldati."

Felisa knocked.

"Come in."

They stepped inside a narrow office. It smelled of dust, paper, old wood, and that boring office tedium that Felisa oh-so detested. Dense bookshelves framed either side of a tiny open window gazing at a nearby tree. Exorcism appeared in a disproportionate number of the titles. The seal of the International Association of Exorcists dominated the opposite wall. A single crucifix decorated the space behind the desk where a man with a gray widow's peak stood, his hand extended.

"Paladin Gaspari. Paladin Aggrey." He motioned to a pair of green leather chairs. "Please, sit down."

Felisa gave the priest a warm smile and took a chair, setting her locking case beside her. Kofi maneuvered into the seat to her right. The knees of his long legs touched the desk.

"Thank you for coming so promptly," Father Soldati said, returning to his own high-backed swivel chair. If there was any sarcasm to his tone, Felisa couldn't detect it. "His Holiness is aware of the situation and has placed me at your disposal."

In your service, you mean, Felisa thought. Since his appointment as the IAE's president, Father Soldati had been quite vocal that the paladins should fall under his jurisdiction. Now it appeared he might be getting his wish. She'd need to speak with the Pope once he returned from Mexico.

"How may we assist?" Kofi asked.

"Archbishop Pablo Sotomayor was murdered three days ago."

Felisa nodded. "I heard this morning. Terrible loss."

"He was very popular," Soldati said. "Quito is reeling from it. Stabbed in his private chambers." He shook his head. "The Ecuadorian government has made catching the killer their top priority. Unfortunately, His Holiness and I have reason to suspect the murderer might not be human."

Felisa and Kofi exchanged a look.

Kofi straightened. "What reasons?"

"Well ..." Soldati turned a laptop toward them. A time-stamped, black-and-white image of a walking priest filled the screen. "This is from the exterior security cameras. We've identified him as Father Eduardo Vasquez, a priest from the village of Girón, about five hundred kilometers away."

"And he stabbed the archbishop?" Felisa asked.

Soldati shook his head. "No. Father Vasquez was found murdered. He died two days before the image was taken."

Felisa's brow rose. "I see."

"That's not all." Father Soldati clicked the keyboard. The image changed to a husky man walking down a path, away from the camera, a rolling suitcase behind him. The time-stamp showed it to be five in the morning. "This is the last known picture of the archbishop. However, he had already been dead for six hours."

"Looks remarkably well for a dead man," Felisa said. "Is there any evidence this Father Vasquez ever left the cathedral?"

"No. He is only seen entering."

"Was either man flayed?" Kofi asked. "Pieces of skin missing?"

The Father shook his head.

"Rules out skin walkers," Felisa muttered. She strummed her fingers on the armrest. A demon that could change appearances without needing the victim's body. There were only so many of those, but they were the most difficult to track. She leaned forward, sliding the computer closer.

Soldati stiffened. Most priests were used to nuns asking permission. But she wasn't a nun, and he needed to remember that.

Felisa tapped at the computer, zooming in on the archbishop's hands. There were rings, yes, quite a lot, but she couldn't tell what they were made from.

"Rakshasa?" Kofi asked her.

"Possibly," she said. "Father, were all the archbishop's rings taken? Were any left behind?"

Soldati's lips tightened, seeming to contemplate it. He opened a folder on his desk. "Um … none were taken, it appears."

"Then where did all of these come from?" she asked, tapping the screen.

He shook his head. "Aside from some clothes and the bag, nothing physical was stolen. Why do you ask?"

Felisa clicked the photograph back to the Father Vasquez lookalike. Rings decorated each finger on his left hand. It wasn't like a shape-changer to keep trinkets between guises.

"Why?" Soldati repeated.

"Rakshasas," Kofi answered. "They're susceptible to gold. Paladin Gaspari is trying to determine if the killer avoided gold rings. Either way, it helps to narrow it down."

The Father nodded. "I see."

Felisa's jaw tensed. Soldati was likely going to assume he now knew everything there was to know about rakshasas, or at least give that impression to make himself look better. Bureaucrats and fools, Rome was full of them.

Stop it, she scolded herself. She ran her thumb along the gold band on her left ring finger. This attitude wasn't befitting an angel's wife.

Kofi ran a slender hand along his chin. "You said nothing else *physical* was stolen."

"Correct. There's more."

Not even attempting to hide the irritation from her face, Felisa lifted her attention from the monitor. Fighting her annoyance, she pressed her thumb hard into the wedding band. *Were you simply waiting for us to ask?*

Soldati drew some pages from the folder. "After the assumed time of his death, the Archbishop's passwords were used to log into the database."

Kofi accepted the pages. "What were they looking for?"

"Among other things," Soldati said. "You. Or at least the weapons. He searched for Ofniel by name."

A sudden rush of fear shot up Felisa's spine. Instinctively, her hand moved toward the case beside her, but she stayed it. "How do you know they were looking for the sword?" She leaned over to read the list in her partner's hand.

"Ofniel was the only angel they looked up by name. Other searched items include *sword, saber, demon blade.* I checked Father Vasquez's recent searches. Same thing, but he lacked clearance to access the deeper archives."

It killed the archbishop for his clearance, Felisa thought, her pulse rising. *It was searching for my husband.*

Kofi handed her the pages. "Do the local police know about this?"

Soldati shook his head. "The browser history was deleted from the computer, but what the killer didn't know is that the Church records all usage, part of the initiative to combat recent … abuses."

"Would Vazquez or Sotomayor have known their logins were tracked?"

"No."

Felisa half-listened as she scanned the list of searches and accessed records. Her eyes paused on a name. Redemptor. Why did she know that? She'd read it before. She searched the list again, this time not looking for anything about Ofniel, but at the words themselves. There! "Hernando de la Fuente."

Kofi paused. He turned to her, his brow's creased. "What?"

"Gran Arbol," she said, reading another line.

"I know that name." Kofi's eyes unfocused, searching his memory.

"Redemptor."

Kofi's expression fell flat. "It can't be."

"What?" Soldati asked.

"Father, we need to go to Ecuador now," Felisa said. "We will require everything you have on these topics, and His Holiness must leave Mexico at once."

"What is this about?"

"We will require security," Kofi said. "Six Swiss Guard."

Soldati gave a surprised laugh. "Six? Tell me what you found."

"Hopefully nothing," Felisa said. "But we can't risk chances."

"I can't have His Holiness cancel his tour on account of nothing."

"Then let us speak with him if you don't have the balls."

The Father stiffened. His dark eyes narrowed. Honestly, this man was in charge of the exorcists? Felisa had once cleaved an eleven-year-old boy's skull in order to save his soul and this man couldn't handle words? Disgusting.

"Father, forgive her," Kofi said, ever the diplomat. "We must act quickly. While I pray we are wrong, we can't afford to take chances."

Soldati's tight lips curled into a forced smile. "I understand." He set his hands on the table. "Please tell me what this is about. What is Redemptor?"

The paladins exchanged a look. Kofi nodded.

"In the battle for salvation," Felisa said, her gaze moving to Ofniel's leather-bound case, "God granted us holy instruments to combat evil. But in any war, Father, there are weapons on both sides."

Is this my punishment, to live as a damned man among the heathens?

Or is this a test?

CHAPTER 4

Atacama Region, Chile

Mei landed in a crouch against the wall, its thin padding cushioning her bare feet.

"Good." Max stood fifteen feet below, or to her side—it was still odd for her to grasp. He picked the red lacrosse ball up off the floor. "Ready?"

Not waiting for a response, the old man tossed the ball into the air.

Mei jumped toward it. Squeezing Lukrasus, she willed the world to spin around her. Her stomach lurched at the movement. Now she was falling, the ball arcing below her. She swung the sword, striking it with the flat of the blade and batting it to the ceiling.

Her feet landed against the opposite wall harder than she'd expected. Letting out an *oomph*, she kicked off and flipped around, keeping her stomach at the center of the spinning gravity. She struck the red ball again, knocking it up. Mei somersaulted and changed gravity's pull toward the floor. Before landing, she reversed it again, but only for a moment to slow her descent, and then landed beside Max with the same force as a light hop. She caught the falling ball in her left hand and turned to her mentor with a satisfied grin.

Max gave an appreciative nod. "Much better."

"I thought it was pretty good." She handed him the ball and wiped the sweat from her face.

"Students always do," he said, his Austrian accent lacing the words. He inspected the ball, rolling it around in his liver-spotted fingers. "No nicks this time."

Mei sheathed Lukrasus. Until two weeks ago, she'd only trained with the scabbard on. Max had been initially worried she might stab herself flying around with an exposed blade. She'd shredded more than a few balls once he let her take it off.

Max sniffed. "I think you're ready."

For a hunt? she hoped. Seven months in Chile and she'd only accompanied the other knights on two hunts, and never once did she leave the van.

He flicked his hand up at the cylindrical tower room. "We'll remove the padding Thursday. Bare walls."

"Oh," she said, trying to hide her disappointment. Picking up a blue towel and a water bottle, she wiped her face before squeezing a healthy gulp into her mouth. There was no question that it was going to be her up there removing it all. Lukrasus' gift of bending gravity meant that a lot of the bitch-work landed in her lap.

"Once you're comfortable on bare walls, we'll start with you in full gear," Max said. "It makes more of a difference than you'd believe. Flips in a bulletproof vest ..." He shook his head. "That's difficult."

Mei rolled her neck and began her cool-down stretches. A lifetime of dancing had made the routine a bit of a ceremony. She half-listened as Max downloaded yet another variation of the same warnings about gear, frequently straying into stories from his own youth when he'd hunted monsters with Lukrasus. The stories didn't bore her. Total opposite. But they did make her long for whenever she'd finally be done with all this training and get to do it for real.

"Come," Max said, opening the door. "Time for lunch."

Mei's stomach clenched at the words. Man, she was hungry. She tossed the damp towel over her shoulder and stepped out into the wide workout room, walls laden with practice weapons and mitts, and then out through a reinforced steel door. A cool gust hit as she stepped out, the dry, dusty air sucking away the moisture. Rocky hills, speckled with scrub brush and browning grass, stretched out as far as she could see.

Huge white wind turbines studded the slope to one side, their slender blades lazily spinning. She'd never really known how big they were until she stood under one for the first time. Her first time atop one had been positively terrifying. Max had already promised that eventually she'd be flying between them like it was nothing.

Following the concrete path, they passed a small parking lot. A pair of sparrows hopped beneath the shade of the metal canopy. Uwe had been wanting to install solar panels along the roof, but Max had said no. The cost was high and they already had more than enough electricity. Uwe argued it would look good for the company having solar panels. Max regularly reminded him that first, no one came out to this godforsaken nothing, that was the point, and second, that their front as an energy company already garnered too much attention for his liking. Personally, Mei loved the idea.

Reaching the blocky two-story building, Mei stopped before a mirrored glass door emblazoned with the logo of a slender, blowing leaf, similar to a scimitar blade. The door read "Employees Only" in Spanish. She tapped her personal code into the keypad and pushed it open.

The employee side of El Sable Energy looked about how Mei figured most high-security offices might appear. Eggshell walls, the paint new and devoid of scuffs, bubble-dome cameras in the ceiling, and shiny sprinkler heads every few feet. But the first thing that seemed out of place, if you hadn't noticed the bulletproof glass door, was the floor. A rainbow of irregular tiles stretched the length of the hall, each consisting of polished stone or metal; it reminded her of a stained-glass window in the church Mei's parents used to take her to.

A pair of plain metal doors stood along one wall. She tapped her code again, opened the right one, and followed a set of stairs up to the second floor. Faint smudges along the wall served as Mei's bitter reminder of the time she'd run up there with dirty shoes, and the hour she'd spent awkwardly kneeling sideways, sword in one hand, sponge in the other, scrubbing her footprints off.

Mei's stomach growled as she caught a faint whiff of frying food. It grew stronger as she reached the second floor.

"There you are," Ester said as Mei pushed open the kitchen door. Her salt-and-pepper hair tied up in a bun, she worked a spatula over a sizzling skillet. A light haze hung in the air. "Hungry?"

"Yeah." Mei inhaled deeply. Cheese. Oh my God, she was frying cheese. Her stomach tightened again in anticipation.

"Always hungry," Ester said with a shake of her head. "Have a seat. It's almost ready."

Mei took a chair at the small table where Gabi was busy playing with a plastic rabbit, trying to feed it the carrots on her plate. The little girl looked up and smiled a gap-toothed grin.

"Hey, Gabi," Mei said, unconsciously eyeing the uneaten food.

Either picking up on the signal or simply frustrated at the toy's unwillingness to eat, Gabi offered the orange wedge. "*Cenoura.*"

"Very good," Mei said, accepting it. "*Obrigado.*"

Gabi laughed. Ester had been teaching them both Portuguese. Gabi, being nineteen months old, was destined to learn it much faster. With a house full of different nationalities, everyone was trying their hand at teaching her something. Mei wondered how hard it would be for her to learn to speak with five different languages being thrown at her at once.

Mei had come down to South America with some rudimentary Spanish, which was improving, but was still really clumsy.

"Any news from Argentina?" Ester asked.

"Nothing new." Max took the third chair at the table. "They'll keep at it for a few more days. But it could be weeks before the eel resurfaces, and there's no telling where that will be."

Ester grunted. "It never gets easier worrying." She slid a sandwich off her skillet and onto a plate with a quick pop and flick of the wrist, almost like some martial arts trick. "Careful. It's hot," she said setting it in front of Mei.

Saliva flooded Mei's mouth, forcing her to swallow. "Thanks."

Ester's head dipped, brow rising in an expectant manner.

"*Obrigado.*"

The old woman gave an approving nod and headed back to the stove. It was times like this, just the four of them, that it felt the most like a family. More like a sitcom, she figured, cast for some weird demographic.

Allowing it about five seconds to cool, Mei picked it up, found the corner that seemed the least hot, and bit into the grilled ham and cheese sandwich.

"Good?" Ester asked.

"Yes," Mei said, her mouth full.

Ester smiled. While never a knight herself, Ester Moreira was the house mother. Technically she was Luiza's mother, but seemed happy applying the role to everyone. She'd moved over from Brazil when Gabi was born, and took care of her while they were off on hunts. Her late husband had been a knight, and she'd even known Max back when he was still hunting.

Ester started the next sandwich. "Max, are you hungry?" Aside from Mei, Ester was the only other person who called him that. To everyone else, he was Master Schmidt.

"I am good, thank you." He played with Gabi, making faces as Mei inhaled the *misto quente.*

Finishing it, Mei came up for air long enough to suck back the last of her water bottle.

Ester flipped the sandwich in the skillet. It sizzled. "You ready for another one?"

"Yes please." She rose and refilled the bottle.

"You're spoiling her," Max said, the concerned tone playfully feigned.

The old woman snorted. "Look at her. She's too skinny the way you have her exercising all the time."

Mei ran her tongue along her teeth, biting back the words. It was like talking to her own grandmother, who instead of saying she was too skinny, warned her that she was going to get fat with the way she ate. Truth was, dancing had given her more muscle than most of the boys she'd gone to high school with. Too much, if you asked her. She was a rail.

"When is your exam?" Max asked.

Mei slid back into her seat. "Friday."

He nodded, seeming to remember. "Then you'll need some extra time to study Thursday."

"It'll be a piece of cake. Nothing to worry about."

"Then I expect a perfect score."

Mei hid her frown behind a gulp of water. After bonding with Lukrasus, she'd given up a dance scholarship to UCLA under the guise that she was going to school in Chile, with a specialized training-education program with El Sable. Part of the deal was that she complete online courses and actually get her degree, which she found annoying. But the other option was severing ties with her family. Some of the other knights had chosen that route, but not her. No way. Max insisted the education was important regardless, but it still felt like a waste of time.

"I'll make a deal," Max said, seeming to read her as always. "If you make a perfect score, I'll take you out to play with the machine gun."

"Really?" she asked.

The old man nodded. "We'll take a few belts, moving targets, have some fun. Does that sound acceptable?"

"Hell yeah."

His frosty blue eyes narrowed. "Then you'd better study."

Mei scrunched her eyes and squeezed the corners on either side of her nose, ball lightning filling the blackness. Reading the monitor hurt her eyes after a while and she had to fight the urge to skim. Most of the other students probably just watched the recorded lectures, broken into nice little fifteen minute segments, but her Spanish still wasn't good enough, which meant she had to read it slowly.

Painfully slowly.

Soft fur brushed her leg.

Opening her eyes, she blinked and looked down at Celeste, Luc's cat.

Her green eyes stared up at Mei, hopeful. She mewed.

Mei reached down to pet her, but the cat slipped away, just outside Mei's reach. She mewed again and lay down on the inlaid floor, teasingly offering her belly two inches too far away.

"Brat," Mei said. "Your dad will be home soon."

The cat only looked at her, as if understanding, but still unhappy with the answer. Mei knew that animals understood a few words. How could they not? But Luc spoke to her in French, so maybe Celeste's limited vocabulary was in that. Mei didn't even know they had black people in France, but then she met Luc and was thoroughly schooled. It had been a stupid presumption. Here she was, Chinese, raised in America, and still thinking that it was somehow the exception. Now they were both living on the ass end of South America together, which was kind of funny when she thought about it.

She sipped her water and spun her chair lazily around, the paintings of long-dead knights and the tightly packed bookshelves moving past. Their colors did little to liven up the coldness of the concrete and steel room. There were no windows in the library, it being twenty feet below ground. A bank of monitors lined the upper wall, showing the wind farm and rooms of the building above. A shiny black mask of a shriveled face was turned toward the metal door.

Max said the ghoul spirit trapped in the obsidian mask would repel demons in case they somehow got down here. If that was true or not, she didn't know. Didn't want to find out. But meeting the little black eyes at the back of its oversized sockets gave her an uneasy feeling, like staring into the face of a chained and pissed-off pit bull.

A huge fire safe with twin combination dials stood below the mask, protecting the orphaned holy weapons still awaiting their mates. Two of the weapons were currently out on loan to museums, a little trick the Valducans did in hope one might bond with someone. That's how she'd met Lukrasus.

Her studying done, Mei clicked the browser. Knowing it was a bad idea but unable to stop herself, she scrolled through social media sites, checked out her old friends from Sacramento. Their freshman year had just ended and they were beginning their summer now. Pictures of laughing faces at parties, clubs, dorm-room study sessions, boyfriends, BFFs, carefree hangouts, and everything else Mei lacked. Mei stopped posting shortly after she'd moved down here. What could she even say?

"Practicing quick draw drills with Matt #hunterlife"

"Soreafteralongdayrunningupwalls#dancingontheceiling"

"Luc showed me how to pull a bootlegger turn ... in a van! #copswontcatchus"

She chuckled at the thought. Once the initial shock of moving down into a compound of paramilitary knights had worn off, Mei had tried to capture some of that party feel herself. She'd driven two hours down shitty roads to Copiapó, the closest thing to a city around here. Of course, carrying a sword into a club was a bad idea, so she'd left Lukrasus locked in the safe. Not willing to let her go unarmed, Max had insisted she carry a small pistol. Free of all the older knights, she tried to have a good time. She even met a few cute guys who seemed real interested in the foreign girl looking for some fun. She even had a few lies Luiza had helped her with, saying who she was, what she did, etcetera. But it just didn't feel right. She was married now. Married to an angel.

But there she was, ditching him in a black steel box as she went out dancing, drinking, and open to getting laid. She loved Lukrasus with all her heart, but the sword couldn't fill *all* her needs. Max was strangely supportive, and *that* was a fucked-up conversation. She was nineteen and wanted to have *some* life, but she couldn't shake the feeling she'd ditched her husband. It reminded her of her friend Jess.

Jess had gotten knocked up at sixteen. After Tyler was born, Jess tried so hard to go out with the rest of the girls, leaving her son with grandma and grandpa, but it wasn't the same. Mei had quietly judged her for shirking her responsibilities, calling her a shitty mom behind her back. And now she found herself doing it to Lukrasus.

Mei only went to Copiapó twice before she gave it up. Like with Jess, that life simply wasn't in the cards for her.

Stop whining, she thought. *You're a knight. You do shit no one ever dreamed of.* Mei squeezed Lukrasus' grip, running her thumb over the octagonal pommel and feeling guilty. She pulled up the Cryptozoo boards. Small photographs of famous, and many debunked, monster sightings framed the list of recent topics.

Forty-three users online, none of them Valducans. It was evening in Belgium, so Sam or Victoria were normally on. Where were they? *Probably hunting,* she guessed with an envious pang. If not, they might be out, enjoying Europe, friends, anything.

Stop it, she scolded.

Mei scanned the site, searching for any mentions of Buenos Aires, hoping no one had spotted Luiza and the others. If she was lucky, she could find a lead on where that eel might have gone. Knights who discovered where demons were hiding were most likely to be on the team to hunt them. Finders keepers.

Nothing.

She moved over to the *Encuentros* website, a South American board, which was way smaller and nowhere near as good. Unlike Cryptozoo, the Valducans didn't secretly run it, so she used a proxy server to mask her location. Most of the threads were days old, with little to no activity. Two glowed dark green, meaning she hadn't read those before.

The first was a conversation starter. First post from a newbie asking about the Nazca Lines, the giant desert drawings in Peru, and its relation to aliens. One of these popped up every month or so. Te-Go, one of the more active members with three thousand posts to his name, had joined in, sharing speculations and offering resources. Mei didn't believe in aliens, at least not the kind that would build pyramids and look at giant spider pictures from their spaceships.

The second thread was another first timer. This one was titled "Nagual?" Mei clicked it open, discovering a wall of text. As it was in Spanish, she read it carefully. Doubly so because the author, a Chico Suerte from Colombia, had written a long, rambling story, rife with misspellings and text-speak abbreviations.

After a long intro explaining how he wasn't doing anything overly illegal, Chico told a story about venturing inside a construction zone two nights before. While he was hanging out on the roof, a car pulled into the drive just outside the fence.

A slender man stepped out, and with his bare hands, tore the lock free from the gate and then drove inside. The man stopped beside an open-top dumpster and hauled something out of his trunk, wrapped in black plastic.

Chico said that even though he was hiding, he got a really good look at the guy. The stranger buried the bundle beneath some scrap and then left. A few minutes later, Chico crawled back down, and despite his trepidations, checked it out. The scrap, which hadn't appeared that heavy by the way the man was moving it, was in fact seriously heavy, but Chico got it aside and pulled the bag open. As he'd thought, it contained a body, his throat slashed and the blood still warm. Chico had seen bodies before, and the man looked to have been robbed. But what freaked Chico out was that the corpse looked exactly like the man who had driven the truck. He swore it was the same guy.

Mei's pulse quickened as she read. If this was true, and not just some stoned idiot's ramblings, this could be her first actual lead.

Finding himself trespassing in a construction site with a corpse, Chico got the hell out of there. Clarifying, yet again, that he wasn't doing anything wrong, he still couldn't call the police. He'd heard about shape-changing witches called naguals, and wanted to know if that was it, and if anything could protect him from one.

No one had replied yet. Either the thread was too new or no one wanted to touch it.

Mei copied the text, then copied Chico's profile information, what little there was. It did say he was from the city of Cali. She PM'd Chico, saying she believed him, maybe keeping him on the hook. Who knew what else he might share if given some support and without it being public.

She opened the Valducan Archives and began searching for shape-changers. Her exhaustion gone, she scoured the database, reading the sometimes archaic text, and began bookmarking, cross-referencing with what she knew: the weather that night, the moon phase, the demonic history of Cali. If this was real, if she had actually found one, she'd show it to Max and insist that once the other knight returned that *she* be on the team to kill it. If they weren't going to give her a hunt, she'd make one. Finders keepers. This bastard was hers.

The dreams continue each night, tormenting me with memories. I find myself again on the deck, the storm raging around me. Paladin Amador stands beside me, Redemptor at his hip. He shouts something, his words lost to the roar of sea and wind. An order? I open my mouth to reply, too afraid to let go of the railing. The ship lurches. A wave crashes down. I lose my footing. Blind from stinging saltwater, I clutch the rail, screaming in terror. Then I waken, soaked in sweat and tears, knowing that Paladin Amador is forever lost.

I'll never know his final order.

CHAPTER 5

Chía, Colombia

The keening grew stronger, a horrible sound like a hundred screeching, out of tune violins. Hernando circled the brick building. One particular note had risen above all the rest, a single instrument amongst the cacophony. A weapon was inside, that much he was certain. But which?

His noticing it had been sheer chance. He'd been circumventing Bogotá, hoping to avoid the shrill wails of the residing demons. Hernando couldn't identify what breeds, or which powers they might yield, only that there were more than six. Although, he reluctantly confessed, he couldn't be entirely sure of how many, if even that. Without Redemptor, he was helpless against them. But once he found her, he'd return to Bogata and reap the harvest.

The single note calling from the museum was too clean to be a demon's. Now that he was close, restricted only by brick and concrete, he could focus on the warbling melody, pushing the insane orchestra aside in his mind.

The maddening sound had been his only companion through those long, black centuries. Stone and earth meant nothing to the songs. They tormented him as he starved and thirsted, his eyes and ears and tongue decaying until the music had become his only stimuli. Past an eon of pain and torment, Hernando rose Christ-like from his tomb.

He studied the hooded camera at the corner of the building, still astounded at the technology. While the memories he'd consumed had considered such things as common, even banal, he couldn't help but marvel. An eternal sentry who never slept, got drunk, or daydreamed. Its unblinking eye always watching. The glass cyclops watched him now, seeing only a man. Victor Rojas—thirty-eight, husband, senior sales representative for Farjay United, father of two, adulterer, and avid cocaine addict. The man himself was gone, buried in a dumpster with the other refuse.

He turned his attention to the door. Tempered glass, stronger than the armor he'd once worn against the savage warriors. Marvelous in its beauty. It seemed a pity to destroy it.

Hernando reared back and punched the pane. White cracks bloomed like a mosaic. He slammed his fist again, his rings clacking against the surface, and the glass exploded into thousands of tiny cubes. An alarm blared, pulsing in high-pitched beeps.

Ducking beneath the crash bar, Hernando stepped inside, glass crunching beneath his shoes. Following the weapon's call, he passed a tiny ticket counter and headed up a staircase, lit by a pulsing alarm light. The copper chupacabra ring gave him sight, rendering those moments of darkness in clear shades of icy blue and red. He passed cases of treasures, some even familiar, but there was no time to entertain nostalgia.

The weapon was close, its song screaming inside his skull.

Incan artifacts lined a small room, each labeled with a plastic white number. Hernando turned to face the left wall and his elation vanished, replaced by something cold and heavy, as if his veins had been flooded with icy lead. A wooden club with a copper, starfish head rested prominently inside. A *chaska chiqui*. It shouldn't exist. How had he not harvested this one before? Now, his failure had blossomed. He could almost feel the weapon's mocking laugher.

Hernando punched the glass, shattering it. Lips curled in contempt, he lifted the ancient mace from its cradle.

"Once I find her," he said to it through bared teeth, "you will pay for this."

My reputation at the forge has resulted in my conscription into Gilberto de Sota's next expedition. We leave in a fortnight.

CHAPTER 6

Buenos Aires, Argentina

"I'm not saying it's perfect," Matt said, "but you have to admit, there's been some—"

"No." Luiza steered the station wagon around a corner, slowing for a pair of young men hurrying across the street. Pedestrians packed the tree-shaded sidewalks outside, talking on their phones and perusing the clothes and jewelry displayed behind shop windows. These weren't the filthy poor of the villa less than a mile away, but the well-dressed women and men of a modern city enjoying a sunny day.

Matt eyed the blood compass sloshing in the dashboard's central cup holder. No hits. "We'll have to train with them. Only select knights will carry them."

"No," she repeated. "You're not getting grenades."

"Just hear me out. Uwe came up with the idea of a sleeve. It's packed with BBs, different metals and stones. Just slip it over the charge and toss it in."

"You know the fact that Uwe came up with it isn't really selling the idea."

"Think about it. If we'd had one loaded with brass or chrome and thrown it down that hole, it'd have taken out some of those skin puppets and then we'd have bagged the eel before it got away. If nothing else, it'd have gotten the familiars."

"And the fact that we killed some of those demons without

killing the familiars means we saved their lives. That means nothing to you?"

Shit. Luiza always got real twitchy when it came to familiars. She considered any that died a defeat, and any freed a victory. Matt chose his words carefully. "I'm not saying that it wasn't great that we saved them. It was. But killing the eel would save more lives overall." Christ, he sounded like Malcolm.

"I see," Luiza said. "So, you think we should have thrown a bomb into a cesspit, blown it, spraying us with God-knows-what, then dropped into it, and shot the demon?"

Matt chuckled. "It might have been messy."

"Messy? That building was held together with good intentions. It probably would've come down on top of us. We would've been buried alive, burned, or drowned in shit. None of which I want to do. I mean, how would we have gotten out if the whole place went up?"

They paused at an intersection. A line of people extended from the doors of a crowded café. Across the street a pair of orange-vested policemen stood by a vendor cart draped in knock-off Disney shirts. Instinctively, Matt slid his gaze away in the same disinterested manner as any other law-abiding tourist. "We'd have crawled out through the drain pipe. Same way it did."

"Uh huh." She continued driving. "Building burning behind us, innocents dying, and we could have suffocated on smoke as we fled down a sewer tunnel. My mommy and daddy choked to death on shit smoke, that's what Gabi would say."

Matt snorted. "I'm pretty sure that's not how she'd say it."

"True. Because we're not going to burn a building down, because you're not getting grenades."

"They don't have to be a big charge. Just enough to spray the shrapnel."

"Matt, baby, I love you, but I swear to God I'm going to slap you if you don't stop. No grenades."

Matt frowned. "You're no fun."

"I know, I know. But not all of us can heal if we blow ourselves up."

He slid his hand on her thigh and squeezed. "Fine. No grenades."

They followed the street around a park. Brightly clothed children played, chasing each other around a central statue. One, a little girl in a floppy red hat, sat on the grass wrestling with a plastic ball. Her glowing smile looked just like Gabi's. Matt squeezed Luiza's thigh again. God, he wanted to go home.

Turning onto Sariento, they drove in silence, the corner of Matt's gaze still on the blood compass. Even if they got a hit, chances were that it wasn't even related to the eel. A city this big harbored many demons. They'd bagged a weretiger their first week here. Good kill, but not what they were looking for. "How long do you see us staying here?"

"Homesick?" Luiza stopped at the gate, showing her permit.

The young guard gave it a moment's inspection before waving them on, the striped bar lifting out of the car's path.

"Me too," she said, pulling into Jorge Newbery Airfield. "I miss Gabi."

Matt grunted in agreement. "The thing is, the eel knows we're here now. Surprise is lost. It'll be careful. Hell, it might have left for all we know, headed off to Africa or something."

She steered past a row of helipads and turned onto a narrow road, concrete wall on one side, white hangars on the other. "And if we up and go only to find out it never left? We'll feel pretty stupid."

Matt nodded. The eel knew how they worked. It wasn't some brainless monster. It knew them. It had been one of them. Anya had known how to hide in plain sight. So maybe she wouldn't have left, because she knew they'd think she would. Shit. The whole thing hurt his head. He just wanted to get home.

They parked behind one of the sheet metal buildings. Pulling the satchel with Dämoren across his chest, Matt removed an armload of bags from the back of the car. Traffic roared on the highway beyond the concrete wall, the sound reflected down from the neighboring building. Luiza shouldered a long, zippered tripod tube and knocked on the hangar's metal door three times, paused, and then twice more. She unlocked it and held it open.

The hangar smelled of grease, solvent, and paint, with a tinge of gasoline. Dusty, rust-flecked girders ran along the curved ceiling. A limp, faded yellow balloon dangled below one of the beams from where it had floated up there, probably a decade before. A single-engine turboprop rested near the big sliding doors.

The Swedish airplane was a serious improvement from the larger and much older one the European team used. Sturdier, faster, capable of landing in a field, didn't shake like it was about to come apart, and had been outfitted with every luxury and gizmo the factory could cram into it. The knights had named it Helen. But leather seats and pretty names didn't change the fact that Matt would rather hitchhike with the Manson family than ride in that thing. And no amount of flying would change his mind. Planes were fucking death traps, one loose bolt away from a fiery end.

Uwe and Luc looked up from their work table, trays of ammunition laid out before them.

Luc craned his neck as if trying to see through the grocery bags. "Please tell me you remembered coffee."

Matt paused mid-stride and shared a look with his wife. "Crap." He sighed, mournfully shaking his head. "I knew we forgot something."

Stifling a snicker, Uwe sipped his Red Bull.

Luc's lips settled into a flat line. "Then you can pick me up some *tatuca* when you go back to get it."

Matt opened his mouth to reply, but Luiza spoke first.

"Don't believe a word he says." She reached into one of Matt's bags and removed a half-kilo of coffee beans, holding it out as if presenting a newly discovered idol. "You can trust that I would *never* forget coffee."

Luc glowered at Matt. "Not funny."

"Fine. Fine." Matt set the groceries onto a battered counter and pulled out a cellophane bag of golden-brown popcorn. "How's this for an apology." He tossed the bag of *tatuca* to Luc, who snatched it midair with one large hand.

"Good start. But you don't get any."

"That better not apply to me," Luiza said.

"Of course not," Luc said.

"Good." She bounced the coffee bag in her hand. "Then be

sure to leave some for me while I go make this." Luiza turned and headed through the door into the hangar's kitchen.

Matt removed Dämoren's satchel and slid into one of the empty seats beside Luc. Eleven fifty-round trays of nine-millimeter bullets sat in a neat row before him, their edges aligned with the table. Brass-jacketed slugs filled one and a half of the trays. The rest were a mix of different metals—copper, aluminum, silver, bronze, nickel, tin, pewter. Most of the bullets had either brass or dull chrome tips. The rest were hollow points with five tiny claws extending from the open noses like empty ring settings. "Looks like the electroplating worked."

"Uwe said it would." Uwe seated a chromed oval bead into the open face of a copper bullet and placed it into what looked like a giant stapler. He lowered the metal arm, gave it a solid press, and then lifted it away. The now-bent claws held the bead against the bullet's nose. He checked the prongs, making sure they were snug.

Not knowing what metals might work against the skin puppets, they'd brought a good assortment, but not many of each. Chrome wasn't one they used much and Uwe's mag back at Villa 31 had been half of their inventory. Since either it or brass was the key, Matt made the call to chrome-plate the other tips they knew wouldn't work. "I'll tell you what." Matt reached for a stack of trays holding unloaded forty-fives. "I'll take these. I'm the only one who'll use 'em."

"Fine with me." Luc's cellophane bag crinkled noisily as he tore into it. "You always have to be different."

"It's my gift."

Luc opened his mouth as if about to say more, but stuck some candied popcorn in instead.

While the rest of the hunters had all adopted HK nine millimeters as their standard sidearm, a decision made by Matt so they could swap mags, he himself still carried the Ingram. It wasn't that he disliked the pistols, quite the opposite, but unlike the other knights, he didn't carry a pistol as a backup. His holy weapon *was* a pistol. No need to carry two. So he figured that the machine gun made a good secondary. Truth be told, that wasn't the real reason he hadn't made the change. The Ingram had been Clay's. Sure, it was older than him. He'd replaced the barrel, firing pin, springs, and silencer baffles, but that didn't matter. It was still Clay's—one of his last connections to him. The others must have figured it out because no one gave him much shit about it.

The whirr of a coffee grinder sounded behind the kitchen door.

Uwe leaned across the table. "You tell her Uwe's idea?" he whispered, voice schemingly hopeful.

"I did." Matt loaded a bullet tip onto a slug and placed it into the cap setter. "No dice, man."

"No?" Uwe sat back, his brows arched in indignant surprise as if Matt had thumped his nose.

Matt pressed the lever down, and rolled his pressure, ensuring he got all of the prongs. "She thinks we're more likely to hurt ourselves and non-targets."

"No. No. You're Arms Master. You can say yes."

"She outranks me." Matt checked the bullet. Satisfied, he prepped another. "She's also my wife. I'm not arguing with her."

Uwe snorted. "Uwe can make a demo one."

"Not gonna work."

"It will once they see it. It'll save us a lot of danger." Uwe wagged a finger at Matt. "Keep you from getting shot so much."

"If you want to make a demo, I'll see it. But I didn't say that." Matt pressed the lever down, affixing the bullet cap.

"Really?"

"Once we get home. Somewhere where we can play with explosives and not have the cops come down on us."

Luc shook his head. "Putting you two together was a bad idea."

"Too late now," Matt said.

"So, you don't like grenades?" Uwe asked.

Luc shrugged his massive shoulders, each one about the size of Matt's head. "I think they're fine in the hands of people I trust won't blow me up."

Uwe snorted. "You don't trust Uwe?"

Luc sighed as if his next words carried the moral weight of the universe. "Back in the slums when you were pinned down, you would have used a grenade then, yes?"

"Yeah."

"And if Luiza and I were on the other side of the wall behind them?"

"That wall was brick," Uwe said. "A small charge wouldn't have penetrated it. It would have simply thrown BBs everywhere."

"Hmm," Luc growled. "But what if it wasn't? What if it were drywall, or tin, or that flimsy plywood that was everywhere? Shrapnel would have penetrated through and hit us."

"But it wasn't," Uwe said.

"Next time it might be."

A muffled cell phone rang from the kitchen.

Matt hadn't even noticed the coffee grinder stopping. Crap. Had Luiza heard them talking? "Luc's right," he said a little louder than necessary. "Too much risk."

"You said Uwe could make a demo," Uwe said, his voice rising in response.

Matt shushed him. He glanced to the door. Luiza's voice came from the other side, but he couldn't make it out. "We'll talk later."

The German's eyes narrowed. "You promise?"

"Of course. Just … later." Matt prepped another bullet for the cap setter. Once they were all done, he'd have to start the actual task of loading the bullets. The press they'd brought was pretty simple. Nothing at all like the sweet setup they had back at the compound. It was going to take forever.

Luiza pulled open the kitchen door, phone pressed to her ear. "Okay, I'll tell them."

Matt spun, a chrome bead still held between his fingers.

"Very good," Luiza said. "Tell Gabi I love her."

"Problem?" Matt asked as she thumbed the phone off.

"Maybe," she said. "There was a museum break-in. University up in Colombia. A man smashed through the glass and stole a weapon. Nothing else was taken."

The knights shared an uneasy look.

"We don't have a weapon in Colombia," Matt said.

"No." She shook her head. "It was an Incan mace. But it

was the *only* thing they stole. Word of the theft spread to other museums, and that tipped off Master Schmidt."

"A holy weapon we didn't know about?" Luc asked.

"No clue."

"So what do we do?" Matt asked. "Do we need to recall the others?"

"Not yet," she said. "We don't know enough."

"That's how it started last time," Luc said, referring to when Tiamat's cultists had systematically stolen and broken any holy weapons they could find, starting with orphaned ones the Order hadn't known about.

"Maybe someone bonded," Uwe suggested. "That's happened."

"That's more likely," Luiza said. "But we don't know for sure if it even *was* a holy weapon. Schmidt said they'll keep an eye out, see if anything looks like a new demon hunter on the prowl. If so, we'd need to find them before they get themselves caught or killed. We're to stay as normal until we know more, but have to be ready to go the moment we hear something else."

The expedition is forty men. Their gold lust disgusts me. They don't know real treasure. They'll never understand the shame of losing it.

CHAPTER 7

Quito, Ecuador

Felisa rubbed her tired eyes and closed the laptop. While comfortable for the first five hours, the airplane's seat had grown tiresome. She swallowed, popping her ears. Across the aisle to her left, Kofi studied his own computer, trying to make sense of the same rambling journal, documenting the author's plummet into madness. Hernando de la Fuente. Could he possibly still be alive? It seemed preposterous. But as experience had taught, preposterous wasn't always impossible.

The private jet's humming engines throttled back, their frequency dropping. Its nose tipped lower as they began their descent.

Corporal Yoder sat in the chair facing her, his blue eyes fixated in a paperback novel. Corporal Gast sat in the seat opposite Kofi, staring out the window. Unlike the others, Gast hadn't removed his black jacket or tie. The crimson wires leading from his pocket to his ears marred the professional appearance. Father Soldati had authorized only four Swiss Guard to accompany them, less than they'd asked, but more than Felisa had actually expected. Only Captain Koehl had even known of the paladins. He'd personally selected the others, and instructed them not to ask questions. He was a good man.

Felisa stowed the computer away and slid the polished

mahogany tray table into its slot. She leaned toward the window. Green mountains stretched below them. Winding rivers sliced the landscape, linking misty valleys and hidden lakes. Beautiful. In the distance to the right, a snow-capped mountain rose high above the jungle, its white peak defiant of the surrounding lushness. They passed a ridge, and a huge city filled the valley ahead: tans and grays, glints of glass windows, the gridwork of streets. A scar in God's otherwise perfect tapestry.

No, she reprimanded, her finger instinctively moving to her wedding band. *The scar is down there, living among God's people.*

The airplane banked into a turn, filling her window with clear blue sky. Felisa didn't look out of it again until they'd landed.

"Any idea how long we'll be here?" Captain Koehl asked as Felisa moved for the open door behind the cockpit. Sergeant Johan Epple still sat in the pilot's chair behind him, his reddish hair smooshed beneath the padded headset.

"Too early to say," she said. "Were you able to secure a helicopter?"

Koehl nodded. "It should be ready in the next two hours."

"Very good." She stepped out and followed the steps onto the tarmac. Green mountains surrounded them on all sides, painted with brightly colored buildings. A brisk wind pulled at her head scarf. Despite being on the equator, the city's elevation made the temperature a near-constant twenty-one degrees centigrade, cool and comfortable. She only hoped they were finished with their business here before the altitude sickness came. Give her coastal. She and mountains never quite got along.

Ofniel's case in hand, she walked to where Kofi waited beside the black sedan with Corporal Yoder. His black tie and jacket back on, the Swiss Guard looked ever the part. Observant, professional, anything but a man who loved cheap fiction. While Felisa had no doubt it was out of politeness they waited, she was certain they both enjoyed the opportunity to stretch those long legs.

The mountains reflected in the twin panes of Kofi's glasses

as he surveyed the surrounding. "Pictures didn't do justice to how beautiful this is."

"They never do," she said.

Yoder opened Felisa's door and stepped aside.

"They call it the City of Eternal Spring," Kofi said.

"Do they?" Felisa slid into the back seat and pulled the long case into her lap.

Yoder closed her door and moved around to the far side, opening the door for Kofi.

The paladin slipped in beside her. He held Salvatio's flat leather case between his knees. "Strange that more don't live here."

Felisa nodded to one of the mountains on the far side of the valley, its peak hidden beneath white clouds. "At a guess, it's the fear of living directly beneath an active volcano. Have you ever visited Pompeii?"

His gaze turned to the mist-shrouded slopes of Pichincha. "Five hundred years. The city is still here."

"Thousand if you count the Incas. I pray it's a thousand more."

Corporal Yoder slipped into the driver's seat. Corporal Gast took the seat in front of Felisa.

"Where to?" Yoder asked, starting the engine.

"Metropolitan Cathedral," Kofi answered.

Gast entered the address into the dash screen, pulling up a map.

"Did you finish the reports?" Kofi asked as they began to drive.

"There wasn't much," Felisa said. "Did you find anything useful?"

"Only enough to pray that we're wrong."

They rode in silence for several long minutes, the GPS map talking Yoder through the winding mountain turns down into the city. Eventually they entered the narrow streets, hemmed in by stone and stucco buildings, the sidewalks congested with pedestrians. There was a European feel to it all, save for the abundance of towering palms. They turned onto a particularly busy street and through the valley of tile-roofed building Felisa glimpsed an enormous winged Madonna atop a hill, her head haloed in metal stars. Definitely not Europe.

"Here we are," Yoder said, pulling to a stop beside a giant, white church. The plain stucco walls were pristine—gleaming. Only a few restrained accents of stonework and green trim decorated the exterior. Even the statues along the roof were painted in the same porcelain white. Hundreds of tourists and students milled and lounged in the adjoining plaza.

Gast stepped out first and opened Felisa's door. Once Kofi and Yoder were out, the two paladins strode up the stone steps, cases at their sides and the corporals close behind them.

Felisa's scalped itched, feeling the cameras as tourists snapped photographs and selfies all around her. She suppressed the instinct to tighten her jaw. Appearing irritated drew notice. Thankfully, no one snapped a picture directly at her.

They passed through the great double doors and into the Cathedral. Gold and vibrant greens filled the interior. Muted voices hummed beneath the elaborate vaulted ceilings. Felisa dipped her fingers into a stoup and crossed herself with cold holy water.

She'd made it five steps inside when she noticed the husky priest hurrying toward them.

"Father Aggrey?" he asked.

"I am," Kofi said, extending a hand.

"It's a pleasure to meet you," he said in heavily accented Italian, accepting the handshake. "I'm Domingo Almeida." He offered his hand to Felisa. "And you must be Sister Gaspari."

"Father," she said.

His attention returned to Kofi. "It's a pleasure to have guests from Rome. No one told us when you were arriving or I would have met you at the airport."

"That's quite all right. We have our own transportation." Kofi motioned to the suited men behind them. "These are Tino Gast and Kent Yoder from the Swiss Guard, our escorts."

Yoder smiled warmly, the dimples in his cheeks giving him a boyish quality. Gast only gave a short nod before returning his attention to their surroundings. His dark eyes searched the cathedral like a hungry jungle cat.

"I see." Almeida clasped his hands. "I hadn't realized the Swiss Guard were investigating this."

"Not in any official capacity," Kofi said, "but with the terrible circumstances, the Holy Father wishes to be as thorough as possible in finding anything we can to assist the National Police."

The priest swallowed and lowered his head. "I pray you can find whoever did this."

Kofi placed a long hand on the Father Almeida's shoulder. The gold wedding band glinted against his black skin. While some might notice the strange adornment on a priest, few questioned it. "We will do our best."

"How can we be of assistance?" Almeida asked.

"First," Kofi said, "show us where the archbishop was found."

When Felisa was eleven, she spent a summer helping her mother clean a hotel. It was a former monastery with lots of wood, and one of her jobs was polishing an intricately carved four-story banister. Once a month, on her knees, she rubbed it down with pungent citrus polish, a synthetic lemony-orange. It always took a full day to get her sense of smell right again afterward.

The heated air fresheners plugged into every socket in the archbishop's quarters smelled almost the same. Even then, they failed to hide the chemical tang of whatever had been used to clean all the blood.

Felisa stood in the dead man's office, her gaze impassively scanning the collection of photographs and humanitarian awards on the wall and mantle. A handmade award from a children's hospital held the most prominent placement. The archbishop had made many friends during his pious life. A good man had died to a monster in the house of God.

Corporal Yoder stood at the back of the room near the door, his hands clasped in front of him. A sprig of his slicked pale-blond hair jutted up in the back, spoiling the perfectly professional appearance.

Kofi's muted voice came from beyond the door, the sitting room where the late Pablo Sotomayor had been discovered splayed out like a frog, seven stab wounds including a slashed throat. Seven sins. Seven virtues. Seven days of Creation. Police were investigating if maybe that was related. Kofi was assuring Father Almeida that they would look into that possible significance but knew that, like herself, Kofi didn't believe there was any. While she detested the charade, posing as a sister did allow the benefit that no one seemed to care about her opinion on such matters. She could leave the awful-smelling room and hide while Kofi played diplomat.

She turned her attention to the wide desk. A high-backed swivel chair sat before the empty space where the computer had once been. Police had taken the machine to recover the deleted history. Felisa touched the chair back, her fingers pressing into the soft leather. The killer had sat here. The monster. She had no doubt it wasn't human. Nothing had been stolen or vandalized. Even with spontaneous crimes of passion, few murderers could resist some keepsake. The computer's search history, the security camera image of the archbishop leaving the site of his own murder, it was too much for her not to believe it a monster. But what kind? De la Fuente? How? And if so, why had he waited nearly five hundred years to make an appearance? She was missing something.

"Thank you so much, Father," Kofi said. "I'll call if we need anything." The office door opened and the lean paladin entered, Gast right behind him, looking every bit the ideal guard.

"Did you learn anything?" Felisa asked once Gast had closed the door, sealing off the newest waft of chemical stink.

He shook his head. "Have you?"

"It's about what we expected."

Kofi drew a breath, his gaze scanning the wall of awards. "If we hadn't come, we'd always worry that we'd missed something."

Felisa checked her watch. "Helicopter should be ready soon. If we want answers, then we'd better go."

"It's not much further," Ortiz said without turning.

Watching her feet, Felisa navigated the mud path behind Kofi. Brown sludge, thick with twigs and leaves, caked her shoes. Her left sock squished with each step. She should have thought of boots.

Captain Koehl walked behind her, his long legs making it infinitely easier to navigate the jungle trail along the creek bed. Sergeant Epple followed closely behind him, and had been the first to slip, coating his slacks up to the knees in mud. Epple had flown the helicopter to a farm outside San Fernando, deep in the Azuay Province. Once, centuries ago, the tiny church of Gran Arbol had overlooked this valley.

Birds squawked in the trees above, taking flight as they passed below. The damp air cloyed with the smell of flowers and rotting vegetation.

"Rains destroyed most of the site," Ortiz said, stepping over a fern-covered log. His neon green and orange police vest looked strange against the fatigues. "Best we can assume was it happened two days before we found them."

Passing a huge leafy plant that looked to have been chewed back with a machete, Felisa stopped beside Kofi. Deep furrows scarred the muddy creek bed. Thick tread imprints showed them to have been from tractor tires. A chain with rusty hooks on the end lay on the ground behind the twin trenches. Its other end ran into the water-smoothed mud beneath an open sarcophagus, its lid half-buried before it. A heavy dread settled in the pit of Felisa's stomach.

"What we can assume," Officer Ortiz continued, "is the two victims pulled it out of the pit back there and cracked it open. The killer, likely a third partner, killed Cortez here. Rains swept his body up under the wheels of his tractor, otherwise we might not have found it. Had a time of it, getting that thing out of there."

"The body?" Kofi asked.

Ortiz sucked air through his teeth. "Tractor. Animals got to the body before we found it. Tore it up pretty bad."

Listening, Felisa stepped down into the creek bed and approached the stone coffin. A shiny blue lizard scuttled away as she neared, escaping out through a hole along the back. *Five hundred years. Could he feel the centuries' passage inside his prison?*

"Do you know how he died?" Kofi asked, following her.

"Couldn't say," Ortiz answered, staying on the semi-dry bank. "Condition was too bad. Now, the second victim, Bernardo Santos, we found him about two hundred meters that way." He pointed off into the jungle. "Killer had taken a crowbar to him. Left it there. After that, they must have taken whatever they found inside and gotten out of here. The only thing we found was a conquistador breastplate. Banged up with a big hole punched through it, but we don't know why the killer would have left it. Even damaged it's worth a lot. Any idea what all was inside? It'll help with the investigation."

"Conquistador. But that's all we know." Felisa knelt and peered through the square hole. *Not even a stake through the heart could kill you.* She turned to Kofi.

He hadn't believed it could be De la Fuente, at least that was what he'd claimed. He'd argued that it was just a shape-changer. Difficult, but not impossible to find. But the paladin's weighty frown told her that was no longer the case.

"I don't know if I can make it through the jungle right now," Felisa said gesturing to her mud-caked shoes. She glanced to the two Swiss Guard and back. "Father Aggrey, would you mind going without me to see where they found the second body?"

"Of course not." Kofi smiled to Ortiz. "Please show me where you found Señor Santos?"

Ortiz shrugged. "Nothing to see there now. Rain got all the blood."

"Please," Kofi said, his smooth voice dripping with charm. "If I report back that I didn't see it … you know how it is."

"Yeah, I know. I'll show you, Father."

"Thank you."

Felisa continued staring at the sarcophagus as the two men trudged off through the forest. De la Fuente was loose. He'd begin hunting them soon, if he wasn't already. Had he heard them arrive, heard Ofniel and Salvatio's songs, as he called them in his journal? If he lived, then did Redemptor as well? A shiver wormed up her spine at the very idea. She'd never worried about her soul once she'd married an angel. Her final destination was known. She'd be canonized after her death, one of the Secret Saints. She only worried for Ofniel and for the lives of others she'd been sworn to protect. But Redemptor … with that damnable sword, her very soul, and that of her husband, risked being devoured. Eaten.

"Are you all right, Paladin?" Captain Koehl asked.

Felisa blinked, emerging from those terrible thoughts. "Yes."

Ridges of concern furled across Koehl's forehead.

She touched her wedding band, reprimanding herself. They weren't supposed to worry about her. She was to worry about *them*. She was a holy paladin, not some frightened girl. Felisa glanced back, making sure Kofi and the officer were well out of earshot. "Captain, I trust you brought all the armaments we told you to."

"Yes, Paladin. Stored in the plane."

"Very good. Call Gast and Yoder. Tell them to ready them. Yoder is a sniper, correct?"

"He is." An uncertain edge accented the Captain's voice. "Is something wrong?"

"Very. Expect a fight." Felisa patted the cold stone box. The Ecuadorian government intended to keep this relic, but she'd make the appropriate calls. Once this was done, she'd drop whatever was left of the Devil's Paladin inside it and destroy them both. "It's time we briefed you on what we're about to face, Captain. I'll explain in the helicopter back to Quito."

We have followed an old Inca road northeast through the mountains. Our priest, Father Liendo, learned of my time in Rome, and has decided I should assist him. I haven't the heart to confess that I am damned.

CHAPTER 8

Atacama Region, Chile

"Careful," Max warned as Mei pressed the stiff latch up in front of the trigger.

The clip's jaws opened and she detached the huge gun from the pedestal bolted to the floor. "Got it."

"Are you sure?" He stood beside one of the metal shutters surrounding most of the semicircular room. When opened, they gave a commanding view of the grounds. Five green metal ammo boxes rested along the single solid wall below an assortment of tools and gear, including a scoped rifle.

"Piece of cake." She slipped into the padded sling and lifted the big rifle. Unloaded, it was still over twenty pounds. No big deal, not after lugging two of those ammo cans down already. Holding it upright, careful to not bump the long barrel, she maneuvered through the open doorway and started down the stairs. Three flights worth.

Closing the door behind her, Max followed Mei down the steps and into the workout area. He hurried past and opened the metal door to the outside.

The morning sun was still low on the horizon, the western hills blanketed in shadow. Not a single cloud marred the perfect blue sky. A hawk or an eagle, Mei couldn't tell, lazily circled in the distance, riding the air currents in search of food. She hoped it didn't wander too close to the turbines. Mei carried the machine gun to the open back of a dusty pickup, set it down on a stack of tarps, and folded the cloth over it.

"Ready?" Max asked, opening the driver-side door.

She glanced toward the compound. The urge to log into Cryptozoo itched at the back of her mind. Shaking the nagging desire away, she climbed up into the passenger seat. "Ready."

Max eyed her as Mei buckled in. His thin lips tightened into a frown. "Is everything all right?"

"Yeah. I was just thinking that maybe something might have come up on that robbery."

"Do you want to go in and check?"

"No." The high tone made it sound completely fake. "I'm sure Victoria or someone will tell us if something comes up."

"But you want to be the one that finds it." It wasn't a question.

She opened her hands in her lap as if she might catch a good answer, but closed them again when none came. "I just … want to be useful."

Max's nostrils flared as he drew a long breath. "I understand. We don't have to go if you don't want to."

Shit. "No. No, of course I do."

"You've been working so hard," he continued as if she hadn't spoken. "I figured it might help to have some fun. Break the monotony of being out here with a pair of old timers."

Mei narrowed her eyes. "You know that's not it," she said flatly. "I want to do this."

"Good." With a smile, he started the engine. "Otherwise I'd have put you in charge of Gabi and taken Ester out for some target practice."

Mei rolled her eyes. The old man was in a strangely good mood. Best take advantage of it.

They rode across the lot to where the pavement led out onto a gravel road. The white metal hangar and airstrip stood off to the far left, barely visible beyond a rise. Max turned right. The truck rumbled along the narrow road, through the wind farm, a white dust cloud swirling in its wake. The great towers loomed around them.

They made Mei think of a field of giant helicopters planted

in the ground, their cabins like onions below the surface, and only their tail rotors visible. While they didn't look like they were going fast, Uwe had told her that on an average day like today, the blade tips spun over a hundred and fifty miles an hour. Her mind turned back toward the raptor she'd seen. *Stay away, little guy.*

As they passed Turbine 43, Mei couldn't help but notice Max's gaze linger on the tower, before returning to the road. Each of the fifty towers was dedicated to a fallen Valducan knight, their names inscribed on a brass plaque at their bases. With over eight hundred years of history, the Order could erect enough towers to power the country and still not run out of names—or at least that's what Uwe said. Turbine 43 was named after Jean Lallement, Max's former student and Lukrasus' previous protector. Jean had been everything: good-looking, smart, a squad leader, and even a renowned dancer. He'd been shot rescuing his team from an ambush. Died a hero. Max never failed to acknowledge Jean's tower whenever they passed it. He even visited it from time to time, but Mei was never invited to those conversations. She suspected the reason Max refused to let her go into the field was because of what had happened to Jean. Mei was chasing a ghost, a knight who had been better than her, and still died. She was the second choice. The alternate.

Passing the towers, they followed the road as it snaked through the rugged hills. They'd been green when she'd first arrived in Chile, the landscape vibrant with green grass and bright purple flowers. Then the rains had ended and the desert reasserted its dominance. Everything browned and withered to dust. Only scrub brush remained.

Finally, they crested a rise and started down into a long valley. The absolute smoothness of the dry riverbed along its bottom stood out amidst this rough landscape of sharp angles.

"You've been busy." Mei eyed the bright orange and red target squares dotting the far slope. A pair of green three-liter bottles stood atop the rusting hulk of a sedan shredded with bullet holes.

Max's mouth creased into a faint smile, the edges of his moustache more telling of it than his lips. "You've earned it."

"When did you do all this? I only got my grade yesterday."

"I assembled it during the week while you studied. I knew you'd do well." He stopped the truck at a flat lookout about halfway along the slope. A dusty unpainted shed and what looked almost like an oversized doghouse stood off to one side. It, like the two others spaced along this side of the valley, housed big electric skeet throwers, their carousels loaded with towers of clay disks. Matt had shown them to her when he'd taught her how to fire a shotgun.

Under Max's direction, Mei attached the machine gun to a pedestal mount bolted into a concrete slab. She heaved one of the big ammo cans up into its side cradle and Max showed her how to load the belt of bullets into the receiver.

Once it was ready—hot, as Max called it—he handed her a pair of bulky plastic earmuffs, which she turned on with a faint click.

"Don't hold down the trigger," Max said, his voice altered by the muffs' speaker. "Video games lie. Your barrel can warp from the heat if you just keep firing. It can explode. Understand?"

Mei nodded.

"Hold it down long enough to say, "Shave and a haircut," then let go of the trigger fully. Then I'll say, "Two bits.""

Mei smirked at the silly phrase, her mind recalling Loony Tunes cartoons on the living room floor, her sister beside her.

Max ignored it. "That gives some time for the barrel to cool and allow you to adjust your aim. Got it?"

"Shave and a haircut," Mei said.

"Good." He nodded across the valley. "Bottom left, by the big rock."

Biting her lip in excitement, Mei leaned into the gun, bracing her shoulder on the stock, peered down the sights at a bright orange square, and squeezed the trigger. The gun roared. Flames pulsed out the vented barrel tip. Brass and loose belt links spewed out the side, landing on a mat of tarps below her. Plumes of dust exploded around the orange target. "Shave and a haircut."

She released the trigger. The chalky dust cloud thinned and the target sat there intact, silently mocking her. She'd expected it to have been mulched, but she couldn't even tell if she'd hit it at all.

"Two bits."

Lining the sights just below it, she squeezed the trigger, leading the bullet stream upwards. "Shave and a—"

The target exploded, spraying smoke and dust. The boom echoed down the valley like a rolling thunderclap.

Max laughed. "That's it!"

Eyes wide, she watched bits of rock and debris tumble back to earth. "What the hell?" She looked at Max who was grinning, his teeth bared in a crazy smile. "Explosives?"

He nodded. "Now shoot the one over there."

Her excitement refreshed and heightened by the new surprise, Mei swung the gun toward the new target, this one no bigger than a shoebox, and two hundred yards away. Electric tingles danced along her skin as she sighted in and squeezed the trigger.

She took out seven of the targets before the first ammo can ran dry. The last target had taken the longest because Max had told her to detach the gun and shoot it from her hip, walking the shots toward it with the puffs of bullet strikes. She'd reloaded the gun by herself and was about to start on the eighth target when a mechanical whine sounded behind her.

A small gray and green airplane, like a World War II fighter, shot across her field of vision. It banked sharply to the right, giving a peek at an orange box about the size of an iPhone affixed to the bottom with blue masking tape.

"Get it!" Max said, his excited voice almost a shout.

Mei swung the gun toward the buzzing toy coasting across the valley. "Shave and a haircut." The gun's handle hummed in her grip, almost saying the words with her.

"Two bits."

"Shave and a haircut."

The plane banked upward and spun as it started back the other way, zipping along the valley trench.

"Two bits," Max said. The plane wove side to side, bouncing, and looping as Mei swiveled the gun to catch it.

It took a few tries before she finally managed to figure it out, shooting a burst just ahead of it and letting the plane fly into the wall of lead. "Shave and a haircut."

Part of the left wing tore free. The plane spun, flashing brief glimpses of its orange payload as it hurtled toward the rocks.

"Shave and a haircut."

The little plane vaporized in a plume of smoke and cheap wood. A wing emblazoned with a white star windmilled into the air.

"That's it, Jean!" Max laughed, slapping his thigh. "I mean, Mei."

A sharp pang shot through her gut. She clenched her teeth, forcing it to pass. Her dad used to get her and her sister's names confused when he was excited. *It meant nothing,* she told herself.

"Sorry," Max said, the joyful gleam fading from his eyes.

She waved it off, but the moment was still tarnished.

Max coughed, just a throat-clearing, and then the shine and smile were back. Casually, he walked to the rear of the truck like nothing had happened and set the remote controller down. "Are you ready for your grand finale?"

"Sure." She rubbed her palms, chasing away the numb tingles the gun's vibrations had left.

He removed a two-foot belt of ammo from a cardboard box and carried it over. "Load these in."

Taking the belt, she easily swapped it out with the one in the can. The only difference she could see with these new rounds was the colored tips. Not the gemstone kind that knights used in the field, but painted with some red enamel.

"Detach the weapon."

Mei pressed the wide clip and uncradled the gun.

"Now," Max said, easing up behind her. "Shoot the bottles atop the car."

Holding the giant rifle snugly to her side, Mei squeezed the trigger. A stream of bright red comets shot from the barrel. "Oh, hell yes!" She fired another *Shave and a haircut,* crimson laser beams coming from the gun like in some science fiction movie. The tracers inched closer, the last few pummeling the car hulk.

"Two bits."

She fired again, this time hitting one of the bottles. It erupted in a spray of fire, splashing and sheeting across the car's roof. The second bottle tumbled and fell as its partner erupted, but Mei hit it before it rolled off the far side. More fire spewed and poured down the dead vehicle. *Suck it, Storm Troopers! That's how you do it.*

Max was grinning beside her.

"What was that?" she asked. Black smoke plumed from the car now painted in orange flames.

"Diesel. What do you think?"

"I'd call that a good end." She looked at the hand-length of belt still hanging from the gun. "Can I finish these off?"

"Of course. Then we'll head back and you can learn how to clean it."

Cleaning and reloading was standard procedure with any shooting day. She'd known it was coming by the big tarp laid out, now thick with empty brass and twists of belt links. Though she'd secretly hoped they'd hold off on that part until Luiza's team got home. Maintenance parties were a lot of fun. They'd pop in some old movie everyone had seen a million times, everyone but Mei, and listen along as they worked, bullshitting and laughing at the movie, usually the bad special effects.

They always rotated who got to choose the feature. Most were action, with lots of guns to go along with the theme. Matt's were always buddy cop movies, one a "by-the-book" character, and the other the "wild card." Luiza's featured a hero going out of their element and visiting exotic locales. Spy and adventure stories, mostly. Luc played sci-fi monster movies. Not horror as much, except he had introduced her to The Thing, but movies where they hunted monsters: *Starship Troopers, Aliens, Predator, Aliens versus Predator*, that type of thing. Uwe preferred World War II movies that took place on submarines. Mei hadn't even realized this was even a genre, but was thoroughly schooled.

She glanced down at the mountain of empty shells. It'd take five movies to reload them all. Maybe more. She'd still have some when they got back. Mei lifted the gun, sighting it in on a shredded propane tank, and squeezed the trigger, adding to the empty casings with a stream of lasers.

Once done, she and Max began the task of breaking it all down. Jean's hovering ghost still lingered in the back of her mind, but lessened now.

"Did you have fun?" Max asked, sweeping the casings into one of the empty ammo cans.

"A lot. Thank you."

"Good."

"One thing, though." She looked at the burning sedan, the fire almost gone. "What's the point?"

"How do you mean?"

Dang it. That sounded bitchier than she'd hoped. She picked up one of the cans, now heavy with brass, and loaded it into the truck. "I mean, why do we even have this? With holy weapons and regular guns we can take out anything. So, is the machine gun just for fun? I mean, I don't mind, but when would we need to shoot a werewolf five hundred times when a few silver bullets would work?"

Max's jaw moved, seeming to chew the question over. He scooped more brass into a fresh can. The smooth dome of his head glistened with sweat. "It isn't for those. It's not feasible to make all the different kinds of varieties of bullets for a weapon like this."

"That's what I mean. So why have it?"

"We keep it for times when we have nothing else that will work. Yes, a brass bullet will kill an ifrit's body, but what if you don't have any brass?"

"Then you use a holy weapon."

"If you had a holy weapon, then why shoot it at all? You can't assume you'll always have it or can use it for every situation. Now, if you can't use a holy weapon, and haven't any brass, what do you do?"

"But what good would a machine gun even do if the bullets won't hurt it? That's what I'm asking."

Max nodded, understanding dawning. "A demon might shrug off one bullet, even twenty, but if you cut one in half with sustained fire, it's not getting back up. Nothing is invincible."

"Oh."

"Years ago," Max continued, "when Alex and I were locked

in the bunker, with a pair of shishi lions clawing at the door and the library on fire, we didn't have any bullets that would work. We were helpless. A gun like that," he motioned to the truck where the machine gun rested, "might have changed things. Two good men died, and several holy weapons were destroyed because we couldn't act. That's not happening again."

Mei swallowed, fighting her anger at even asking that question. She'd known of that attack. Jean had died that same night. The reason for the panic room, the turret, the escape tunnels, were all because of what had happened then. Why in the hell would she even bring up anything that would remind Max of that? "I see," she managed.

They finished cleaning in silence, Mei too terrified of spoiling the morning any further and Max with that distant-eyed look that she never quite knew what he was thinking, but knew it wasn't good.

She offered to drive the way back. Max was looking tired, but she didn't want to call him out on it.

He handed her the keys without protest.

A growing anxiety gnawed at Mei's guts as they rumbled back up the hills toward the spinning turbines. This was a good day, at least it should have been. Was Max actually glum or was she simply projecting it on him? Maybe he was responding to her, picking up on it. They were both bonded to Lukrasus, which meant that they were bonded too, was that it? He'd spent days readying this just for her, and here she was pouting that she wasn't his first and only apprentice as if either of them could have helped that.

Turbine 43 came into view. Max's pale blues slid toward it.

"So there's something I've been working on," Mei blurted. "I want to get your opinion."

"What's that?" His gaze unmoving from the white tower.

"I might have found a shape-shifter, or at least it could be. There's definitely a body."

Max turned his head, breaking the tether to Jean's memorial. "Where?"

"Colombia. Cali," she clarified.

"Colombia? The museum break-in."

"About three hundred miles off, otherwise I'd have brought it up right away. But yeah."

"When?"

"About five days ago. Some guy posted about it on the boards. I got to talking to him. The local news reported finding a body at the same spot, so I know it wasn't all BS. Then with everything else, the robbery, the Buenos Aires team, I got distracted. But would you mind looking at it?"

Max's moustache twitched. Not a smile, but close. "You were keeping it quiet, weren't you?"

"No, I just didn't think it was enough of a lead to bring it up, yet."

"Mm-hmm. You just forgot?"

"Well ... no. I got distracted."

They passed 43, but Max didn't seem to notice it. He *looked* at her. "You were hoping that if you found one by yourself that I would let you hunt it."

Mei's fingers tightened on the wheel. It was no use lying. It'd only make it worse. "It ... had crossed my mind."

The old man snorted. He bobbed a slender finger at her. "That is why Lukrasus chose you. Initiative. None of his protectors could stand being complacent. Leaders, every one. You know you should have told me."

"I'm sorry."

Max turned his eyes back to the road. "You can tell me all about what you found as you clean the gun."

The highway led us to the edge of a deep ravine. The rope bridge that these savages use had been cut, preventing our passage. De Sota, proclaiming this an attempt to stop us from finding their treasure, intends to lead us through the jungle and across the river into their domain.

CHAPTER 9

Quito, Ecuador

"That was enlightening." Corporal Yoder set the tablet down onto the table and slid it away like a diner finished with his meal. He'd been the last to complete the journal reading, short as it was. Captain Koehl and Corporal Gast had read it earlier and were now off gathering final supplies. Sergeant Epple remained at the hangar, his standing orders to be ready to fly out with little notice.

Felisa looked up from her laptop. "Any questions?"

Yoder rose from the sofa and approached the large window looking out over the city. "Hundreds." He huffed a humorless laugh. "Did you know when we left Rome? Is that why you brought us?"

"No." Felisa glanced to Kofi, quietly watching from his chair. "We had our suspicions."

He stared out the window, eyes searching, but for what Felisa couldn't guess. "What purpose? Can we even kill him?"

"Everything dies," Kofi said with that sage-like authority. "That is God's will."

Yoder turned. "But can *we* kill him? He said bullets didn't work."

"There's an enormous difference between an arquebus and modern firearms." Kofi said. "He'll fall. Though it might take a little more than it would for a normal man."

Felisa nodded. "Hence the reason we asked for a sharpshooter. None of you will be asked to engage close quarters."

Yoder looked back at the window. "Never thought I'd be tasked with shooting the Devil himself."

"You aren't," Felisa said. "De la Fuente isn't the Devil, although Redemptor might be."

The corporal grunted.

She returned her attention to her computer, opening a new attachment and scanning the photographs. Swords, so many it was difficult not to skim. But each one she stopped and looked at, saving possible candidates to a separate file, noting their locations. While Redemptor, the divine instrument of God, was well documented in sketches and even one painting, no one truly knew what Redemptor, the abomination, looked like. While they could ascertain that the second sword looked like the original, albeit with more gold, that was only a guess. The sad truth was that no one but De la Fuente knew what they were even looking for.

Once they'd returned from viewing the empty sarcophagus, Felisa had called His Holiness, spoken to him personally. The Pope had placed Father Soldati in charge, but she bypassed him. This was too important. Once His Holiness heard, he promptly agreed and forgave the breech of protocol.

That day a message was sent to every church, monastery, abbey, and convent, instructing the recipients to visit every local museum and photograph any and all swords displayed. It had been over a hundred years since such a secret order had been given, activating the Vatican's immense network. Once, such orders would have come in wax-sealed letters to be burned upon their reading. Now it was email. It was faster—probably no more or less secure than the old method. Either way, receiving an order directly from the Pope himself was nothing if not motivating.

Felisa had joked, referring to it as God's spy collar instead of spy ring. Kofi hadn't seen the humor in either term.

In the three days since, over 400 replies had come, with more arriving every hour. Thousands of photographs. Too many for two people, even twenty people, to scour. She kept her search within two thousand kilometers, which encompassed everything between Guatemala and Bolivia. Even then, this might very well be a fool's errand. Redemptor might not be on display at all. It could be hidden away, stored in an attic in Iceland for all they knew.

Yet it was their only option.

De la Fuente lived, and if so, so did Redemptor. They had to find it first.

Two more men vanished last night. Father Liendo was one of them. Our watch didn't hear or see anything, but as dawn's light broke, we discovered blood dripping from the trees. The men fear it was a monster that came from the jungle. I pray that they are wrong. I have seen monsters, and without Redemptor, we are doomed.

CHAPTER 10

Goiânia, Brazil

Hernando slowed the automobile as he neared the white concrete wall. A solid metal gate sealed the driveway, its glossy blue enamel the same as the trident spikes along the wall. Manicured trees, underlit by white lights, stood beyond it and behind those, the straight-line edge of an enormous flat-topped house. The *tre-le-la-le-le-la* of a weapon's song called from somewhere inside.

Desire mounting, Hernando forced himself to drive on, parking a block ahead beside a recently cleared lot, a backhoe looming above a rubble pile like a victorious warrior. Once, men constructed edifices to last centuries, monuments of achievement to stand against time. Now, buildings rose and fell like weeds, ugly and unmemorable. A flowering tree shaded the truck from the nearest street light.

He waited.

Hours rolled by, but Hernando knew patience. He'd waited longer than empires had lived and a little longer was nothing of consequence. The occasional vehicle turned onto the street and he lowered his face from the brilliant beams of their lights.

Some pulled into their own drives, the metal gates swinging open or sliding away on steel rails. Almost no one parked on the street.

The accursed *chaska chiqui* had made it impossible to hear other songs over its infernal melody. He'd hoped to bring it to the sacred mount that Atik had shown him five centuries before. But the site was still buried deep within the jungle. He was thankful that it hadn't been absorbed into this new world, a place of smoke and asphalt. A world of lotus eaters. Nor had it been leveled into the sprawling farmlands that were once dark, impenetrable forest. God was truly generous.

However, he did hide the mace, wrapped in plastic beneath rocks a hundred paces off of a long and empty highway. When the time came, he'd return and silence its song.

Time.

He pressed the button in the dash, awakening the green clock. 00:32. The time for waiting was done.

Hernando stepped outside into cool, dry air. Thin, pebbly clouds floated high above like the sliding scales of a great monster. They glowed silver-gray from the million lights of the city, this strange non-night of the lotus eaters. Two shimmering threads crisscrossed the sky, only visible if he didn't look at them directly. *Cequs*, Atik had called them. Rivers of God. Even without seeing them, men had erected their hideous city beneath their intersection.

Insects whirred and droned their familiar, tireless song, but Hernando felt more than heard it. The only songs he heard were those of the two demons in the city and the overwhelming *tre-le-la-le-le-la*.

He followed the sidewalk along the walled properties, some painted and smooth, others of crude brick. The path before each house was as different as the walls protecting them. Most were plain concrete, others paved in stone or tile. Status symbols, hints of the wealth hidden behind the fortifications. Fruit trees grew along the path, jutting from neat holes in the concrete. A sun-dried crust of rinds and bird excrement skirted each one, their bounties plundered before they'd even ripened.

Scratching his short hair, Hernando stole a glance behind

him as he neared the white-walled home. The streets were empty. He studied the wall: three meters high, the spike tips adding a hand's length to that. Once, he could have climbed it as easily as a tree lizard, in a blur of color and motion and then gone. But the leaden ring that enabled such power was gone, severed with the hand that clutched Redemptor on the night of his deception. His remaining rings, those he'd kept on his left hand, were spread across his ten fingers. But there were no rings that could bypass this barrier. With the power of his silver-pearl necklace, he leaped, clearing the barrier and spikes, and landed in a moist, mulched flowerbed.

The stink of cat shit curled Hernando's nose. Evidently, the thick blanket of wood chips served as its toilet. Tiny beads of water, glistening like stars with distorted reflections, dripped from the oval leaves and thick grass. A faint hiss and the wet splatter drew Hernando's attention to the black, telescoping sprinklers now watering the far side of the yard near the closed garage doors. Clouds of tiny bugs swirled in the beams of upturned spotlights. The shadows cast by tree trunks and manicured shrubs crisscrossed the open grass, reminiscent of the invisible beams above.

Unlike the courtyard, the house itself was hideous and cold. Glass and steel, like stacked cubes, slightly offset. Enormous plate glass windows, some with gossamer curtains, others with tight, slatted blinds, and all in various shades of cream. Most of them were dark. Hernando's gaze moved to the wide door, painted the color of half-dried blood with polished gold hardware, the only color to this tasteless monument.

Keeping to the shadows, Hernando stalked around the house to the nearest lit window. The wedge of light spilled across a narrow alcove paved in pale travertine. A knee-high statue of a baby riding a tortoise sat off to one side as if it were charging into a bed of long-leafed plants.

The weapon's song grew louder with each step. Hernando bent his head, peeking around the corner. Through a glass door, he spied a shirtless man, the black hair of his temples and chest graying with age. The man knelt before a stainless-steel refrigerator and removed a cardboard tub from a bottom drawer. The light caught off a small gold crucifix and twisting rope chain around his neck.

Hernando's eyes moved to the sliding door. Would a man who locked himself in a fortress behind steel and concrete leave his back door unlocked? Doubtful. The man might go to bed soon, or at least leave the kitchen. Hernando could check then. But even if unlocked, a man with such fear of theft must surely have an alarm. A tone announcing Hernando's entry would spoil the purpose of waiting.

The man with the golden cross scooped ice cream into a small clear bowl. His head bobbed in a subtle rhythm, his lips, though restrained, mouthed words. Lyrics. There was a song in this man, albeit not of the same melody as the one shrieking through Hernando's mind.

He could not wait for the man to go to bed. He needed Redemptor *now*.

The man slipped the spoon into his mouth upside down and pressed the ice cream lid back on. Hips moving to his personal song the man turned away and returned the carton to the freezer drawer. As he turned to face his late-night treat, his eyes widened in shock, seeing Hernando outside his door, the tortoise-riding statue lifted in one hand. His mouth opened in a cry, the spoon tumbling from his mouth as the concrete figure flew through the plate glass. The window exploded. Shards rained down, skittering across the polished wood floors. Hernando dashed through the cascade. The knife in his other hand lifted and slashed across the screaming man's almond-brown throat. Blood fanned across the kitchen, splattering the glass-fronted cabinets, the granite countertop, and the two large scoops of nut-speckled ice cream.

Like a jaguar, Hernando was on his prey, mouth latched to the sputtering wound, he pulled his victim to the floor. He sucked the hot blood. Energy coursed through him, swelling within him. The man's fists pounded against his back, each blow growing weaker.

Hernando drank. He needed to taste it the instant life fled the dying man's body, or the soul might escape.

The man's arms fell limp, one arm around Hernando's neck

as if holding him in a friendly embrace. Hernando slid the knife blade into the flesh below the raised arm, puncturing lung and heart. An alarm blared somewhere in the distance.

The pulse slowed.

Stopped.

Hernando sucked the open throat.

An unseen brilliance erupted in the back of Hernando's skull, like a sunrise. Memories sprang from the light like flowering plants, their roots and branching arms weaving themselves into his brain. Eyes closed, Hernando lifted his mouth from the dead man's throat and savored the rush of knowledge, a lifetime all at once.

His muscles swelled and shrank, the bones shifting in the deepest massage imaginable. Hernando looked down at the dead man's face, the face he now wore. Ricardo Garcia, forty-nine, owned ten auto dealerships, husband, father, and lover of golf. They were now one. Feeling a moment's pang of guilt, Hernando flipped the crucifix on Ricardo's chest around. While important, Christ should not witness this work.

Ricardo had been a good man. He wouldn't be the last to die by Hernando's hand. Archbishop Sotomayor had also been good, though Hernando hadn't expected that. There, in the house of God, he'd wanted to force a confession from the priest, hear of his sins. But why bother? One taste of the archbishop's blood and Hernando knew the man's transgressions, his memories, his dreams, desires, and fears. It was all there and Hernando now knew that the archbishop's only true sin was that of ignorance.

He'd laid the body out regardless. Posed it Christ-like on the floor. While the man was innocent, Rome was not, and Rome would see its first taste of the coming storm.

Rising to his feet, Hernando strode to the alarm unit near the door. He tapped the six-digit number, leaving Ricardo's bloody fingerprints on the lighted screen. The alarm ceased. Nine more seconds would have resulted in summoning the *Policía Militar*. A break-in at a house like Ricardo's would most definitely bring helicopters, automatic rifles, and a small army that Hernando didn't want to kill.

A woman's voice shouted. "Baby? Baby, what happened?"

Hernando turned. A woman stood halfway up the stairs, her shiny black hair tucked into a sapphire-blue silk robe clutched tightly at her neck. Esperanza—Ricardo's wife of twenty-three years, mother of their two children.

She gasped, her mouth open in terror – whether it was the sight of her husband slathered in crimson blood or the knife still in his hands, Hernando didn't know. Not yet.

He sprang toward her, the blade coming up before him. It was a good knife. He'd purchased it in Colombia. A solid piece of flat metal, its grip made of tightly braided cord, its chisel tip cut in the tanto style. Hernando knew fine craftsmanship and the blade's was superb.

Esperanza took a step back, a scream rising from her lips. The tanto blade slammed into her chest so hard that Hernando felt the crack of her sternum like a splitting log. She fell limp, her body carried backward by the blow and onto the steps. Hernando pulled the narrow blade free and tore the robe open. He dipped his head and pressed his lips to the triangular slit and drank.

It didn't take long and a new sun exploded within his skull. A fresh garden bloomed, intertwining with her husband's still-growing branches. He shivered. His balls slithered up inside him. The gray hair dissolved and withdrew back into his chest as his nipples pressed against his tightening, blood-wetted shirt. The breasts weren't as large as Esperanza's. Hers contained 250cc of silicon, the procedure performed by Doctor Olivera of Rio in 2009. Hernando's rings loosened on the now slender fingers, manicured but not painted. Without Redemptor, he couldn't control these changes. He always took the form of the last person he'd tasted, but soon that would remedy.

Tucking his long hair behind his ear, Hernando looked around. The house was empty. Thiago, their eldest, was away at school. Architecture. His parents were proud. Almir had moved away two months ago. A falling out with his parents, but they both still loved him despite his terrible decisions.

The memories of sons he'd never met flickered in the back of his mind as Hernando walked up the steps toward the song.

The now oversized shoes rubbed his heels and he kicked them off. He threw open the doors to Ricardo's study and stepped inside. Antique weapons lined the walls. The weapon song filled the world, making his teeth sing like tuning forks in their sockets. But it wasn't Redemptor's song. He didn't turn on the lights. There was no need.

Already knowing the terrible truth, Hernando looked at the curved, silver-handled knife on the wall. Rage flooded his veins. Would he ever find her? Clenching his fists, the long nails digging into his soft palms, he clenched his eyes, wishing that this had been her and not this terrible siren. He hated this knife. Hated abomination within it. He wanted to smash it, cease that terrible song, but knew that was what it wanted. It wanted to escape him, but he would make it submit. That was God's will.

He needed Redemptor to rule it, but where was she?

Hernando's heart seemed to stop, the fury abating. He saw her. He saw her in his memories. Not his, but Ricardo's. This man had seen Redemptor.

"Thank you, God," Hernando breathed. He understood now. This was part of the Almighty's plan. The song of this evil knife had called him here, and now he knew where Redemptor was.

We have reached a city. Though there were only twenty-three of us, the natives bowed to our superior might. We have two hundred prisoners. De Sota has ordered me to interrogate the old man that killed Luis before we brought him down. I believe he is their holy man. I have never seen anyone move as he did.

CHAPTER 11

Mei squeezed a glass in her right hand, enjoying its cold smoothness against her burning skin. The morning's practice had been her first with bare walls. The steel of the tower gonged every time she came down too hard. Max had ridden her ass about that.

"You need to land silent. Like a hawk, not a squirrel hurling itself onto a branch."

She hadn't realized how dependent she'd been on a lousy half-inch of padding, but her knees were telling her that they definitely missed the cushion. The worst had been when she came down wrong and slammed her hand against the side. It wasn't anything bad, just a little skin off the palm, but it hurt like hell and she'd nearly dropped Lukrasus. Of course, dropping the sword would have meant that his power would have ended, and she'd have fallen ten feet onto the floor. A skinned hand would have been the least of her problems.

Max hadn't been very sympathetic. He had his own collection of scars and calluses to back it up. "Keep going. We have twenty more minutes."

Silently cursing him, she kept at it. She'd been dancing since she was five, and a little pain was nothing.

Once that was done, and she was fed and showered, it was straight back to research. She sat in one of the corner offices up on the second floor, a wide panoramic view of the rocky desert and the practice tower with its top-floor machine gun nest beside her. It wasn't much to look at, but it sure beat sitting in the windowless library. It always made her feel like some nuclear survivor down there, locked in a bunker with a bunch of books while the world outside burned. Gabi sat on the floor playing with an assortment of plastic cups. She had toys aplenty, but stacking those cups was her favorite.

Ester had gone out for groceries, an errand that took most of the day just to get there and back. Max was off doing something around the compound. He'd loaded some tools in the truck right after practice. So, until either of them returned, Gabi was Mei's responsibility.

Mei had sealed the doorway off with a collapsible swing gate so Gabi couldn't make a break for it once she'd lost interest with her cups. Celeste lounged in the hall outside, loudly licking herself *just* beyond anyone's reach. Cartoons played quietly on the wall screen, but no one was watching them.

Ever since the museum break-in, her daily ritual included scouring news reports on any suspects or strange killings in the area. If a weapon they hadn't known about had bonded with someone, then they needed to find the new protector before the police did or before they got themselves killed.

She clicked a new article and Mei's chest tightened. The university museum had released the security footage, including some stills. There, on the top of the screen, the thief stared directly at the camera, his face perfectly clear. She saved the image and pulled up the picture of the late Victor Rojas from Cali, the man Chico has seen thrown in a dumpster. The obituary photo showed a clean-cut man with a neat moustache and perfect, parted hair. He wore a pale yellowish suit the color of crème brulee and a bright blue tie. The man in the black and white security picture was unkempt, his hair tousled and button shirt untucked. The hard, studying eyes were the same, as were the slender nose and plump lips.

Mei stared at it for a solid minute, her stomach twisting

knots between joy and horror. She'd found the thief, but it wasn't human. She had the lead, but had kept it to herself. What had her inaction cost? It had over a week's head start now.

No. There was no way we could have known. The picture only came out today. If I hadn't been following up on Chico's lead, then we wouldn't know what it is.

The words didn't help. Truth be told, *she* didn't know what it was, only that it wasn't human. Unless Señor Rojas has some evil twin brother no one knew about. Mei needed to share this with the Order, but she wanted to give them something more, something to prove that she'd been working on it during those lost days. So, what did she know?

Mei leaned back in her swivel chair, her gaze on the shifting colors of the television, but she didn't actually look at it. The monster had killed Victor Rojas and taken his form. Most demons possessed the body, and transformed that into their bestial shape. So, what stole the body without possessing it? Her research had yielded only a few suspects.

Rakshasas for one. Those could assume the guise of anyone they wished. They could turn invisible and duplicate their image, appearing in multiple spots at once like some funhouse mirror maze. Matt called them "Million Dollar Demons" because only gold bullets worked on them. They were bad news.

It could also be a doppelganger. Those had to consume part of a victim to steal their form, usually some hair. They could also liquefy, or at least squish their way through openings like an octopus. Weaknesses included pyrite, Alpine roses, and whale ivory. But doppelgangers rarely killed those they mimicked, preferring instead to destroy their lives.

The other option would be an incubus. While they didn't change their form exactly, they could cast a glamour, like a hologram, to make themselves appear as someone else. Mei doubted that one. Incubi made their guises incredibly attractive, the kind of impossible sexiness reserved for movie stars or magazine covers. The Victor Rojas staring at the security camera was strikingly less appealing than the real one had been.

Gabi's laugh pulled Mei from her thoughts. The child had constructed a wobbly tower six cups high, a bobble-headed toy stood atop it. Gabi yanked the yellow cup out from the bottom and the tower collapsed with a hollow clatter. She stared at the cups rolling across the floor, her lips drawn into a deep scowl, seemingly angry that the rest had fallen.

Mei suppressed a snort. "Fall down?"

Gabi laughed again and said something Mei couldn't begin to understand. Mei bent and rolled a blue cup back toward the little girl, but its tapered shape caused it to curve off path. Gabi lumbered to her feet and began gathering her fallen cups, and Mei returned to her thoughts.

The other thing Mei knew was that it was working alone. There hadn't been a second culprit in either Chico's story or the security footage. The sightings were about three hundred miles and only days apart. Demons didn't normally move that far that fast. They were drawn to areas with lurid pasts. Demonic gravity, Max called it. Of course, some could escape it if they tried hard enough, maybe just orbit it, but then they'd simply get caught in the next spot and then the next. They moved in curves, kind of like that rolling cup. Never a straight line.

No, to move three hundred miles, a demon normally had to jump bodies by seizing control of another victim they had possessed that was now in a different location. But then why would it still appear like Victor Rojas? Why keep the same form? Was that particular body important to it somehow? Maybe Rojas had somehow wronged it, and the demon was now off committing crimes to spoil Rojas' reputation even after death.

But why travel hundreds of miles to do that? It could have done that in Victor's home town, not break into a university exhibit and steal a single weapon. Obviously, the thief didn't care if anyone saw it. Why bother? It could just change its appearance and throw off the authorities.

She glanced over to where Gabi had now constructed a pyramid, three cups high. She marched the little toy up the giant steps, one, two, three, and stood it atop the peak like a triumphant Everest climber. Keeping her brown eyes fixed on the toy, Gabi's hand snaked out and pulled the middle cup out from the bottom. The pyramid fell and Gabi laughed.

Mei continued to watch as Gabi began constructing her next tower to destroy.

Destroy.

If it was a holy weapon that the demon stole, and Mei was pretty certain that it was, why did the demon take it?

She knew that demons could see holy weapons for what they were. Matt had told her that to them, holy weapons glowed, sort of like an aura. So the demon would have had to have seen the weapon, or have known it was there, and then it broke in after hours and took it. That was weird, but shouldn't the demon have just broken it there?

Max told her that Tiamat's cultists stole weapons and destroyed them in sacrifice, summoning more powerful entities. Was that what it was doing? Maybe the Incan mace was only one of several weapons to be offered up?

A sudden chill tickled up the back of Mei's neck. Her hand moved to Lukrasus at her hip. If she was right, the demon would need more weapons. She squeezed the handle.

Don't get paranoid. She needed to give the Order *proof,* something to validate the suspicion. One stolen weapon was hardly a trend. But what if there were more? Not all weapons were in museums.

Mei turned back to her computer and began searching news stories. If she was right, and she prayed that she wasn't, there would be more thefts. Maybe even more murders.

I've come to enjoy this man Atik. The old priest knew of the monster that had killed our men. While his people lacked weapons to fight it, he assured me that the demon was no threat for anyone in the city. I must learn how.

CHAPTER 12

Buenos Aires, Argentina

"Here we go." Slowing the van, Matt flipped a switch below the steering wheel, killing both the headlights and brake lights. He clicked a monocular down from his helmet, displaying the world in shades of black and green. Beside him, Luiza strapped her helmet on, her face hidden behind a black mask.

They rode in silent darkness, the only sounds being the low rumble of tires along the packed earthen road. He turned onto an even rougher path slicing a canyon between walls of high grass and even a few trees.

"Everyone stick together," Luiza said, her words echoing a moment later in his ear bud. "Uwe on point. We have no way of knowing how many are corrupted, so hold fire until they pose a threat. If they do, drop 'em, but don't slow down. Be ready for anything."

A pair of capybara, looking like rats mated with hippos, sat in the road ahead. They waited until the last moment before darting off into the brush.

Matt glanced at the bottle in the dash cup holder. It appeared black in the night vision. Instead of only a few drops from a pricked fingertip, he'd squirted 10cc of his blood into the water. Maximum range and potency. There was no holding back tonight. It was only luck that they'd gotten a second chance and there was no way they'd get a third.

The narrow road ran alongside the Costanera Sur Ecological Reserve, a marshland park built atop a former dump. There, hidden in the wild emptiness between cycling trails and the shadow of a wealthy marina packed with sailing yachts, a ghost slum had taken root. It had no name, and probably never would, the city fathers refusing to admit its existence. Once it became a nuisance, they would quietly excise it, scatter the residents, and pray for a few peaceful months before its inevitable recurrence.

Even with all of their scouring of the city, the Valducans never would have found it on their own. A conversation overheard on the police radio had tipped them off. A boater had seen a man's head erupt. Such reports had occurred every few weeks now. Squid Heads, as the police jokingly referred to them on their private channels. It was considered nothing more than an elaborate prank. Public reports were suppressed out of fear of prompting a mass hysteria or encouraging the demented pranksters. They investigated it of course, halfheartedly, and as expected no bodies were ever found.

But if all went well, there would be more than a few bodies to be discovered once dawn's light broke on the horizon. Matt only prayed none were their own.

A faint glow welled beyond the grass and trees ahead, diffused with the haze of campfire smoke. Sharp irregular shapes emerged into view, tiny one-floor shacks and lean-to shelters piecemealed from broken scraps, patched tarps, and sticks. A rust-crusted cylinder, like part of an old smokestack or industrial fuel tank, stood at the heart of the shanty town. Only twelve feet high, it loomed above everything else like a junkyard fortress. Figures moved among the buildings or huddled around cooking fires. A few glanced up as the van's tires crunched closer.

The water in the compass went clear, all the blood condensing to a single large sphere, pointed directly at the rusted tower.

"We're here," Matt said, pulling to a stop.

A scraggly-haired teen with a wispy beard rose from his fire and took a few tentative steps toward the vehicle. Squinting, his mouth opened in a questioning expression, he moved his head side to side, owl-like as he came closer.

"Do it," Luiza ordered.

Matt flipped up the night scope and hit the twin toggles on the console. All at once, the van's high beams shot through the encampment as a light bar on the dash strobed red and blue. A siren began wailing, shattering the silence.

The bearded youth stumbled backward and fell. Eyes wide in terror, he scrambled and ran away.

Luiza was already out the door, her pistol up and its under-barrel light shining a brilliant beam across the rickety village. She clutched the blood compass in her off hand. Uwe and Luc were right behind her, Uwe with his spear and Luc with a shotgun. They moved forward and Matt hurried out to join the formation, Dämoren in hand. His slung Ingram bounced against his Kevlar vest.

Shouts erupted, barely audible above the siren's wail. Most of the residents scattered, fleeing into the darkness, abandoning whatever few worldly possessions they owned. Whether it was fear of the police themselves or rumors of the Villa 31 Massacre, Matt didn't know. But their escaping this demon nest would save their lives.

A woman dressed in a mustard-yellow shirt ran from a nearby shack, clutching a serrated knife. Her head burst open with a wet pop, the swollen brain unraveling as she neared. Luiza shot her twice, once in the head, and the woman crumpled.

More filthy residents and skin puppets charged from the shadows. Luc's shotgun blew an old man's head clean off as the demon erupted. Instantly the boy beside him began to transform, but a second blast sent him down before his skull had finished swelling. The knights didn't slow as they fired at the closing mob.

The chrome-brass loads worked as they'd hoped. Sure, they only killed the bodies, allowing the demons to "respawn" as Uwe called it, but the skin puppets they could kill later. The eel was the prize.

Matt fired Dämoren as a skin puppet hurdled over a fence made of shipping pallets. It stumbled as the blessed slug tore through its chest. A second shot blasted its squirmy head open and golden teal fire sprayed across a chipboard wall. *No respawn for you.*

"Reloading," Luiza called. They didn't stop. Matt lifted the Ingram in his off hand and laid a burst of fire across a trio of closing familiars. Beads formed and vanished in the blood compass as fast as the knights could shoot, but the single bead aimed at the tower was all that mattered. They were close enough now to see the sloppy corrugated tin roof covering its left side.

A skin puppet, its body that of a boy no older than eleven, leapt out from behind a blackened steel drum as they moved past. One bone-tipped tentacle wrapped around Matt's left wrist, jerking it aside. Matt twisted in time to get the plate of his ballistic vest in the way of the second tentacle before it speared him. It snaked up toward his face, but Matt hacked with Dämoren, chopping the pink tendril with the blade affixed below the revolver's barrel. Hot, coppery blood spewed across his neck and chest. He rammed the barrel between the demon's bulging eyes and fired. The blood on Matt's chest ignited as the monster fell. He yanked the greasy tentacle from his arm and hurried to keep in formation.

A transforming skin puppet slammed into Uwe's invisible shield. Uwe shoved it like a battering ram knocking it back as the tentacles lashed toward him. Luc took it down with his twelve-gauge.

They reached the rusted tower. Three feet of weedy earth ringed the outside like an impact crater. They followed it around, searching for the entrance. The blood bead rolled along the inside of the compass, tracking the solitary demon inside. That didn't mean it was alone. Familiars or un-transformed skin puppets might be protecting it.

"*Don't trust that compass too much,*" Clay used to say. "*You grow dependent, and it'll leave you a blind spot.*"

Matt kept his eyes on the open roof. If the eel tried to fly out, he'd nail it with Dämoren.

A long, shoddy shack with stacked brick walls extended from the south-most side. Luiza drew Akumanokira from the scabbard along her back.

Uwe crouched and shined the light strapped to Tuerie's shaft inside. "This way."

They hurried through behind him. Luc's helmet banged into one of the beams supporting the low ceiling.

The inside reeked of salt and rust. Matt glanced behind him through the shrinking door. The grounds appeared empty, lit by the fires of dead demons and flashing police lights.

Uwe was the first into the metal tower. Rapid gunfire thundered in the enclosed space, the shots thumping off Tuerie's force field.

"Down!" Uwe yelled.

Matt dropped into a squat, duckwalking deeper inside. The flashing gunfire came from behind a makeshift barricade of stacked cinderblocks, a single hole in the middle where the barrel protruded.

Uwe pushed further in as the rest followed single file. Matt was the last inside. Once the shooter stopped to change mags, or stuck their head out, he'd take them out.

The shots continued.

Even a hundred-round drum would run dry eventually.

A crash boomed just behind him. Matt whirled as the front bumper of the pickup slammed through one side of the brick tunnel and into the next. Dust and bits of broken brick surged out as the entrance collapsed.

"Matt!" Luiza shouted. The firing had ceased. He turned back just as a skin puppet leapt out from behind the bunker and caught the upper rim of the tower with its tentacles. Matt raised Dämoren and fired. The metal gonged as the bullet struck an inch to the left of the demon's head. He cocked the hammer and fired again as it reached the top, hoisting itself above the lip.

Teal-gold fire ignited as it fell back to the earthen floor.

Luiza sprang forward, catching and swinging herself over the brick bunker, katana raised. "Where's the eel?"

Their lights played off the walls. The room was twenty-five feet across, thick welds framed the curved sections of steel plate. Bits of trash and a few dry weeds littered the hard-pack floor. The only way out was the rim at least twelve feet up.

Son of a bitch. Matt looked at the low entrance now sealed with rubble. "It's a trap."

"I can get that," Luc growled, starting toward it.

Something thudded. Matt whirled to see a thick, tape-wrapped tube lying on the ground. A sparkling fuse ran down into the top.

"Behind Uwe!" Uwe dropped to his knees, bracing his spear toward the bomb.

Shit! Matt scrambled behind him, slamming into Luiza as they both hunkered behind the shield. Scrunching his eyes, he wrapped his arms around Luiza, pulled himself on top of her, and buried his face against the back of her neck.

The deafening boom shook the world. His bones jarred with the sudden concussion of pressure and sound. Metal pinged on all sides. Rock and bits of shrapnel rained down, stinging his curled legs. Something hard slammed into his back. Matt gasped, tasting the dust even through the tight cloth mask.

His body ringing, he rolled drunkenly off Luiza. A shrill hum screamed in his ears. Matt tried to sit up, but only managed to fall on his side. Smoke and dust filled the air. The stars above flickered red and blue. He blinked and realized the flashing stars were the police lights now visible through the hundreds of tiny holes perforating the bent half-roof above.

A silhouette rose into that section of exposed sky. Someone had climbed the outer edge. Man-shaped, but Matt couldn't tell if there were head tentacles. He did see the rod clutched in the figures hands. Gun! They were going to finish off any survivors.

Matt had dropped Dämoren, but he clawed for the Ingram still slung to his vest. The would-be killer must have heard him and the rifle swung Matt's direction. Matt lifted the Ingram, not really aiming, and pulled the trigger.

Nothing.

Matt's chest tightened in horror. Debris had gotten into the open bolt, jamming it. *No!*

The figure lifted the rifle to it shoulder.

No!

Three quick pops sounded to Matt's left. The silhouette jerked, the rifle going off with a bright flash, and then a fourth shot sent a spray of mist from the shooter's head. It fell and landed inside the tower, though Matt couldn't hear it land with the ringing in his ears.

He looked over to see Luiza on her back, her pistol raised in both hands. *Damn, I love you.*

She kept her aim up on the rim in case more attackers might climb up. "Everyone okay?"

"Uh ... Uwe's alive," Uwe groaned. An eight-inch-high wall of debris marked the edges of Tuerie's invisible shield. Had it not been there, those chunks of brick and shrapnel would have torn right through them.

A gloved hand lifted from the dusty lump behind, bits of rock falling with the movement as Luc gave a thumbs-up. "I wasn't ... ready for *that*," he grumbled, the words coming in through the ear bud.

"I'm okay." Matt stumbled to his feet. He wobbled as the world seemed to teeter like being on a ship. He caught himself and looked around. Small gold-teal fires burned all around them, bits of the dead demon Dämoren had shot caught in the blast. Matt staggered to a severed leg sheathed in demon fire and almost fell as he bent down. He pulled off his glove and pressed his fingers into the pulped, burning meat. A silky wave rolled up his arm, spreading through his veins. The fog and ringing in his ears vanished. His mind clear, Matt stood and let the limb plop back to the ground. "How are you?"

"I'm fine," Luiza said, still covering the tower's upper edge. She had the least dust on her. "Just get us out of here."

Matt helped her up. Luiza never broke her aim.

"The bitch led us into a trap," Uwe growled.

"She knew." Luc panted and rose into an unsteady crouch, hands on his knees. Dust cascaded off his back. "She knew we were coming."

"Honeypot," Uwe said.

Matt nodded. Anya had led many knights into ambushes during her time with the Order. She knew how they operated and they'd walked right into it. He picked Dämoren off the ground and cleared the dust off her. A shredded plastic bottle rested a few feet away, the blood compass' contents already drunk up by the dry ground.

"Discuss it later," Luiza ordered. "Luc, can you get the door?"

The giant nodded. "I need a second."

"You don't have one. God knows if they have a second bomb."

Luc blew two deep breaths and stood. He drew Velnepo from his belt and approached the rubble-filled doorway. He pulled a few of the looser bricks from the tumbled pile and lifted the mace high. "Get back."

Matt lifted his hand to shield his eyes as Luc slammed Velnepo into the remaining mound. Shards of masonry exploded outward. He hit it again and again, each blow as devastating as a wrecking ball.

Uwe crept forward, his spear before him. The cloud of red dust deflected and swirled around the shield's unseen edges. Luc struck again, reaching inside as far as his arm allow.

"There," Uwe said. "I can see through."

"Where's the compass?" Luiza asked as they began clearing the rubble.

"Gone," Matt answered. He loaded fresh shells into Dämoren. "Doing this the old-fashioned way."

Uwe probed his spear through the hole, knocking aside a large block. "Uwe goes first."

Matt snapped the revolver's loading gate closed and cocked the hammer. "I'm right behind you."

"I'm team leader," Luiza said.

"And I'm completely fine. You're all half-deaf, still yelling everything. I'm after Uwe."

Luiza's lips moved beneath her mask as if to say more, but she gave a decisive nod. "I'll be after Matt. Luc, take rear."

Uwe crawled into the small opening, Matt right on his heels. The sharp corners of brick dug into Matt's knees. The short tunnel only extended a couple of feet before the top opened up. They peeked above the trough rim and looked about. Several bodies littered the empty shanty town, a few burning with demon fire. Nothing else moved. Matt strained to hear anything above the still wailing police sirens, but couldn't. He was at least grateful none of the demons or fleeing residents had trashed the van.

Slowly, Uwe pushed over some more debris and climbed out. Matt scanned behind them, making sure it was still clear, and followed the hunter out, his weapon ready.

The village was empty.

Once Luiza and Luc were clear, they hurried back to the vehicle. A long crack ran across the windshield where someone had thrown a rock, but it was still usable and the tires appeared intact. *Thank God for small favors.*

They gave a quick inspection, making sure there were no more bombs hidden under or inside it.

Matt killed the flashing lights and siren. "Let's get out of here."

They rode in silence for several minutes. Once they reached paved road, Matt pulled off the helmet and peeled the dusty balaclava from his face. The cold air felt amazing against his sweat-slicked skin.

"Forget any griping I did about the helmet," Luc said, inspecting a long, pale rent along one side.

"I knew it was too good to be true," Luiza grumbled. Her nostrils flared. "Played right into its trap."

Matt rested a hand against her leg. "What do we do?"

"We need to ditch this vehicle. Then figure out a new way to hunt for it that it won't expect."

Matt nodded, choosing not to ask what that could possibly be. For all they knew the eel was long gone, just setting a distraction while it made house a thousand miles away. He'd mention that once tempers had cooled.

"Uwe says we fly out of here tonight."

"You want to run?" Luiza asked, a dangerous edge to her voice.

"No," Uwe said, sounding like it was the stupidest question he'd heard, "but we must move. If that eel laid a trap, then it might know where we are or be figuring it out soon. So, we leave. Make it see us leave. Then come back, set up somewhere else, something like we've never done and won't expect. Maybe rent a warehouse."

"He has a point," Luc said, his voice the volume of a man half-deaf.

"We could bring a new team in," Uwe continued, starting a roll, his words coming faster. "Hunters the eel wouldn't recognize. Chaya, Victoria, Taras. We've lost the element of surprise, but *they* could reclaim it."

"Give Mei a shot," Matt added.

Uwe snorted. "Master Schmidt won't cut the cord for these sons of bitches. You know that. First thing, we go back to Villa 31. I bet they moved back the moment we cleared it. Best hiding place in the world is right were you thought you checked."

Matt shrugged in agreement and steered them onto the highway back to the city. A buzzing rattle sounded in the console. Luiza didn't seem to notice it, either still deaf from the fight or unable to hear past Uwe's talking in the back. He lifted the little plastic console door to see the light of Luiza's phone as it vibrated again.

She pulled it out and gave a gusty sigh. "Schmidt."

Uwe went silent.

"Probably anxious to see how we did," Matt said. The Valducan Masters almost always watched the teams' progress via GPS during hunts. Though making first contact right after was a bit strange, even for Max. He normally waited until the next morning if he hadn't heard anything yet. Matt held out his hand. "I'll take it."

"You're driving," she said.

"Yeah, but my ears aren't ringing. I'll give him the bad news."

She handed him the phone and Matt answered it as it buzzed again. "This is Matt."

"How did it go?" Schmidt asked, his voice harsh, even for him.

"Bust. Led us into an ambush and tried to blow us up."

A pause. "Is everyone all right?"

"Fine. Just banged up and pissed. Uwe shielded us from the worst of it," he added, throwing the German a bone.

"Good. Is everyone there?"

You know they are. You're watching the GPS right now. "Affirmative. We're all here."

"Put me on speakerphone. There's been a development."

Matt's irritation washed away with a sudden chill. Was someone dead? Was Gabi okay? Maybe Master Turgen or one of the other teams. He thumbed the screen and held out the phone. "You're on speaker."

"Can everyone hear me all right?" Schmidt asked, his amplified voice carried that too-loud metallic quality. "There's a change of plans. A family was murdered in Brazil two nights ago. A wealthy collector in Goiânia. A Tibetan knife was the only thing stolen. Dealers and auction houses were notified to look out for it."

Matt swallowed.

"Not again," Luiza breathed.

"This is the second weapon theft in less than two weeks," Schmidt continued. "The Order is recalling all holy weapons on loan to museums. This is now Priority One."

"What else do we know?" Matt asked.

"First victim's throat was cut. The wife was stabbed. No bites. No one missing. Mei linked the first theft to a murder victim some days prior, also with a cut throat."

"Prior?" Luc asked.

"Correct. We suspect the killer is a shape-changer."

Luc growled.

"Those are a bitch to track," Uwe muttered under his breath.

"Once the weapons are safely back at the compound, we'll begin our next move. The Takaira Clan has already been informed. We'll begin reaching out to any independent hunters we know of. Luiza, tomorrow you'll fly to Rio and fetch Fuertod. Matt will go to Montevideo and secure Ozkareen. I'll inform the curators in the morning. Keep them under constant watch until they're released into your care."

Luiza's hand was at her chest right above where her pendant of Feinluna rested below her vest. Her sword had been broken when Tiamat's cultist had systematically destroyed all weapons they could find. "Understood."

"Very good. All knights will report in twice a day without exception. We are under attack."

"What about the eel?" Matt asked.

Schmidt waited several seconds before replying. "We'll revisit it once we have the weapons home."

After hearing of Redemptor, Atik has promised to teach me his secrets. He says she can be reforged. First, I must bring him the beaded necklace that was taken during his capture and a golden mask that De Sota has claimed as his prize.

CHAPTER 13

Montevideo, Uruguay

Trying his best to appear official without standing out, Matt strummed his fingers along the brown calfskin satchel as he gazed across the wall of glass cases. Rather than focusing on the relics inside, he studied the reflections of museum patrons. He'd grown so accustomed to boots that the dress shoes with their paper-thin black socks felt weird, and he had to keep himself from shifting his stance. A young couple, though they probably weren't more than a year younger than he was, strolled past. Between ogling the relics, and fawning over each other, they snapped a thousand pictures and selfies.

Matt stepped back, allowing them room, his nose curling at the black-haired boy's musky cologne.

"Look at that one," the girl said, gesturing to a silver and black suit of armor with feathered wings rising from the back. The manner in which she held her hand up and the fresh sparkle to the diamond ring on her manicured finger screamed *newlywed*.

She snapped a picture of herself before the armor and continued her perusal of Hussar artifacts. Neither paid more than a moment's attention to the Polish war pick nestled among the other weapons. Just as well. Today would be a poor day for Ozkareen to bond with someone.

A tall man with a narrow head, and a light-colored suit stepped into the room. Despite his slender features, the pronounced belly poking out from the jacket made him look pregnant. He smiled in that well-practiced salesman way that all curators did and strode toward Matt.

"Señor Hollis?" he said, offering his hand. "Claudio Alamilla, I'm the … Assistant Curator while Señora Benitez is away."

Matt accepted it. Alamilla had a much stronger grip than he'd expected. "It's a pleasure to meet you."

"Please." He swept his hand toward the door. "Let us discuss this in my office. Would you care for a coffee?"

Matt eyed the long-handled pick resting behind its glass. While Master Schmidt had specifically instructed him not to let Ozkareen out of his sight, neither of the previous weapons had been absconded with during daylight hours. At least he was in the same building with it. Uwe sat in the car outside keeping watch. Tuerie was too long for the German to simply carry inside and leaving it in the car, especially while a weapon thief was on the loose, was simply out of the question.

Alamilla coughed lightly, his question still unanswered.

"Please." Matt sighed. "It's been a long morning."

"Did you arrive from Chile this morning?" Alamilla asked, leading him through the narrow museum, its walls trimmed with European moldings and peeping cherubs. The Galería de Monterrosa occupied a three-story building within Montevideo's oldest district, the Ciudad Vieja.

"Buenos Aires." Matt glanced down the wide staircase to the front doors where a tour group, evident by the yellow stickers on their shirts, clustered by the counter. "We took the ferry."

Alamilla inhaled deeply, nostrils flaring as if he liked what he smelled. "Beautiful drive." He pulled open a small iron and glass elevator door and offered it to Matt.

"It was." He stepped inside, having to slide Dämoren's bag a little behind him to allow room for them both to comfortably fit. The tiny cage groaned as it started down. They passed the first floor where the tourists were already shuffling past the rope gate as the elevator continued downward toward the basement.

"Do you intend to stay in our country very long?"

Either Alamilla was terrible at small talk or he was feeling Matt out, readying him for a delay. "Unfortunately not," Matt said, adding a hint of impatience to his voice. "I assume you spoke with Max Schmidt about our situation?"

Alamilla nodded. The elevator halted with a light jolt and he opened the door. "Yes, we spoke this morning. But as I explained to him, releasing the artifact requires more than a phone call. We have never met. There's liability involved."

"I see." Matt sat in a brown leather chair at Alamilla's desk. It was organized like a showroom, the papers, pen holder, a glass award, and a stack of wood inlay coasters all arranged with meticulous precision. It was the office of a man who did everything by the numbers. The fact that he'd taken Matt alone into this office at least meant that he didn't think this was a scam, or at least that Matt wasn't dangerous. He could work with that. "What will you require?"

Alamilla poured coffee from a stainless pot into a heavy porcelain cup. This guy took his coffee seriously. Matt liked that. "Cream? Sugar?"

"No, thank you."

The assistant curator gave an approving smile and offered the steaming cup. He sat on the opposite side of the desk. "With Señora Benitez on vacation, and without my being able to reach her, I'll require a physically signed order for release from your company, specifying you as the recipient, as well as identification for yourself."

Matt sipped his coffee with an understanding nod. "Understandable. Your attention for the relics is why we selected Galería de Monterrosa. I have my passport and company ID, so there's no problem there."

Alamilla drew a long, nasal breath. "However, the transfer paperwork from El Sable will require more time. Señor Schmidt said he would expedite it at once, but even same day delivery …" Another sniff. "It might not arrive until tomorrow."

Shit. If Schmidt drove like a bat out of hell to Copiapó, and

Matt knew the old man could, it'd still take him hours to deliver any paperwork to a courier. He likely had to send a similar release to Rio. The knights hadn't been able to reach him that morning, and Ester said that he'd left well before sunrise, so maybe the papers were inbound. Matt hid his frown behind a sip. The coffee was good. Not amazing, but still pretty good.

"Do you have a place to stay?" Alamilla asked.

Matt lied with a nod.

"I do apologize for the inconvenience, but had we warning …" He gave another annoying sniff. "The contract stipulates a week's notice prior to a display's removal."

"And we sincerely thank you for accommodating us," Matt said, ignoring the not-so-subtle blame-throw. "It is a legal issue with the previous owner's estate. It has gotten rather messy and we've found ourselves in a rushed situation. I promise this will not affect any of the other Hussar antiques on loan. Those were not part of the disputed estate. Only the nadziak."

Alamilla's shoulders seemed to relax at that. He drank some coffee. "Since it appears we will be waiting, I can call you once the release papers arrive and we can settle the transfer then."

"That won't be necessary. We're eager to collect it as soon as possible, so I'll stay until everything is in order."

After a week in the jungle, I can finally distinguish the faint line
stretching across the heavens, more slender than a spider's strand and
only visible at dawn or dusk. I cannot perceive it directly, but only in
the corner of my eye. Atik says it will become easier with practice. He
calls it a river of the gods. Once it intersects with many more, we will
have reached the holy place.

CHAPTER 14

Uwe twisted in his seat, adjusting his position. He'd been sitting in the car for two hours. Three, counting the drive up from Colonia. On the ferry ride across the Rio de la Plata, Uwe'd at least gotten to stretch his legs, walk across the deck some, but once they'd made landfall he'd been stuck here. It wasn't so bad. He wasn't one for pretending to be some museum official. Uwe preferred surveillance. He was built for it. No one noticed Uwe.

He'd always had the gift that no one took Uwe seriously. Luc was always serious. Serious to the point that when he wasn't, everyone was delighted, as if it were some rare celestial event. Luiza was as no-nonsense as they got. Always business with her. Uwe suspected that being a beautiful woman in a machismo family made her compensate too much. By default, Matt had to be serious, too. Otherwise he'd live in Luiza's shadow. Master Schmidt, well, Schmidt was probably born old. Part of why no one took Uwe seriously was that he was small. Small for a man. He was larger than the other women, except Ester, but she was fat and that wasn't really fair to her because she wasn't a knight. But that was beside the point. The point was that Uwe had always been small and he'd learned early on that people underestimate those they don't take seriously. So, Uwe had made an art of it. Whenever they all entered a room, all eyes moved to those he was with, and simply rolled past him. Optical Teflon. Uwe got to see how people really were when they weren't posturing to impress. Uwe liked that. It gave him the advantage.

He sucked the last dregs of melted ice from his plastic cup and wondered when he might get the chance to take a piss. *Hopefully soon.*

Pedestrians strolled past, a few glancing at the parked, silver sedan. The Ford stood out among the smaller Fiats and Suzukis. It looked official, a bit classy, but nothing too flashy— the kind of car the emissaries of an energy corporation might use, driven by boring-looking Uwe. Open magazine in his lap, Uwe scanned the mirrors, watching the streets outside.

Scaffolding encased the building behind him. The sidewalk tunneled through the construction zone. Movie posters completely plastered the tunnel's walls, the same one over and over again just in case someone missed the first fifty, maybe the fifty-first identical poster might catch their attention. Black fabric stretched over the upper floors, giving it a strange tent-like appearance with all the scaffolding poles pressing beneath it. No, not a tent, Uwe decided. A cocoon. Soon it would open and the restored building would emerge. Uwe smiled at that.

Uwe reached for his cup, remembered it was empty, and was about to return to pretending he was reading when a big, black Renault sedan pulled in front of him, a little crooked since there wasn't enough room for it. The front passenger door opened and a suited man stepped out, his eyes scanning the streets warily. Bodyguard?

Attention still on his surroundings, the man opened the rear door.

Curious as to who the important or self-important passenger might be, Uwe gave a surprised snort as a very tall and very slender priest stepped from the vehicle. The white rectangle of his collar seemed to glow against his black suit and black skin. He held an equally black case at his side, narrow, but a little bit longer than a briefcase. A strange disquiet rustled at the back of Uwe's memory. What priest travels with an entourage?

His suspicion flared in full-blown alarm when a small nun emerged from the opposite side with another bodyguard. The nun habits Uwe was familiar with had white at the throat and along the inside of the veil, but this one didn't. The only hint of color on her all-black attire was a deep burgundy, like dried wine, along the inside of her head scarf. The locking case at her side was narrow and long, and Uwe knew, *knew* in his bones what was inside it. "Oh, shit."

Scarecrow and Sister Gaze. The Order had but a single image of them, a ten-second black and white video captured in the Paris Underground the previous year.

But this couldn't be them. Why would the Exorcists be here? Why now?

There was one way to be sure. Uwe picked his phone up from the console, activated the camera, zoomed in on the pair and snapped a picture.

The nun's head swiveled instantly around, narrowed eyes locked on Uwe. The priest and the bodyguards looked up as well.

Say cheese. Uwe snapped a second picture and looked up from the phone's screen. He smiled that goofy half-grin that tourists get, the one reserved for bumbling past social etiquette. Not giving the Exorcists time to recognize him, if for some reason they might, he turned his attention to the side window and photographed a man walking a pair of dogs. Still playing it cool, he resisted the urge to look back at them as he took another picture, this one of some of some disheveled woman in a long, leather coat, staggering like she was high or drunk. She was glancing at the priests, too, like she was worried God might notice she'd been up to no good all night long.

He braved a peek back. The nun had turned away. Uwe scratched his chin, sucked the straw of his still-empty cup and pulled up his phone's contact list.

"Tourists," Felisa grumbled as the bug-eyed photographer smiled stupidly and began taking pictures of something else. Dogs? There was something about him. Something familiar with that round head and wavy brown hair.

"Is something wrong?" Captain Koehl asked.

"Nothing." She turned her attention back to the stone-faced building with ornamental columns framing its windows. A café occupied the building on its left, a boutique to its right. The brass letters across the door read, "Galería de Monterrosa." While it fancied itself a museum, the Jesuit brother that had investigated it had said the business served as a retailer. Many of the artifacts inside were also for sale. Felisa prayed that was the case for the gold-hilted *spada da lato*. A simple purchase would make things much easier.

Kofi gave a nod and Corporal Yoder drove away to find a suitable parking space. He removed his sunglasses and looked down to Felisa. "Ready?"

"After you, Paladin."

Kofi strode toward the entrance, holding the door for her, Koehl and Gast in tow.

The small mountain is unlike anything I have ever encountered. As we cleared the grass and trees along its slopes, I realized it to be a solitary, flat-topped pyramid. The enormous blocks that form it are all unique in size and shape and perfectly fitted in a maddening pattern as if once solid, but now shattered, a puzzle hewn from stone. I can just make out God's rivers crisscrossing high above. We will begin work at dawn.

CHAPTER 15

After his first hour standing watch over Ozkareen, pacing around the room as tourists shuffled past, Matt had come to the decision that El Sable Energy would donate chairs, or at least a few benches, to any future museums displaying their weapons. He could hike or run for hours, yet thirty minutes of standing, especially in these shoes, and he was in agony. He thought of bankers standing behind a counter all day and wondered how in the hell they did it. As one hour bled into another, his strolling perimeter widened, stretching across the entire museum's second floor, but never leaving it.

Schmidt had phoned, saying the release forms were en route. He also said that once this affair was over, the Order would begin grooming Matt to be the American museum liaison, a position he'd dreamed of for years. Clay had taught him the antique business, using it as their cover and also making some good money on the side while doing it. He knew Clay would be proud.

Matt couldn't wait. He'd travel and visit museums from Chile to Canada. Maybe make a road trip out of it. Take Luiza and Gabi and spend a few months living on the road, seeing the sights, living in hotels, hunting along the way, just like he and Clay used to do. The image of Gabi's face as she looked over the Grand Canyon made him smile and he dreamed of more for her to see.

Matt's phone buzzed loudly in his jacket pocket, interrupting the fantasy. He drew it out and saw a message from Uwe. He probably needed to take a leak. Matt felt tinge of guilt that he'd forgotten to offer first. He was already moving toward the stairs when he opened the text, and froze.

"Huge problem!"

A second message arrived a moment later. A picture.

Matt opened the attachment and stared at it for a long second, eyes widening as he realized what it was. A group of dark-suited men stood before a building, their backs to the camera. In the foreground, a young nun turned her head, the dark shawl billowing with the movement. Fierce eyes stared directly into the camera. Behind her, above the men's heads was "Galería de Monterrosa" in large letters.

"Son of a bitch."

A second picture came through, this one where all the suited men had turned toward the camera, two gazing past it; the third, a slender African with a white priest collar, looked at the nun. Her piercing eyes were still locked on the camera. Matt knew who she was before he even registered the black cases in hers and the priest's hands. The goddamn Vatican had arrived.

"What the hell are you doing here?" Matt looked up from his phone to see them below, moving past the ticket counter and starting up the stairs. The priest, the nun, and two men who looked like government spooks. The corners of their jackets didn't swing naturally, meaning they'd sewn weights into them to keep pistols concealed.

Oh, shit. Averting his eyes, Matt turned and walked toward Ozkareen's display, forcing himself to look as casual as possible. Reaching the side room, he risked a peek behind him. The priest, Scarecrow they called him, had broken off. One of the suits headed up to the third floor. The other suit and Sister Gaze stopped on the second floor and started in his direction. Matt hurried into the display room. There were no exits here. A pair of middle-aged woman were quietly perusing the displays, completely ignorant of the massive shit storm that was about to come down. Matt maneuvered himself between the doorway and Ozkareen. He slipped his hand into the slit along the side of Dämoren's satchel and gripped the revolver.

There was no way this was chance. The Church had to know what the nadziak was. Were they the ones stealing the weapons, or were they here to take it before anyone else could? Either way, it wasn't theirs to take. Matt coughed, cocking Dämoren's hammer as he did. Three soft clicks and the gun was ready. Christ, they couldn't have a shootout here. The museum knew his name. They knew El Sable. What the fuck was he supposed to do?

Think, Matt! Think!

The nun and the suit rounded the corner, their eyes scanning the cases. As her name implied, Sister Gaze spotted him first. Picking up on her, the suit froze as well, and turned his attention on Matt, his hand not so subtly inside his attaché. The man's hand started toward his jacket, but Matt swiveled the satchel toward him.

The man tightened his jaw.

"Careful, Gast," Sister Gaze said. Matt didn't recognize the language, but that didn't matter for him. "Hands at your side."

"Who is this?" Gast asked.

She smiled, predatory yet respectful, like a tiger nodding to another, a disputed kill between them. A creepy expression for a nun. Her gray-green eyes studied Matt, sizing him up. "This is the gunman."

Hernando's guts roiled at the overwhelming songs. Long before he'd even reached the city, he'd known that this was the place. Demons, more than he'd ever encountered over all his years, an army of the damned, gathered to the west. A smaller force of accursed weapons staged themselves within the city, their chaotically shrill songs calling and taunting him. How many there were, he couldn't say. At first, he thought four, but then six. Six weapons, all in the same city. He'd never imagined such an amassing of power.

With the silver dagger in his vehicle, shrieking its horrible *tre-le-la-le-le-la*, he'd worried that he wouldn't hear Redemptor's call. It didn't matter. He knew where she was. But now, among this symphony of madness, the dagger's song was only one of many. Unable to think above the cacophony and his vision blurring, he'd left the car and its singing occupant in Toledo, an outlying village unworthy of its namesake. Like himself, Redemptor, the first Redemptor, had been born in Toledo, Spain. How dare these peasants soil its great name. Once he had her, and the monsters had been harvested, Hernando would return, reclaim the dagger, and destroy this imposter Toledo. Its citizens would feed Redemptor's hunger.

At first, the weapons were spread out, but as Hernando neared the museum, he could hear them converging, their united songs becoming one. Rome knew he still lived. They were readying for him. Fools. They did not understand. He'd told them, but still they denied the truth. Denied God.

They could never block him from Redemptor. They'd tried to kill him and failed. How many more must die before they confessed the truth?

His head swimming from the songs, he stopped at a corner. Across the brick-paved street, a priest and sister exited a black car. Paladins. Even if he couldn't hear the wailing of their pathetically concealed weapons, he would have known. They were warriors. Their statures dripped of arrogance. Pride was a sin and all sins were equal in God's infinite wisdom.

He thought of the tanto hidden beneath his lambskin coat. He could kill these two before they even knew that he was here. Even with their devil's blades and his weakened state, he could best them before they could draw. He was faster, stronger. But no. No, like the blades, like the Church, the Paladins were deceivers. They'd deceived him once, cut off his hand, stolen Redemptor, impaled him, and locked him in a box. They would never trick him again.

Hernando sensed their trap. Heard it. There was a third weapon outside the museum. He had noticed the automobile behind the paladins but now focused on the man fidgeting with his mobile. Hernando hadn't registered him at first, but now he recognized another warrior. He too had a weapon.

Hernando smiled. He could play the game of deception. No, he wouldn't take this easy kill, this pathetic trap. The paladins were looking for a man, but he still wore the face of Esperanza Garcia. The advantage was his.

The paladins walked into the museum, followed by a pair of stewards. Hernando straightened, suppressed his pain and discomfort, forced the music to flow past him, and followed.

I have completed construction of the forge atop the pyramid. While well crafted, the original was inadequate for my needs. Atik has spent the days grinding the powder he says will contain the spirit until we can bind it.

Once the ceremony has begun, we cannot sleep or leave the circle until Redemptor is resurrected, otherwise the entity will seize us.

CHAPTER 16

"There are cameras all over us," Matt said, keeping his voice confident and steady. "So we're going to behave ourselves, right?"

The little nun stared at him for five full seconds, her dark eyes large and calculating. Finally, she gave a single nod. "Agreed."

"Hands away from the radio, Gast," Matt said to the suit whose posture showed he'd been considering it. The man gave a tiny wince at hearing his name. Good.

"Do as he says," Sister Gaze ordered, her plump lips completely expressionless.

The two women in the room had ceased their perusing and now watched the little standoff with increasing attention. Matt relaxed his grip on Dämoren, but didn't remove his hand from the satchel. "Fancy meeting you here," he said in friendly Italian.

Picking up on the cue, Sister Gaze smiled warmly, revealing white teeth, a small gap between the front two. "Indeed it is. May we step inside? No need for us to block the entrance, is there? We are friends, after all." Despite the pleasant smile, her eyes were anything but warm.

Gast wasn't even trying to act.

"Of course." Matt took a single step back, maintaining his position between them and Ozkareen's display. The phone in his pocket began buzzing. Probably Uwe freaking out. Matt ignored it. Uwe was too smart to come charging inside. He'd notify the Order, wait, and worry.

Placing her hand on Gast's arm, she led him into the room, stopping only a few feet from Matt. "So what brings you to Uruguay, Mister...?"

"Davis," Matt said.

"No." Her brows drew together. "That's not it. Hollis, correct?"

Matt nodded. If the nun wanted to shake him up, she'd have to try harder than simply knowing his name. The Order had taken that honor when they'd first tracked him down three years ago. "I don't believe we've met. Sister...?"

"Paladin," she corrected. "Paladin Felisa Gaspari. And you haven't answered my question. Why are you here?"

The two women strolled from the room, leaving them alone. If this paladin and her partner were going to try something, now was the time.

"Just enjoying the sights," Matt said. "Wonderful seafood. There's a café along the boardwalk. I highly recommend you try it. You should go there now. They fill up fast."

Her mouth curled into an approximation of a smile. She stepped to the side, leaning to peek behind Matt. "What are you hiding?"

"Nothing that's yours," he said, repositioning himself to block her view. She and Gast were now standing too far apart for his comfort. If they made a break to get on either side of him, he'd only get one before the other could get their weapon out.

"This is a dangerous game, Mister Hollis. Whatever you believe that is, I swear to you that it isn't."

Matt snorted. He took another step, his back now against the glass case. "You'll have to try harder than that. The Order has—"

Gast cocked his head. "Captain Koehl has found it."

Felisa broke eye contact for the first time as she glanced at her partner. "Are you sure?"

"Are you instructing me to radio for verification?"

"Stay off that radio," Matt growled. "Found what? Why are *you* here?"

Felisa looked at him again, seeming to reappraise him, more curious than cautious this time. "You're not here for the sword."

Matt blinked. Now *that* shook him. What sword, he was about to ask, but then the alarms began to blare.

His jaw clenched, Hernando slid his money across the marble counter. "No change," he said as the middle-aged woman reached into her till. Weapon songs shrieked in all directions—the man in the car outside, the black priest strolling into the gallery ahead, the nun ascending the stairs, the blond man atop the stairs, and two more above him. Their merging melodies roared in his mind, a single maddening song. He had to be careful. Enemies were everywhere.

The woman offered a pink ticket in her loose-skinned fingers. She said something, but Hernando didn't hear it. She was already looking at the next person in line as he accepted it.

He started up the stairs, gripping the brass rail to steady his shaking hand. The nun and the blond man were on the second floor, gathering near one of the unseen weapons. Surely this was the one, but as he reached the landing, Hernando recognized a familiar melody. *Dee-o-ri-la. Dee-o-ri-la.* His heart seized and began pounding harder, thumping in his ears. Redemptor was here! She called to him from the third floor.

Resisting the mounting desire to run, he continued up. Sweat poured down his face. His pulse hammered with each step, falling in time with her song. How could he have ever mistaken another for her melody?

He pushed past a quartet of tourists, lost in their guidebooks at the top of the landing. His wrist throbbed where it had been severed the last time he'd held her.

Stepping through an arched doorway, he found himself inside a large room. Armor, crossbows, cooking utensils, powder horns, a hundred other relics of the Great Conquest filled the cases along the walls and long tables at the center.

Redemptor's song roared from an upright glass case.

A suited man stood before it. One of the Paladins' stewards. He spoke into his black lapel. "This is Koehl. I've located it on the third floor."

Hernando moved behind him. There, on a glass shelf between mortal weapons, he saw her, his heart leaping and aching at once. Rusted spots pitted her blade. Her gold hilt gleamed, but a warped bend in her branch showed that the knuckle guard had been damaged and ineptly corrected. A long split ran along her wooden grip now dull with age.

He stifled a moan. *Oh, what have they done to you?*

Redemptor's song rose with demanding fury. She hungered.

The steward's head turned as if sensing the woman standing directly behind him. Hernando slammed the man's head through the glass. The man fell to the floor, blood streaming from his face. Deaf to the screams and wailing alarms, Hernando reached inside and reclaimed his love.

The terrible music ceased. Chaos washed away in one glorious instant. With perfect clarity, he could hear each of the devil blades around him with laser precision, where they were, how they faced. He could almost see them through the walls. Redemptor was in no condition to face them. She required sacrifice.

The injured man on the floor reached into his jacket. Hernando plunged Redemptor into the steward's chest, feeling the ribs crack. Pale light sprang from the wound like luminous vapor, visible for only an instant before the thirsty blade drank his heretical soul.

Redemptor shared none of the man's strength. She was too weakened to spare any of the meager essence, but a tingling shock flowed up Hernando's arm and burst within his skull.

The life of Captain Lionel Koehl of the Swiss Guard opened within Hernando's mind. All his secrets and passions were now Hernando's. But there was no time to explore these blooming memories. The weapons were moving. He had to escape.

The necessity for stealth now gone, he ran at his full speed. Moving faster than any human, he knocked one man down the stairs as he raced to the second floor before his enemies could cut him off. A woman screamed behind him, but Hernando didn't look. He ran down the second flight.

A blue-uniformed security guard hurried out from behind the counter, clawing for a baton at his belt. Hernando threw his open hand toward the closing guard. Cold power surged down his arm, gathered in the steel cuff on his wrist, and a released with a blast of air from his open palm. The guard launched back as if he'd been kicked by a horse and went sprawling across the floor, the baton skittering away.

A young woman dove away from the door and Hernando closed in. He wrenched the door open and stepped outside into the cool afternoon air. Cars moved along the street, ignorant or indifferent to the ringing alarm. A few pedestrians stood on the opposite sidewalk with open curiosity.

The warrior stationed outside had emerged from his vehicle. He stood beside the open car door, eyes wide with shock or befuddlement. Lionel Koehl had no memory of this man, who he was, or what accursed blade he wielded. Obviously, the Paladins had kept their men ignorant of their full numbers out of fear of Hernando harvesting their memories. Their pathetic attempts at subterfuge only disgusted him.

The other weapons were closing in behind him. But this man, who had failed his task at spotting him, was alone. Vulnerable. Hernando lifted Redemptor, still stained with Koehl's blood, and charged.

Three days without sleep. My mouth is numb from the leaves Atik and I chewed as we worked, my hammering in time with his ceaseless chanting. Redemptor lives! She is more beautiful than ever, and I have been reborn with her. I cannot mourn Atik's death. He is part of me now.

CHAPTER 17

Matt flinched from the sudden clanging of alarm bells. Instinctively, he glanced back long enough to verify that Ozkareen was still in its case behind him. Felisa and Gast seized that moment to turn and run.

What the hell was going on? Part of him suspected the Exorcists might be trying to lure him away from the holy war pick, but a woman's scream overrode that idea. Still gripping Dämoren inside her satchel, Matt hurried out after Felisa and Gast.

Most of the museum patrons simply stood looking around in confusion and getting in the way. Others, following the hunters' lead, ran toward the exits. Matt rounded the corner in time to see a man in a green shirt tumbling down the stairs and crashed into the floor. A woman in a flapping leather trench coat streaked down behind him, clutching a blood-stained sword. She turned at the landing and raced down with impossible speed, like an Olympic sprinter on fast-forward.

What the hell?

Shouting patrons scattered. The two women from earlier almost plowed Matt over as they clambered to escape the sword-wielding woman.

"Move!" he shouted, shouldering through the crowd. Matt started down the stairs just behind Felisa and Gast. Ahead, a security officer rushed to intercept the thief. The swordswoman threw out her open hand and the guard flew back as if he'd been hit by an invisible car. His cap flipped straight up into air before falling to the floor.

The woman yanked the door open and fled out into the street.

Matt raced to keep up with her, but knew there was no chance. Scarecrow was the first one to the door. Matt leaped down the last four steps and charged after him.

The clanging of metal greeted him as he reached the door. Uwe and the swordswoman were in the street. The woman hacked and thrust her blade into Tuerie's shield with a machine gun fury of blows, each one jolting Uwe back against the car.

Matt froze. A lifetime of Clay's training battered his instincts. If he fired Dämoren here he might save Uwe, but witnesses packed the street. The gallery knew who he was and police were probably en route. He wouldn't escape. *No!* Uwe needed him.

Scarecrow didn't have such scruples. Before Matt could act, the slender priest reached for the flat case in his hand. There must have been some kind of trigger in the handle because it seemed to pop open automatically. A short, engraved axe with a narrow, chisel-like blade launched into the priest's open hand. He hurled it, not at the sword woman, but off to the side. The weapon spun through the air, nearly across the street and began curving its flight around.

At the same instant, Felisa charged forward, her own leather case springing open. She drew a broadsword that looked half a size too big for such a little woman and raised it high.

The swordswoman spun away from Uwe's spear thrust. She sidekicked Tuerie's force field, knocking the German back. Her cheeks puffed as she blew at the closing paladin. As if anticipating it, Felisa sprang to the side, dodging the distorted cone of air bursting from the swordswoman's pursed plump lips. Ice crackled across the rear of a black car, cracking a tail light as the woman's breath hit it.

Matt drew Dämoren from his satchel and lifted her. But

there wasn't a clear shot with all these damn people gawking at the swordfight. Gast had a black automatic out. He raised it, but scowled. He moved to the side to get a clear line of sight but Matt couldn't see one.

Scarecrow wrenched his empty hand like he was pulling a rope and the flying axe shot toward him, dipping its arc toward the swordswoman's back. The woman wheeled to face it, and batted it aside with her sword. The deflected axe smashed into the windshield of Matt and Uwe's rental, flipped up, and sailed into Scarecrow's empty hand.

Seizing the opening, Felisa dove forward, thrusting her blade at the swordswoman's back. The swordswoman leaped away, landing on the hood of a car that had stopped to watch. Metal buckled from the impact. A car horn blared.

Matt brought Dämoren up, placing her chest directly in the revolver's sight, but then the swordswoman was running, dodging between cars at easily fifty miles an hour.

"Son of a bitch," Matt said as she shot around a corner and was gone. Who the hell was this? Praying that all eyes had been on her instead of him, Matt tucked Dämoren back into her satchel and out of sight. He jogged to where Uwe was crawling to his feet.

"Shit!" Felisa shouted.

Matt offered Uwe a hand. "You all right, man?"

Panting, Uwe pulled himself up to his feet. "The fuck was that about?" He gripped his spear as Felisa marched up, her sword at her side. The museum alarm was still ringing.

"Why didn't you shoot him?" Felisa demanded.

Matt straightened. "Because he's with me."

"Not him!" She pointed down the street. "The woman … she's not a woman."

"Could have fooled Uwe." Uwe glanced at the priest and Gast closing in. "Matt?" he said, a wary edge to his voice.

"I don't think they're after us." He looked at Felisa. "You're not after us, right?"

"We need to go." Scarecrow said, his accent sort of British, but not really. He bent and picked up Felisa's dropped case. "Where is Koehl?"

Gast got on his radio. "Captain? Do you read?"

"Find out where Yoder is." Felisa winced. "Tell him to get here. We have to go." She winced again, and Matt noticed the man aiming his phone camera at them. "You need to come with us," she said to Matt. "Both of you."

Matt laughed. "You need to tell me what in the hell just happened. Who are you and who the hell was that?"

Scarecrow was looking at them. "Valducans?" It sounded like *Valdookhanz*.

"That a problem?" Uwe asked.

Felisa shot Matt a glare that Luiza would have envied. "Whatever rivalry you imagine we have, you need to put it aside. We have a bigger problem and the authorities are on their way."

"The Captain isn't responding," Gast said.

"Then find him!" Felisa snapped, and Gast went running back into the gallery.

"We're not leaving," Matt said. "I shouldn't even be talking to you right now."

"Please," Scarecrow urged. His axe was already back in its case. "There is something terrible coming. We must stick together."

"Tell me why."

"Because," he said with the calm, regretful manner of a surgeon delivering the news of a loved one's passing, "as of right now we are being hunted."

"Hunted by that woman?" Matt asked.

Scarecrow shook his head. "That was no woman, and yes, it is hunting you and the angel you protect."

"Matt," Uwe whispered. "We should go."

"What?"

Uwe swallowed. "You didn't fight her. She would have killed Uwe if they hadn't chased her. And if they wanted to attack us, they would have by now."

"Finally, one of you understands," Felisa said. "We'll explain everything, but we need to leave and get somewhere safe."

"You're the one who isn't listening," Matt said. "I. Can't. Leave."

Understanding dawned in Felisa's gray-green eyes, cooling the anger. "There's another weapon inside."

Matt didn't answer.

Scarecrow's eyes widened. "We need to get it away from here."

"I was working on that when you showed up," Matt said.

"Just in time to save your partner," Felisa said. Matt was about to reply but she cut him off. "Stay then. Get the weapon out. But it's vital that we talk."

Gast raced back, his face grim. "Captain is dead. Yoder is on his way."

"How soon can you recover the weapon?" Felisa asked.

"After this?" Matt laughed humorlessly. "I have no clue. It should have been another hour, but now … I just hope it's today."

"Very well. We'll contact you once you have it."

I slew a jaguar today. Redemptor drew in its soul, that sliver of divinity, and offered it to me in communion. I can feel its power inside me. Its memories are mine. If I consume a jaguar and become a jaguar, what else might I become?

CHAPTER 18

All things considered, Matt decided as he adjusted his cuffed wrists, was that going back inside Galería de Monterrosa had been a mistake. It wasn't that Uwe hadn't tried to talk him out of it. He had. The problem was that Matt had been pissed off at the situation and couldn't bear the idea that a simple mission was bust. Bombshell, Clay used to call it.

First, they'd had to scrap the eel hunt. That had started it. Then a simple pick-up and retrieve had been delayed because the curator was on vacation. The appearance of the Exorcists and a public swordfight must have just scrambled his brain. Because all he could think was the inarguable fact that a holy weapon was in danger, and he had to get it out.

On some subconscious level he must have known what was going to happen. Before he'd walked back in, Matt had done something so rare that he could count the instances on his fingers. He'd handed Dämoren to another, entrusting her to Uwe for safekeeping. It was a good call because the police hadn't seized her. But it was stupid as all hell because Uwe was now all alone with two holy weapons, a car with a busted windshield, in a city with two Vatican hunters and some batshit murderous swordswoman who might not be a woman or even human.

Now Matt was sitting in a police interrogation room as the only suspect in a murder and theft.

The room was about eight feet by ten, walls the chalky color of a yellow SweetTART, wire-reinforced window in the door, and a heavy-duty camera up in the corner. It was clean and about five degrees colder than comfortable. It smelled of some bleachy cleaner and the lingering cigarette smoke on the officer seated across from him.

"Señor Hollis," Detective Alonzo said as if summoning some deep reserve of patience, "we have you on video speaking with a nun and a suited man. You don't know who they are?"

Matt shifted his handcuffs. The right shackle was cutting off circulation. His hand throbbed with each heartbeat. "No, sir. I've never met them before."

Alonzo nodded. Most people looked silly in berets, but this guy was born for it. He looked great. The thick moustache was a nice completion to the image. "You had a disagreement?"

"A misunderstanding." Matt sighed. He'd perfected it during traffic stops when he *really* didn't want anyone to check his trunk. Endearing, yet resigned. "They evidently knew my company. The suited guy said something rude, not realizing that I spoke Italian."

"What did he say?"

"He referred to me as a testicle."

Alonzo's moustache twitched with a momentary amusement.

"I overheard it," Matt explained. "My company is very involved in the antique trade, and there are more than a few rivalries."

"El Sable?"

"Yes," Matt said. "They mistook me for a potential buyer and things didn't start off too well."

"And a Catholic nun referred to you as a testicle?"

Matt chuckled. "I'm sure you've met a few nuns with a mean streak before."

The moustache twitched again. "So, they were there to purchase a sword?"

"I assume so. I was there to retrieve a Polish war pick we

had on loan there. The man said that the sword they wanted was on the third floor."

"And the sword that was taken and used to murder Señor Koehl was it?"

"I wouldn't know. I was only there to pick up our property. Claudio Alamilla at the museum can verify that. I'd planned to have left long before the incident, but there was a delay in paperwork. You know how that goes?"

Detective Alonzo's eyes narrowed, seemingly immune at Matt's attempt to bond over red tape being a common enemy. "Tell me why you chased the murderer."

"Honestly, I have no idea. At first, I thought it was a fire alarm, but then I saw the woman strike the guard, so I chased her. Swept up in the moment, I suppose."

The detective nodded, but nothing about him looked like he believed him. "One witness says that you had a firearm."

"I'm … sorry." Matt opened his palms resting on the table. "I didn't have a gun."

"You had a shoulder briefcase in the video. What happened to it?"

Shit. He'd really hoped they hadn't noticed that detail. "I don't know. I must have dropped it during the confusion."

"Dropped it?"

"I suppose."

Alonzo snorted. The interview continued for another hour, the questions varying from repetitions of earlier ones, looking for holes, to very pointed attacks on Matt's crumbling lies. Matt suspected, more than a little, that had he not been established as being with a foreign energy corporation, and therefore well connected, that the interrogation might have included more than just words. Finally, after Matt had accidently admitted that he had spoken with the man seen outside holding a spear, Detective Alonzo left to make some calls.

Matt cursed to himself, trying to hide his obvious irritation from the watching camera. Master Schmidt had to have known by now that he was in custody. But what could they do? This might take more than a few bribes, and Matt was well and truly fucked. Luiza was going to kill him.

On the bright side, there were probably worse jails he could be in. It might have been Colombia, or Mexico, or Kentucky. So there was at least that.

His stomach rumbled. When was the last time he ate anything? It was near dinner time and he'd skipped lunch and had a very early breakfast. Matt wondered what sort of food they had here. Would they let him have dinner, or was he going to have to wait for morning breakfast? His stomach actually growled again at the thought of South American prison food.

The door opened and a new officer walked inside, this one wearing a suit, which wasn't a good sign because it obviously meant he'd upgraded to management.

"Señor Hollis, my name is Captain Edgar Silva. I deeply apologize about your treatment." He removed a long handcuff key from his pocket.

"Um … that's all right," Matt said, wondering where this little game was headed.

Silva unlocked the unlocked the cuffs and slid them into his pocket. "We had no idea who you were, but once the President's office called …" he chuckled reticently. "Let's get you processed and out of here."

Matt had no idea what this guy was talking about, but decided to go with it. "It's understandable. No harm done." He followed the captain out of the interrogation room and through the station. Detective Alonzo sat at a desk, phone to his ear, and pointedly not looking in Matt's direction.

Once his effects had been returned, including a small staghorn knife that had raised a few eyebrows and several questions during interrogation, Silva offered Matt a ride to his hotel or wherever he needed to go.

"Back to Galería de Monterrosa," Matt said.

The two officers in the front of the police car didn't utter a word on the drive back to the museum. Red and yellow tinged the western clouds and the streets were notably less busy than they had been earlier, the fleeting reprieve between day and night traffic, separating business and playtime.

Not willing to check his messages while still in custody, Matt watched the road for any sign of Uwe, the Exorcists, or the swordswoman, but seeing none. He still wasn't entirely convinced they'd released him. What the hell had Schmidt done to get the president involved? Offered a percentage of El Sable? No, there was no way.

A single squad car sat outside the gallery's entrance when they arrived. The officers pulled in behind it and they let Matt go with nothing more than a simple, "Have a good evening."

Matt unlocked his phone. Eight missed calls in the last three hours. He started with Luiza—she was probably worried sick—but it went straight to voicemail. Judging by the time, she and Luc were probably already in the air, flying back to Buenos Aires, Feuertod under their protection.

"Hey baby, it's me. Police let me out. Not sure what Schmidt or Turgen did, but they let me go. Call me once you land. Love you."

Next, he called Uwe. No telling how freaked out he was, and Matt really wanted to be sure he and Dämoren were safe.

Uwe picked up on the second ring. *"That was quick."*

"I suppose that depends if you were the one in custody or not."

"Perhaps. Where are you?"

"Back at the museum." Matt headed toward the door, phone to his ear. He doubted he would even get inside with the investigation and everything that had happened, but he had to try. His stomach growled, telling him what the next stop would be with a dull pang.

"Good. Uwe's on his way. They should be expecting you." Uwe hung up before Matt could even ask what in the hell had happened.

A sign on the door read, "Closed until further notice." White plastic covered the windows, probably to keep tourists or media from peeking inside. There wasn't any buzzer, so Matt knocked.

A corner of the improvised curtain pulled back, and a man's dark eye peered at him. The lock clicked and Claudio Alamilla opened the door.

"Señor Hollis." His tie was gone and the bags beneath Alamilla's eyes and ruffled hair made him look like he'd been up for days. "Please come inside."

Matt stepped in from the cold. He wasn't sure what he'd expected when he walked in. Maybe tripods of lights and paths of colored tape like in cop shows, but aside from a line of half-empty coffee cups on the ticket counter and a brown cardboard box, the lobby appeared perfectly normal.

Alamilla glance up and down the street, and shut the door, locking it. "I'm terribly sorry about the confusion earlier." Sniff. "Horrible business."

"Hardly your fault, Señor Alamilla. I realize it's been a bad day, I can't imagine how difficult it's been, but did the courier—?"

"He did," Alamilla blurted. "The release papers arrived while you were, um, detained. I have it ready for you." He stepped over to the wide flat box and opened it. "I haven't fully packed it because you'll need to complete the final inspection."

Still not sure what in the hell was going on, Matt followed him to the counter. There, inside the box, Ozkareen rested between taped bundles of bubble wrap. Intricately engraved lines accented with silver ran along its narrow handle and crisscrossed at the head, decorating the square hammer and tapering pick.

He lifted it from its recess and turned it over in his hands. While elegantly crafted and in miraculous shape for its age, he couldn't feel the entity residing within it. Malcolm was the only knight who could do that with aid of a tattoo on his palm, but Matt knew Ozkareen and this was him. "Looks good to me. Thank you."

Alamilla gave a polite smile. He offered a metal clipboard. "These are some forms I need you to sign and that should be everything."

Matt filled in the appropriate forms while Alamilla carefully wrapped the war pick in bubble wrap and began taping the box closed.

"Are there any leads in the theft?" Matt asked.

Alamilla sighed. "Nothing yet, but the case has been dropped." Sniff. "Police are still searching for the killer."

"Dropped?"

"Yes, the payment arrived an hour ago. Quite generous."

"I see. So, El Sable purchased the sword?"

The curator paused in his taping and gave Matt a puzzled look like he should know this. "No. The Archdiocese. Cardinal Larrosa delivered the payment personally."

"I see," Matt said, hiding his surprise with a smile. He licked his lips. "I hadn't realized it would be so prompt." Detective Alonzo had said the sixteenth century gold-hilted *espada ropera* was valued at five hundred thousand pesos, or a little over sixteen thousand dollars. Except for a few pictures, he knew nothing about it. "What was the agreed price?"

"Two million."

Matt blinked. "Very generous indeed. And the church is not pursuing the theft?"

"I don't believe so, but as I said, the murder investigation is still ongoing."

"Of course." Matt needed to talk to Master Schmidt immediately, find out what was going on. He was becoming more and more certain that it hadn't been the Order who had arranged his release with the Uruguayan president. Catholic nation, a cardinal personally buying a stolen sword; Matt was beginning to feel like a pawn on a very big chessboard. He scratched his final signature onto the forms. "Is there anything else?"

"This is all. Once again, Señor Hollis, I am terribly sorry for these events."

Matt thanked him and accepted the taped box. The pick's weight made it incredibly off balance. Tucking it under his arm, tight in case some running thief tried to snatch it away, he left. Wet, chilly wind coursed along the brick road, sweeping up papers and leaves in its passing. The sunset hues had brightened in the western sky and soon night would come. He'd hoped to have been back in BA by now.

"Matt!" Uwe emerged from a black sedan, one hand raised, Dämoren's satchel in the other.

Matt headed toward him. His guesses as to where Uwe had gotten the new car and who the figure in the driver's seat was were instantly confirmed as the door opened and a man with strawberry-blond hair and a familiar cut of black suit stepped out.

"Mister Hollis," the man said extending his hand. "Sergeant Johan Epple of the Swiss Guard." The late Lionel Koehl had also been Swiss Guard, or at least the ID police discovered on him had said so.

Matt glanced at Uwe who gave an assuring nod before he accepted the sergeant's hand. "I thought you guys wore orange and blue with silly hats."

Epple smiled weakly. Probably not first the time he'd heard that one. "Not always."

Uwe handed Matt his bag.

"Thanks." Matt unclasped the flap, making sure the revolver was still fine. *Sorry to have left you, girl.* "So how did you two get together?"

"He was following Uwe around. Uwe spotted him, of course." He shrugged. "Figured it would be easier if we rode together, and he has an intact windshield."

"So why were you spying on us?" Matt asked Epple.

"I wasn't spying," Epple said. "I was tasked with protecting Mister Rachow. Now that you've been released, I am to escort you to Paladins Aggrey and Gaspari."

Rachow? No one called Uwe by anything but his first name. He was like Sting or Beck. "And you were protecting him from what? Police? That swordswoman?"

"Apologies, sir, but that woman was no—"

"Woman. Yeah, I heard that one. So, it was a demon?"

"It is ... best if the Paladins explain the situation."

"So, no." Matt looked to Uwe. "Can we have a word?" He and Uwe stepped a few feet away.

Epple turned his attention to the street, scanning the windows and rooftops, hands clasped before him.

"Do you trust this guy?" Matt whispered, keeping the Swiss Guard in his peripheral.

The German shrugged. "Uwe called Master Schmidt. He says no, but told Uwe and you to find out what they have to say. We know someone stole the other weapons."

"So, they want us play diplomats." Matt sighed. The two of them were probably the last knights Schmidt or any of the Masters would have selected for this.

"Just a simple talk."

"Yeah, but the Vatican and the Order never really got along. This could go south."

Uwe shrugged again. "Uwe trusts him."

"Why?"

"Because Uwe isn't dead. And that bitch nearly killed him. They want the bitch dead and so does Uwe."

"Enemy of my enemy and all that?"

"That's how Uwe sees it."

"They tell you how they got me out of custody?"

"No. He just said it was taken care of."

"Presidential order to release me. Some cardinal bought the stolen sword for four times the value and the robbery charges went away."

"Must be nice. Uwe once had to ride out of Stockholm in the car trunk. They just make a phone call. Schmidt will have Luiza and Luc hold back until we say it's okay. Uwe has his tracker on. Yours ..." His eyes glanced at Dämoren's bag. "... in there."

Matt patted Uwe's shoulder. "Good man."

"Uwe knows this."

Matt turned back to Epple, still surveying the street. "So where are we headed?"

"Mister Rachow suggested Colonia."

That was just right across from Buenos Aires. *Good job, Uwe.* Matt motioned to the vehicle. "Can we grab food on the way?"

Only after I became one with Atik did I learn that the golden mask is all that protected his village from the monster prowling the jungle. He had prayed Redemptor would slay it once and for all. I will fulfill that prayer.

CHAPTER 19

Colonia del Sacramento, Uruguay

When Epple had told him that the Paladins has secured a church as their base of operations and home for their clandestine meeting, the first between the Order and the Vatican in centuries, Matt had expected something grand. Most likely the basilica in Colonia's historic quarter, something old and heavy, a place where history had been made. So when the car turned off Route 1 and started down a narrow asphalt road and not the cobbled streets he'd expected, he'd been a little surprised.

Low cinderblock homes lined the narrow street, many of the windows dark and empty. They passed the industrial park with its high, barbed wire fences, and rows of identical steel warehouses, and turned onto an unpaved street. Dust swirled in the car's tail lights as the tires rumbled over hard-packed dirt and rock. Homes dwindled fewer and fewer, and each less inviting than the last, some with dogs leaping and barking inside their questionably sturdy kennels.

A single yellow light glowed ahead like a beacon between scraggly trees. The road curved around and a small stone chapel came into view, sitting alone on the marshland, the lights of river boats moving in the distance beyond it. Scaffolding encased one half of the building. Stacks of lumber rested beneath it, blanketed with a fluttering paint-speckled tarp. A three-foot wall surrounded the property with a trio of small outbuildings off to one side. None of them had doors or roofs. It looked like every rundown, haunted church in every horror movie Matt had seen. If the paladins had wanted privacy, they'd most definitely succeeded.

If they want to pop us and roll our bodies into the river, they found the right place, too. The lingering itch that this was all some elaborate trap flared up again. He pushed it aside. If the Church intended to kill him, they'd have done it in Montevideo or on the road, not driven him a hundred miles to do it here. The itch persisted. Matt imagined being tied to a chair, some Inquisition-level shit being performed on his flesh. He tried to ignore it.

Epple stopped the car before a rusted gate. Gast stepped out from the shadow of a tree. His black suit with white shirt was so clean and pressed that it looked like he'd just put it on. The night vision monocular and suppressed MP7 submachine gun were new additions. Gast opened the gate and waved them on with a sweeping gesture that said, *Around back.*

Epple maneuvered the sedan past pallets of red, terracotta shingles and a rust-streaked water tank. He parked between a second car and a blackened burn pile, littered with half-melted bottles and the charred ends of tree branches. Insects orbited a tall light post near the back of the yard. "Welcome to Sagrada Sangre."

Sacred Blood, Matt thought. *Not the most comforting name at the moment.*

The chapel's rear door opened and Felisa and Scarecrow started down the crude ramp. Their weapons hung at their sides. Scarecrow appeared much the same, though the white collar was absent. A simple silver cross glinted below his neck. Felisa had abandoned her nun's uniform with its grandma shoes for tactical boots tucked into black pants. The black shirt was snug, but not tight. Simply comfortable and practical. Only the burgundy shawl betrayed her as a woman of the cloth and not some sword-swinging soldier. Almond-brown hair peeked from under the covering, her hairline coming to a sharp point at her forehead.

Matt stepped out. The tang of swamp tinged the chilly, humid air. He stood straight, trying to look confident. Last thing he needed was them to see insecurity.

Scarecrow extended a long-fingered hand. "Mister Hollis, I am Paladin Kofi Aggrey, husband to Salvatio. On behalf of His Holiness, thank you for coming."

Matt shook it. The rough calloused hands were those of a man who had worked hard his entire life. "Matt Hollis, protector of Dämoren. This is Uwe Rachow, protector of Tuerie."

Kofi inclined his bald head in a single, respectful bow. "A pleasure to meet you both. It is unfortunate that such circumstances were required to bridge the gap between us. And this is my colleague Paladin Felisa Gaspari, wife to Ofniel."

"Nice to see you again," Matt said, shaking her hand. Felisa's grip was hard. Crushing, even. Clay would have liked that.

"A handshake should be firm enough to squeeze out all the bullshit and let you get down to business," he used to say.

Felisa only nodded. "You have a third angel with you, yes?"

"We do."

"Good. Bring it inside with us. We have much to discuss."

"Who else is here?" Not moving, Matt scanned the shadows.

Felisa's lips drew into an impatient line.

"Corporal Gast at the gate," Kofi said. "Corporal Yoder is manning the belfry. You have met Sergeant Epple."

Matt glanced at the narrow steeple, highlighted with silvery moonlight. He didn't see anyone, which was probably the idea. "You always travel with bodyguards?"

Kofi smiled. His teeth were extremely white. "The Swiss Guard are a military regiment. We rarely use them, but circumstances have warranted it."

"And that man who was killed, he was Swiss Guard?"

The smile vanished. "Captain Koehl," he said, regret weighting his words.

"So, what circumstances warrant four soldiers?" Matt asked. "That woman?"

"Please," Kofi said, gesturing to the door. "Let us explain it inside. There isn't much time."

Matt glanced at Uwe. The German gave an agreeing nod. *We better be right about this.* Matt removed the cardboard box with Ozkareen and followed the paladins up the plywood ramp and into the church.

The smell of sawdust, age, and dampness permeated the old building. Passing a pair of small rooms, they entered the chapel. Clear plastic tarps hung from the walls like dusty tapestries. A tiny balcony, probably for a choir, overlooked the room. Plywood covered the round window behind it. There were no pews, just empty floor, the mismatched planks consisting of old, not as old, and fresh, alluding that the restoration had been started, abandoned, and recently been taken up again. A tile strip ran up the central length, most of the small, colored pieces missing. A big manual cutter sat off the right beside a stack of fresh tile. An underlying scent of garlic and tomato drew Matt's attention to a folding stove and dishes on a sawhorse table off to the left. Beside that, several wooden chairs, black canvas gun cases, a dog-eared paperback, and various other items had been arranged. *Looks like they're staying awhile.*

Felisa removed an open laptop from one of the chairs and began arranging them, two facing two. Matt grinned as he took the uncomfortable chair opposite her. No, the first conference between the Valducan knights and the Catholic Church since the Second Crusade wouldn't be held in grand surroundings, but in a place of restoration. There was an elegance to that.

"Can I offer you something to drink?" Kofi asked.

"Please," Matt answered before Uwe had time to think about it. Matt needed a drink and this situation called for one, maybe three. It had been a shitty day and he didn't see it getting better any time soon.

The paladin opened an Argentinean Malbec, and poured a healthy dose into four clear plastic cups. If Matt had known there was going to be such a meeting he'd have loved to have brought a bottle of the Valducan's blend, Château d'Épées. Most ended up in local cafés, but Matt enjoyed it. The Order had all but ceased production two years ago, but this was definitely the time to pop a bottle.

He lifted his cup in salute and sipped it. Definitely better than the Valducans' wine. "Before we begin, I have a question."

"Only one?" Felisa asked.

"How did you know who I was?"

She grunted. "We first became aware of you eight years ago. There was an incident in New Mexico."

"Albuquerque." Matt nodded.

"We tracked you for two years before losing the trail. I'd suspected the Valducans had recruited you when we heard your description in Paris last year. Mister Rachow we were aware of, but never knew his identity."

"Sir Uwe," Uwe corrected. He never liked going by titles, but Matt suspected the German might be feeling the need with paladins and their bodyguards.

Felisa gave a respectful nod. "My apologies. We had a photograph of Sir Uwe in Mumbai from 2014, but that was all."

Uwe shot Matt a sideways grin. "Uwe covers his tracks better."

Ignoring the jab, Matt sipped his wine. "How long have you been bonded to Ofniel?"

"Five years last March. I was twenty when he called to me."

Matt looked at Kofi.

"Four," he replied. "I was a steward under Paladin Egbo for the previous three."

"How many more Paladins are there?"

Felisa and Kofi exchanged a look. Conferring how much they should divulge. Matt was about to call them out on it, but Felisa answered first.

"Only ourselves."

"I see." He'd expected as much. While the Order knew almost nothing about the Vatican's hunters, they'd suspected no more than four weapons under the Church's protection. That meant two were likely sitting in a display or buried in a vault somewhere.

"And yourselves?" she asked.

Now it was Matt and Uwe's turn to share the look. If they were serious about opening a dialogue, then they should say it, but Matt wasn't going to make that call. Though he rarely acted the part, Uwe was technically in command, so Uwe could deal with it.

"We have five active knights in South America," Uwe said. "Two nearby waiting to hear from us."

"How many in total?" she asked.

Uwe licked his lips. "It's only our first date."

Felisa smiled, the gap in her teeth peeking for only a moment. "We should work on our trust."

"Our previous ... breakup didn't go very well."

"Does your order still cling to that old enmity?" she asked. "Things have changed, Sir Uwe. Whatever grievances we had were a long time ago. The men clutching those grudges are long buried. Paladin Kofi and myself have never held them and neither has His Holiness."

"Uwe is here." He gestured around the empty chapel. "First step is complete. Uwe thanks you for your help, but Uwe still doesn't know why we're here or who that bitch with the sword was."

Felisa's demeanor darkened. Those gray-green eyes studied Uwe, reassessing. "That *bitch* was no woman."

"Uwe has heard."

As if considering her next words, Felisa moved to sip her wine, but gulped back half her cup. "In 1532, the Holy Church dispatched Paladin Bartoli Amador to the New World. His ship was caught in a storm and Paladin Amador and his sacred sword Redemptor were lost at sea. His steward, Hernando de la Fuente, survived. He later worked as a blacksmith in Lima. He sent several correspondences during that time, begging to return to Rome but ..." She shook her head.

"No one wanted him?" Matt asked.

"He was excommunicated for the loss of Redemptor and his master."

Matt snorted. "Bit harsh."

"As I said, things have changed. In 1539, he joined an expedition, venturing deep into the jungle. Two years later he returned the only survivor and carrying Redemptor."

"So ..." Matt started, considering the gravity, "he reforged it?"

"Or so he claimed. He'd located a pyramid, an Incan holy place, but what he made was an abomination, powered by Hell itself. This false Redemptor twisted his soul, turned him into a monster."

"And you're sure it wasn't the same Redemptor remade?"

She scowled. "Impossible."

"Not really. Dämoren has been reforged twice. That's sort of her gift."

"No," Kofi said. "The sword he brought back was in no way Redemptor. Hernando's letters claimed that all of God's weapons were fueled by demons, that angels and demons were the same, and he could bend them to his will. He murdered men and took their souls. He could steal their likenesses. And when he found a true Weapon of God, he destroyed it, and took the power for himself."

Uwe's grip tightened on Tuerie leaning against his knee. "How?"

Kofi lifted his hand. A smooth, gold wedding ring glinted on his slender finger. "Jewelry. He bound demons and angels alike into jewelry, bracelets, rings, even his armor, though that was later destroyed."

Matt was lifting his cup for another sip but froze, the plastic rim just below his lip. Demon jewelry. He'd heard of this before. Hell, he'd experienced demon-bound masks several times. *I need to call Mal.*

"He destroyed holy weapons?" Uwe asked.

Kofi nodded. "Three that we know of."

"So, what happened to him?"

"After the paladin sent to stop him was killed, there was no one to protect the people from De la Fuente's wrath. He murdered priests, officials, anyone with power. In 1545, a Franciscan monk named Pedro Bernal forged a letter requesting negotiations between The Holy Church and De la Fuente. He arranged the meeting at Gran Arbol, a small church far outside of Quito, where De la Fuente was residing.

"De la Fuente had become paranoid, delusional, and the letter assured that no paladins would attend the negotiations. De la Fuente could sense sacred weapons, so he would know if it were a trap. Mortal weapons had yet to kill him. Once he arrived, he was ambushed by several farmers and soldiers. Some died, but they managed to sever the hand holding Redemptor. They locked him into a stone sarcophagus, and drove an iron spike through his heart. They then buried him in an unmarked grave."

Matt refilled his cup. "That's one way to do it." He offered some to Uwe but the German shook his head. Felisa accepted the last of the bottle.

The corners of Kofi's lips tightened into a frown. "In 1553, an earthquake and resulting mudslide destroyed Gran Arbol. Wiped it away."

"What happened to Redemptor?" Uwe asked.

"Lost. After De la Fuente was buried, Bernal realized it was gone. He believed one of the locals who had joined in the ambush had taken it as a prize. It was only now that we learned it was still intact."

Uwe grunted. "So, who was the bitch? She knew what it was."

"That," Felisa answered, "was Hernando de la Fuente."

"The woman?" Matt asked.

"Yes."

"So, he's undead?"

Felisa opened her hand in resignation. "We don't know for certain. We know he ate like a normal man, however his sleeping habits are unknown. We'd assumed he was mortal."

Matt grunted. While some demon-possessed could age slower, nearly all of them would succumb to time after five hundred years. "Why now? Why wait so long to make a move? And how did you know he was going to be there today? It seems a little odd that he just *happened* along at the same time we were there."

A hint of anger ignited in the young woman's eyes. "A pair of farmers found De la Fuente's sarcophagus in a creek bed. Their mangled bodies were discovered several days later. We first became aware after the Archbishop of Quito was murdered. We knew the killer was looking for Redemptor, but only learned of De la Fuente's escape once we arrived. Through … channels we learned that the sword might be in Uruguay. We'd hoped to purchased and destroy it before De la Fuente arrived. But you've never told us why *you* were there."

Matt held the Paladin's accusing gaze. "Two weeks ago, an Incan mace was stolen from a Colombian museum. Few days later, someone murdered a family in Brazil and took an antique Tibetan knife. We figured out that there was a shape-shifter involved, so we came to Uruguay to retrieve a holy weapon that we had on loan. After that, we planned to find out who was stealing them."

"Now you know," Kofi said, his voice doleful. "We had not known De la Fuente had already begun collecting divine weapons. Surely it was God's intention we meet when we did."

Matt shrugged. The first god he'd met was a horrible dragon-snake-thing with eels squirming out its back. He'd killed Tiamat with his bare hands, even licked up part of her brains. The next gods he'd encountered had been a pair of drunk homeless men squatting under a New Orleans bridge. One of them stole a truck and gave Matt the scariest ride of his life. He figured it was best not to mention that in a room of armed Catholics. "Works in mysterious ways."

Kofi lifted his plastic wine cup in agreement.

"What do we do about the weapons?" Uwe asked. "How do we find him?"

"He'll come to us," Felisa said.

"How do you know?"

"He can hear them, he said. Like music. Even across kilometers, demon or weapon alike, none can hide from him. He wants our weapons. He's probably heading here right now." She finished her wine, eyed the empty bottle by Matt's feet, then set her cup on the floor.

A cold shiver ran along Matt's spine. That's why they'd set up here, someplace remote, armed lookouts on the road and in the tower. He needed to make a blood compass. Luiza and Luc were out there somewhere, waiting to hear from him. He had to warn them.

"What else can you tell us?" Uwe asked.

"We'll give you what we have," Kofi said. The paladin's

calm demeanor while waiting for this monster to show up suddenly struck Matt as creepy as all hell. "His letters, his journal, everything."

"Electronic files?"

"Of course."

Uwe turned to Matt. "We need to make some phone calls."

"Are you certain we can trust them?" Luiza asked.

Phone to his ear, Matt scanned the shadows, spying Epple patrolling near the out-buildings, SMG at his side. The sergeant's attention was focused outside the low wall, and not on Matt hanging out by the cars. "Certain enough. Uwe definitely does, and he never trusts anybody."

Luiza was quiet, probably conferring with Luc. *"You better be right about this."*

"Agreed. Just don't forget my stuff."

"Already loaded, baby."

"Good. Uwe's checking out the paladins' files, making sure they're clean before sending them out."

"I thought he trusted them," she said, with a sarcastic hint to her voice.

"As much as Uwe trusts anyone. Look, once you see the church, flash your lights three times. The guy at the gate is named Corporal Gast. He'll let you in. Message me when you get close so I can meet you."

"Got it. Ferry lands in twenty minutes, so we'll be there soon. Love you."

"Love you, too." Matt clicked off the phone. Leaves rustled as a cold wind blew in from the Rio de la Plata. Pools of pale moonlight shone between the shuddering branches. A pair of birds broke from the high grass. Matt checked the fresh blood compass on the roof of the car.

Still pink.

He wasn't sure if the compass would react to demon jewelry or not. It did for demon masks, so he hoped that it would. Still, he felt naked out here. Exposed. Dämoren hung from her nylon shoulder rig. Twenty-three spare, bronze-cased shells filled the loops of his old police belt. But he'd left the Ingram back in BA, and while it probably wouldn't offer much in the way of protection, its absence was unsettling. It was a totem, a good luck charm even more then the staghorn blade strapped to his ankle. He'd left his warding powder back at the hangar, too. It'd probably do shit against jewelry, but there was still a chance. If he was going to face this immortal, evil paladin, Matt wanted every trick in the book. Especially any hints as to what they were about to face. Fortunately, he knew someone who might know.

Matt scrolled through his contacts and selected a number.

Doctor Malcolm Romero, voodoo priest, former Team Leader, and part-time Valducan knight, picked up on the fifth ring. The rapid beat of drums thumped through the speaker. *"Hey brother, what's going on?"*

"Hey, Mal. I got a problem."

"I figured. You've never called just to shoot the shit. Give me a minute, okay. It's a little loud here."

"Where are you?" Matt asked.

A distant, primal whoop sounded over the phone. More voices joined as the drums grew faster, but then muted as if a door closed off between them and Malcolm's phone.

"Sorry about that."

"Where are you?" Matt asked again.

"Oh, just a little celebration at Saints of Light. Nothing huge."

Matt recalled his first and only visit to the New Orleans voodoo church. Surreal didn't even begin to cover the night Malcolm banished a werewolf from his own body, the only person Matt knew of who had ever done that. But what Mal had done with the demon afterward was what interested him now.

"So what's going on? Any update on that weapon thief?" Malcolm asked.

"Yeah, you could say that," Matt said. "It's not Tiamat's cult, but that's the only good news."

Matt downloaded the day's events, the Exorcists, Uwe's attack, the truce with the paladins, and the tale of Hernando de la Fuente. Malcolm didn't utter a word as Matt laid it out.

"So, in short, this five-hundred-year-old motherfucker is

gunning for us," Matt said. "Now, you once told me about the idea of demon jewelry and even a demon weapon, remember?"

"*Intimately. But the idea of capturing an angel ...*" He blew a long sigh. "*That one's new.*"

"So?"

"*I guess it's possible. You're the one who says the beings in the weapons are some kind of higher demons, so why not? It's just trickier, that's all.*"

"Trickier how?" Matt asked.

"*Because a weapon isn't a living host. Break a weapon, and the spirit just gets away. Also, the spirit is way more powerful than any demon. It'd take some serious power to hold it long enough to bind it.*"

"Could you do it?"

Malcolm snorted. "*Doubtful. Best case, it'd escape the binding. Worst case, it'd probably kill me and still escape. Trapping a lamia laid me out for days, and that's nothing by comparison.*"

"All right," Matt said, a little comforted at the thought Malcolm couldn't trap weapons. "So, this jewelry, what can I expect? Does a vampire ring make him a vampire or what?"

"*Possible, but not exactly. The item wouldn't necessarily take on the specific powers of the entity within it. It's more of a focus.*"

"How do you mean?"

Malcolm was quiet for a few seconds. The muted drums played in the background. "*A demon mask can repel other demons, right? But a ghoul by itself could never force a more powerful demon to cower. But placing it into a focus, in this case a mask, gives it that power. Trap a more powerful demon and the mask is more powerful.*"

"So, it's a battery?"

"*Precisely. An electric battery could power a light, or a motor, or magnet. It doesn't matter as long as it's got enough juice to do the job. You bind a demon to a necklace, you're powering the necklace. Now what that necklace can do, I have no idea. I never tried it and don't plan to. It's too dangerous.*"

"Yeah," Matt agreed. He'd seen what happened when someone put on a demon mask. It seized possession and transformed them into a monster in mere seconds. No way would he put on anything trapping one of those. "Anything you can tell me about the jewelry itself?"

"*Not without seeing it. But demons can only be bound to the substances that weaken them. Jade for oni, silver for werewolves, etcetera. If you break the item, the demon's spirit escapes.*"

"So, unless we want to face the demon later on, don't break the jewelry."

"*Maybe,*" Malcolm grumbled. "*But leaving them in jewelry is simply delaying the inevitable. It's like holding on to a time bomb. Eventually someone is going to put it on.*"

"So says the guy who's made demon masks."

"*Point taken.*"

"What about my blood compass?" Matt asked. "Think it'll read them?"

"*I'd imagine so, but no promises.*"

"Good enough for me, I suppose." Matt noticed Epple coming around the churchyard again, having completed a full circle. He still wasn't paying the knight any attention. "So, you're not coming down?" Matt asked into the phone. "Schmidt said he was calling everyone back."

"*Just finishing up some affairs here first,*" Malcolm said. "*I'm heading down Thursday.*"

Uh-huh, Matt thought. *Don't rush yourself, or anything.* "Look forward to seeing you."

"*Me too, brother,*" Malcolm said, either not catching the sarcastic edge to Matt's voice, or choosing to ignore it. "*You be safe.*"

"Always am."

Malcolm snorted as the call ended.

Pocketing his phone, Matt surveyed the property again. Lots of shadows for someone to hide in. Too many for the three Swiss Guard, especially if the target could move like De la Fuente. They'd need to set up shifts if they were going to stay here. Hell, they needed to even if they weren't. They needed to be ready.

Already planning their arrangements, Matt walked back up the ramp and into the comforting light of the church. Uwe was off in a corner, leaning over his laptop. Felisa paced nearby, a phone to her ear. Kofi stood at the front door, hands clasped behind him as he stared out the window.

Matt peered over Uwe's shoulder. Looked to be a text file, but he couldn't read it. "They're on their way."

Felisa's hand shot up to shush him. She clamped the hand over her other ear. "I apologize. Can you repeat that?"

Uwe looked up from his screen, and whispered, "How long until they arrive?"

"Half an hour, I guess. You get a hold of Schmidt?"

Uwe nodded. "Uwe emailed him the files and also to Allan and Sonu. Maybe they can find something helpful."

"That what you're looking at? The journal?" Matt squinted, struggling to read the words on the screen. It appeared to be Italian. *Figures.*

"Yes, we will," Felisa said, her voice echoing around the vaulted room. "I'll let him know."

Uwe nodded. "It'll take hours to read it all."

"Can you translate it to English? My Italian isn't so hot."

"You speak it fine."

"I speak everything fine," Matt said. "Reading … different story. I have to hear it."

"Then read it aloud."

"I've told you, it doesn't work like that."

Uwe shrugged. "It might eventually."

"Maybe," Matt said, playing along. "But we don't have time."

"Good point. Uwe can run a translator on it."

"Thanks."

"Yes, Your Holiness," Felisa said. "Yes. And also with you." She hung up the phone.

Your Holiness? Matt turned to the small paladin pocketing her phone. "Was … was that the Pope?"

She shot him a flat stare. "Of course. He's requested regular updates."

Matt blinked. He'd been in the same room as someone talking to the actual pope. Had the pope heard him when he'd spoken? Probably. If Matt had farted loud enough, the pope would have heard that, too. He wondered if the pope would have laughed at hearing it. Matt chuckled at the image of the pope in his white robes and pointy hat giggling at a fart.

Uwe's brow crinkled. "What's so funny?"

"Nothing," Matt said, fighting away the smile. He doubted Uwe would have seen the humor in it, anyway. *Luiza will, though.* "Run the translator on it. Let's see what we're dealing with."

I should reach Atik's village tomorrow. Strange music thrums in the distance, igniting some primeval anger. It haunts my dreams.

CHAPTER 20

Buenos Aires, Argentina

Deep beneath the earthen floors of Villa 15, also known as the Hidden City, Sicthwa coils and swims within her private sanctuary. Few know of, and less have ever seen, the chamber with its uneven, red brickwork and tiered, concave floor. Who had built the cistern is unknown even to Sicthwa. The date scratched into the mortar reads, "1938." But she is grateful for it. The roominess and blackness provide her ample room to play.

Her children will lock victims in here with her. She enjoys watching them stumble in the dark, disoriented, hands stretched out before them as they whimper and search for escape. A splash of her tail or whispered word brings the terrible realization that they're not alone. *Swish, swish.* Sometimes she touches them, sliding her body across the backs of their legs, just for an instant, but long enough for them to know that they're alone in the dark with a monster. Wide-eyed and blind, they scream or beg. Some boast hopeless threats, swinging fists at the darkness. Others fold themselves into corners, arms hugging their knees, and piss themselves. Once she tires of her little amusements, she feeds. Twice a month, providing her hunger is satiated, she blesses one, impregnating it with her child.

Sicthwa prefers this den more than her previous one in Villa 31, though the despair was more exquisite there. She should have foreseen the Valducans finding her. While she has never spoken to her sisters since the night of their hatching, Sicthwa knows some of them are no more. In her dreams, she has felt them, and whispered untold secrets. Three of them have fallen silent. They were the same flesh, but not spirit. Sicthwa doesn't mourn them, but fears what their deaths mean. The Valducans are coming.

After violating her sanctuary, decimating her children, they'd survived her little trap. She'd seen them with her own eyes and knew their names. Anya had known them. Anya, who had given herself to the Great Mother and whose face Sicthwa now wears. Anya had understood the Valducans, brought them to their knees. Anya knew their weaknesses and therefore so does Sicthwa.

Hiding wasn't going to work. It has failed for three of her sisters and has nearly cost Sicthwa her own life. No, if she intends to survive she must attack. The Order is not invincible. Their refuge is their weakness: the archives, the Masters holed up as the troops perform their murders, the orphan weapons.

She smiles to herself in the darkness, lips drawing away from venomous fangs, as a plan begins to crystallize.

A shout yanks Sicthwa from her thoughts. A man screams and gunshots erupt somewhere above.

They're here! Sicthwa swims out from the pool and into the air, water pouring off of her long body, and she wriggles into one of the two concrete tubes leading from her sanctuary. The tunnel extends straight forty feet, ending abruptly at the base of a half-built hospital, its construction abandoned in the 1970s. A break in the concrete wall will allow her escape.

Another shot echoes behind her.

A corroded metal sheet blocks the exit. Sicthwa presses against it, but the barrier doesn't move. She coils behind it, pushing her formidable strength against the obstacle. It yields a metallic groan, but nothing more. How the Order knows of this escape baffles her, but they have blocked it. She considers hiding in the tunnel. No one can reach her here, but Matt Hollis and his damnable revolver could simply shoot down the tube, killing her like a sniveling dog. *No. They can't have known of both exits.*

Sicthwa twists her body around and swims back toward the cistern chamber. Her children can hold the Valducans at bay long enough for her to escape. She'll rebuild, and once ready, she'll crush them for this second violation.

Color glimmers in the chamber ahead. Not light. Light would fill the flooded room, reflect, pierce shadows, yet color still shines in the blackness ahead.

Sicthwa reaches the edge of the tube. A stranger stands on the steps above the waterline. A curiously archaic black beard juts from his chin, slender and pointed. Vibrant hues halo the rings on his fingers, a thick steel cuff, and a trio of necklaces. They glow not with light, but souls. Sicthwa's gaze transfixes on the sword in the stranger's hand. It isn't an Oppressor. Those shine with an unmistakable light, but this one is alive. Blackness, like liquid smoke, swirls along the blood-streaked blade. Threads of teal-gold drift around it like spider webs in the wind. They pass through the living blade and up into the swordsman's hand, reeling them in like ethereal fishing strings. She knows those lights. She knows which of her children they belonged to.

Fear melts into rage as Sicthwa's children are devoured before her.

"The other escape is blocked." Despite the lack of illumination, his eyes are directly on her own. "Cower in your hole or face me, demon."

"Who are you?" Sicthwa asks as her length draws up behind her, the muscles tensing.

The swordsman doesn't reply. The teal-gold strands dwindle.

"*What* are you?" Sicthwa doesn't wait for a response that she knows won't come. This hunter is not a man of words. This hunter is not a man at all. She strikes, stretching her full twenty-one feet, mouth wide.

The swordsman blurs to the side so fast it's almost as if he'd vanished. Her jaws clamp empty air and a sudden icy shock pierces her side. Sicthwa tries to scream, tries to turn to face the attack but can't. Eyes frozen in silent horror, the world rips away as she's torn from her flesh and spins into hungry oblivion.

Brilliant amber light swirled around Redemptor's blade, brighter than any demon fire Hernando had ever witnessed. He'd known this one was different long before he'd arrived, the melody wrong, a thousand instruments in one. The memories he'd consumed of the bizarre tentacle-headed monsters outside had reverently referred to this as *mother*. Hernando hadn't dared to believe what that meant, Mother of Demons, but now as her foul essence spun into a vortex of threaded light, he knew it to be true.

Liyliyth.

Redemptor shared the beast's power and Hernando's mouth opened in awe. No, not Liyliyth, not the Serpent of Temptation as he'd first assumed, but something equally as amazing. A glowing forest of memories filled his consciousness. Hernando marveled at the untold knowledge, the answers to secrets he'd never fathomed. Before, he'd always seen them divided in strata. The lower demons—the imps and monsters that killed the helpless—and arch-demons, the deceivers within the weapons, the so-called *angels*. Arrogant and demanding, yet God set his angels below man. They were to serve, not control his favored children.

Now, Hernando had something new. A devil capable of propagating its foul line. What could this mean? He searched the blossoming forest but discovered only holes, vacancies in the new memories. Redemptor had kept secrets, things even Hernando, Paladin of God, couldn't know. Hernando could not be angry at this. The thirst for forbidden knowledge was the first sin.

More songs called in the distance as the swarming power drew further inside him. With each kill, his ability to hear the songs had grown. Now, with this devil eel and the multitude of spirits within it, the range of his awareness expanded not by miles, but hundreds of miles. Thousands. Even transcending physical distance and into the realms beyond, the barriers becoming less tangible. Weapons and monsters sang to him from far across the globe, lands he'd never heard of during his life. He could now hear the songs beckoning him, challenging him.

Across the bay, where his pursuers had stopped, he could hear the music of eight arch-demon blades. They were no threat to him now. He would crush them and those heretics who foolishly worshiped them.

The spinning amber strands tightened and Hernando felt Redemptor's beautiful voice, like storm winds beyond the horizon.

A crown.

Yes, he thought. This false Liyliyth would become more than a simple ring or bauble. He would not need to go to Atik's pyramid to craft it. She had been no arch demon, yet she was special. Hernando would craft a crown of bronze to rule his new army.

Praise be to God.

In my absence, the demon had laid siege to the village. Its fury had slain all but a few. The song beckons me. I will fulfill Atik's prayers and destroy this monster.

CHAPTER 21

Atacama Region, Chile

"The mask is the key to understanding it," Master Sonu said. His narrow face occupied the left half of the screen. The thick, snowy eyebrows and moustache stood out drastically against the old man's brown skin. Technically, his title was Master Rangarajan, but everyone just called him Sonu.

Aware that all the Valducan Masters could clearly see her on their own monitors, Mei stifled a yawn, her chest unmistakably rising with the action. Exhausted, with no makeup and hair pulled back in a haphazard ponytail, she couldn't escape the self-conscious unease of being the only knight in a teleconference with all four Valducan Masters.

"The Incan mask?" Master Alex Turgen asked, his hoarse voice coming through the television's speaker. The feed on the right half of the screen showed the old warrior seated in a leather chair beside Master Allan Havlock. Unlike the rest of the Valducan Masters, Havlock was younger than most of the other knights. He'd served as a hunter until last year. His gray slacks and black shoe hid the prosthetic leg. Mei wouldn't have known it was there by looking at him.

A small window at the bottom of the wall monitor showed Max, seated in the compound's media room, papers spread on the folding desk before him, and a laptop occupying the desk of the empty seat to his right. Mei sat at his left, dark bags below her eyes.

She'd spent the last day poring over De la Fuente's weird journal, his letters to Rome, and various accounts of those who had witnessed him. It wasn't entirely boring, at least not after he'd met the Incan priest Atik, but the style of it forced her to read slowly. The masters had all finished the records, but she still had more to go.

Sonu nodded. "According to the reports, De la Fuente used the gold to create Redemptor, harnessing its power."

"But Mal said you can't alter a demon mask without destroying it," Master Havlock said.

"Doctor Romero said that he doesn't know how," Max clarified. "Not that it was impossible."

"Listen to this," Master Sonu said, his eyes moving to a tablet in his hand. "'Its artistry is entirely incongruous to that of these people. There is an unfinished quality to its features, an unsure masterpiece. At one angle, it appears male. Another female. Atik warns me not to stare at it too long, lest I enrage the entity inside it.'" The old man looked back at the camera. "I believe Lady Mei's original theory of a rakshasa is correct. But not as she had assumed."

Mei's lip twitched in an attempt to smile. Somehow, he'd managed to both compliment and demean her, though he probably hadn't intended it.

"The mask is almost certainly a demon mask. Rakshasas thrive on deception more than any other breed. If a rakshasa is what controls Redemptor, that would account for why De la Fuente believes himself on the side of righteousness."

"Which begs the question as to where the Incans got the mask," Master Turgen said.

"I believe they made it," Master Havlock said.

Shaking his head, Turgen turned to the younger Master. "De la Fuente himself noted the style wasn't Incan."

"It doesn't matter where they got it." Max huffed. "Not now. It happened. This creature poses a threat to not only ourselves, but to the weapons. What are we going to do?"

Master Sonu nodded in agreement. "What do you suggest?"

"We have four knights with two orphan weapons and a pair of Vatican hunters with three soldiers. Even without this … thing coming for them, I'm entirely uncomfortable with it. We need to bring the orphans home. They're too much at risk."

"All right." Master Havlock strummed his fingers on his desk. "One of our knights should leave with the orphans and bring them back to Chile? Luiza's the only one who can fly, so they'd be without her. Personally, I'd prefer her on the front line."

Max shook his head. "I don't want to take any of them off the front line, but there's too much risk in having the orphans there. Perhaps I should go to retrieve them, and meet with these paladins."

"Absolutely not!" Turgen said. "You're Master of that house. Your knights are away. You can't simply charge off, leaving it with a single, inexperienced knight."

Max's cheeks reddened, his jaw muscles rippled. He drew a purposeful breath and let it out. "Mei," he said, his voice even. "Could you make some more coffee, please."

A familiar pang rose in Mei's chest. An irritation she'd thought long behind her. "Of course." She closed her laptop, took Max's empty, sixteen-ounce coffee mug, and quietly left the media room.

Max's voice started up once the door had closed behind her. For the briefest moment, she considered listening, but discarded that idea. At dinners growing up, when the topic turned to money with questions of how her parents would pay for her dance classes, she was always asked to go do the dishes, change out the laundry, some other menial task that only meant, "the adults are talking." She was done listening at doors.

Lukrasus swinging at her hip, she walked down the hall, brooding on her anger. Turgen's voice echoed in her mind. *Inexperienced knight.* It wasn't *her* fault she hadn't made her fist kill. *She* was the one who discovered the trail. But they didn't even think she was good enough to oversee a near-empty compound in the middle of nowhere. In that case, why not send her after the orphans?

Mei already knew the answer to that. *No way would Max let*

you near the front line with Catholic knights, and some Conquistador lich with a demon blade—yeah, right.

A metallic rattling of pots came from the kitchen ahead. The lights were on. Pushing open the door with her hip, Mei found Ester standing above the sink, washing dishes, her long, gray hair tied in a bun.

The black, rubber handle of a short-barrel revolver peeked from the holster at her waist. Ever since they'd recalled the weapons, Max had insisted that all of them were to remain armed at all times. Even after learning what the Vatican knew, he hadn't changed the order.

"I can get that if you want to go to bed."

Ester spun at the voice. Wide eyes relaxed as they fell upon Mei, laptop under one arm, giant mug in hand. She pressed a damp hand against her chest, leaving a print. "You frightened me."

"Sorry. I was just saying I could do that if you want to go to bed." It had been Mei's night for dishes, but she'd been distracted. Ester shouldn't be doing it.

"That's all right, dear. I'm almost done."

A guilty weight settled in Mei's stomach. "I'm sorry I hadn't washed those yet. I should have—"

"That's all right. I can't sleep. Are you hungry?"

"No. No, thank you." Mei shook the mug, the bead of cold coffee rolling around the inner rim. "Just coming for a refresh."

The old woman smiled and returned to her sink.

Ignoring the mega-sized espresso maker the other knights favored, Mei loaded the old-fashioned Mister Coffee to the top, and hit the button. She realized that in her rush to escape the videoconference that she'd left her own cup by her chair. She opened the cabinet and removed Matt's big mug shaped like an Easter Island head. He wouldn't mind.

As the coffeemaker began to burp and gurgle, she sat down at the table and opened her laptop. The personal journal of Hernando de la Fuente stared back at her in black and white, patiently transcribed into digital by some unknown Vatican priest, and translated to English by Uwe. She'd perused scanned copies of the original, hand-written pages—old and yellowed—but couldn't read them if she wanted to. Hell, she didn't even want to read the translations anymore. She'd read them all day.

Page after page after page of self-deprecation. Christ, maybe that was why she hated it. Her feeling sorry for herself and reading "poor me" from five hundred years before. *That's what you look like,* she reprimanded. *No wonder they treat you like a noob.*

Only after De la Fuente had met the Incan priest did the mood change. Then, once Redemptor was forged, did she see the darkness worming in, eating the man's sanity with long diatribes about the farcical angels and "tearing the veil aside" that stretched for pages at a time.

Ester finished the dishes and sauntered off to bed, leaving Mei alone as the coffee maker continued its gurgling.

Mei read the account of Hernando facing Paladin Marco Bencivenni, who carried a mace named Eremiel. While a battle between a paladin and the anti-paladin should have made for some good reading, De la Fuente reduced it to simply, *"He fell before Redemptor's might."*

The next entry, weeks later, said that he had bound the arch-demon Eremiel to a steel cuff. He continued, describing the power the cuff granted, *"God's holy breath."* But Mei paused on a single line in the text. "Upon my return from the mount, I dispatched a letter to Rome, informing them of Bencivenni's redemption."

Returned from the mountain? What mountain? De la Fuente had been in Quito. There were several mountains there, but which one had he gone to and why? Why had he been there so long?

Mei searched the document for the word "mount," hoping to find some reference to this mountain. It came back with 119 hits. She clicked through them slowly, reading the adjoining text.

The coffeemaker beeped, announcing its completion just as Mei found it.

The pyramid.

It was the only mountain he ever spoke of specifically. The rest had been obstacles he'd crossed. The pyramid, the hewn stone mountain, was the only destination. He'd gone back to the pyramid. It would account for the gap in the journal, but why?

Pondering it, Mei filled the two cups. She added cream to hers and five heaping spoonfuls of sugar to Max's. While the Masters were debating the significance of the mask, they'd only given passing comments about the jungle pyramid, putting more significance in the ley lines De la Fuente had described. But even after Redemptor was made, he'd gone back to it. That was important.

There was no map in the journal. That'd have been too easy, but page after page describing the expedition from Lima might do the trick.

Leaving Max's coffee on the counter, she carried hers back to the laptop. He probably hadn't wanted it, anyhow. He'd just been getting her out of the room. Mei opened up Google Earth and found Lima. The landscape had changed a lot over the centuries with man's intrusions, but mountains were mountains and rivers were rivers. Sipping the hot coffee, she opened the journal in a neighboring window and began searching for the path De la Fuente had described.

The demon's terrible song silenced as I plunged Redemptor into its black heart. Pale orange light sprang from the wound, encircling the blade in luminous threads reminiscent of God's rivers. As the power filled me, I heard a voice, Redemptor's voice, commanding me to touch the glowing blade to a ring, a loop of tin, to commemorate our victory.

CHAPTER 22

Colonia del Sacramento, Uruguay

"I'm out." Luc dropped his cards onto the table, which was really a door laid across a pair of sawhorses.

Uwe scooped the mound of tiny tiles serving as chips toward him. "Uwe wins again. That's what, three now?"

Luc pursed his lips into a scowling smile. "You keep bragging and you'll be playing alone."

"You're just a sore loser," Uwe said, shaking his head. "Another game?"

"No, thanks." The huge man sighed. "I think I'll hit the sack."

Uwe snorted. "Sore loser." He turned to Felisa who was half-watching the exchange as she paced the chapel. "How about you, Paladin? You want a game?"

"I'm on patrol," she said, dryly. "And you should be going to bed." With luck, maybe he would. These knights prattled more than anyone she'd ever known. While the laughter and conversations were initially refreshing, she missed the silence.

Luc smiled, a real one this time, and gave Uwe a "there you have it" gesture with his open hands.

"Everyone's a poor loser," Uwe mumbled, gathering the cards.

Rising to his feet, Luc bid Uwe good night and gave Felisa a polite nod before heading to the back rooms where they'd set up the cots. For two full days now they'd slept in shifts, two hunters awake at all times, keeping watch for the guest of honor.

He was late.

Felisa hated waiting. She wanted to do something, anything to stop De la Fuente. But she couldn't. If they split up, dividing their forces, De la Fuente would strike. She had no illusions that she could face him alone. Despite the Valducans' bravado, Felisa suspected they felt the same way. None of them had left chapel grounds since their arrival.

When they needed supplies—food, propane, cots—they'd send the Swiss Guard. Two at a time. De la Fuente wouldn't be able to impersonate them both. It was a sound strategy, they all agreed, but would it work? Would he come for the weapons? Maybe he was out there now, wreaking havoc while they hid. *Fiddling while Rome burns.*

"Night," Uwe said as he started toward the back, spear in hand.

"Good night, Sir Uwe." She watched him go, still unsure what to make of the strange little man. Despite his oddities, he wasn't a fool. He pretended to be. The knight may have even been a little crazy, but watching him plan contingencies and ideas proved that he was extremely bright.

The rear door groaned. Felisa turned as Luiza stepped inside. A copper-handled samurai sword, a relic from the second World War, hung at her hip. They shared a polite smile, though Felisa recognized the mistrust in the Brazilian's face— the tension at the corners of her lips, a narrowness to the eyes. It was the same smile Felisa reserved for Father Soldati.

"Is there any coffee left?" Luiza asked.

Felisa nodded. She wanted something to say to her, something interesting, something that might open an actual dialogue. Apart from discussing De la Fuente or their patrol assignments, they'd only shared simple one-sentence exchanges. "How long have you been married to Akumanokira?"

"Three years." Luiza set down the plastic bottle of faintly pink water and poured a cup from the stainless percolator atop the folding stove.

"Really? And in three years you've risen to a leader. Very impressive." The woman appeared to be late twenties, maybe early thirties. It was difficult to tell. "What did you do before?"

Luiza's lips puckered in a kiss and she blew steam from the mug. She drank it black. "This is all I've done. My father was with the Order. I grew up with them. My mother brought me to mass twice a week, though I never understood why none of my other family came." She tongued her cheek, a shadow settling beneath her eyes. "When I was fourteen, my father brought me on my first hunt, a vampire outside Madrid. After that, he offered to train me with his sword, my grandfather's sword, Feinluna. But he warned me that joining the Order would excommunicate me and break my mother's heart."

Felisa bit her lip. Centuries before, when the Valducans had broken from the Church, they had been declared *vitandus*, the lowest form of excommunicate. "I don't believe the vitandus proclamation applies to you or your family."

"Oh," she said, one brow arching. "Has the order been rescinded? I thought it applied to all members forthwith until the *Day of Judgment*. We still have the letter declaring it."

"I ... I can speak to His Holiness about that oversight."

"Mm-hmm. And if he does correct that, might he also send a letter to my mother, begging forgiveness for all the tears she shed for her daughter and husband, and my little girl?"

Felisa pressed her thumb against her wedding band. How in the Saints had this gone badly? "I'll speak with him."

Luiza's hard eyes softened. "I'm sorry. I'm ... I'm a little on edge."

"It's understandable." Smiling her best "nun smile," the one reserved for consoling families, Felisa turned and continued her patrol. After another minute, Luiza headed back outside. Two more quarter-hour radio checks and they'd switch. The air in here was stuffy. Her cheeks felt hot. She wanted out now.

Felisa ground her teeth, cursing herself for letting the words hurt her. She'd never once met a female hunter. She was always surrounded by men with their ideas of how she should behave and when she finally meets another woman, a sister-in-law, she finds herself again on the outside.

What did she want? Luiza's approval? What was that really worth? Luiza, bride of an angel, was married to the American who was also wed to Dämoren. Was the union to an angel not enough? Polygamists. That's what they were.

No, she scolded. Who was she to judge them? Judgment was a sin. If their weapons hadn't approved of the union, then the weapons wouldn't have allowed it. They were bound to angels. Angels only accepted the purest of souls.

She thought of the bottle Luiza carried with Matt's blood. Was there significance to the blood of an angel's husband bringing protection? *Yes.* Blood was sacred. *This is my blood,* she imagined him telling Luiza, *may it protect you.*

Still reprimanding herself for her harsh judgments, and her needy desire for their approval, Felisa stepped through a narrow doorway and started up a tight stairwell. The smell of old wood and the tang of mouse pee filled cramped space.

Paladin Kofi hadn't tried to win the Valducans' approval. He hadn't fluttered around Luc, hoping to build some bond over their shared race. No, as always, he'd been a professional. He was everything Felisa should strive to be.

The creaking stairs ended at the choir balcony where crude ladder rungs continued upward to the belfry. The buzz of nighttime insects called from the opening above. She continued up.

"Good evening, Paladin," Gast said as she reached the top. He huddled on the narrow ledge, his back against one of the corner supports. Yoder's scoped rifle rested across his lap. Without the long-absent bell, the perch allowed a commanding view.

"Pardon me, Corporal. I needed some air."

"Nice night for it." The words sounded clumsy. Pleasantries were not the corporal's forte.

Felisa closed her eyes, enjoying the cold breeze play across her face.

"Do you need me to move?" he asked, sliding closer to the edge. "We can both fit up here."

"That's all right." Felisa scanned the horizon. Colonia's lights glowed across the treetops. Behind the church, far across the bay, the bright towers of Buenos Aires shone like beacons. Taking another step higher, she could see the grounds below. Over two dozen electric lamps illuminated the perimeter, their shadows crisscrossing over the grass. While such a thing might bring unwelcome attention to their presence, Luiza had insisted, saying the lights would help with Akumanokira's gift.

Felisa touched a slender, blue feather wedged between two of the rough boards, upright like a sail, and vibrating in the steady breeze.

"Yoder put that there," Gast said. "I believe it's to gauge wind."

Or because it's beautiful. She stroked the soft feather lightly, careful not to dislodge it. Closing her eyes, she sighed, releasing a morsel of the pent tension. Later, when she could be alone, she would make confession to Ofniel and purge herself of her petty insecurities.

She opened her eyes and smiled.

Something glinted at the edge of her vision. A truck bounced down the road, dust whirling in its wake. A sedan followed closely behind it. Neither had their headlights on.

Rounding the bend, their engines roared as they accelerated toward the gate. The little hairs along Felisa's forearms prickled upright and pressed against her sleeves. *It's him!*

"Contact!" Gast radioed. He lifted the rifle and peered down the scope at the oncoming truck.

A sudden shock zapped Felisa's skull, just behind her ear— harder, more focused than a camera's snap. Instinctively, as if burned by a hot plate, she ducked into the ladder shaft. A gun boomed. Meaty pops and cracking wood sounded above. Hot wetness spattered her cheek and forehead.

Gast let out a hoarse groan. The rifle tumbled from his fingers. It clattered and fell over the side. He clutched at his collarbone, blood streaming from several holes. His hand exploded as a second shotgun blast struck. Gast jerked against the support behind him and then crumpled forward. Felisa dropped lower as the dead man landed atop the hole, one arm hanging beside her ear.

Metal crashed outside.

Someone screamed into the radio.

Felisa scrambled down the ladder. Gast's blood rained from above, spattering her head and hands in sticky warmth. Ofniel's warning had saved her. Had she not moved, the first shot would have hit the back of her head. But she'd been looking at the truck. De la Fuente wasn't working alone.

She reached the balcony to see Luc, shirtless, charging across the chapel, his mace held high. A man with a strangely bulbous head ran to meet him. The stranger raised a machete, but Luc smashed the mace into his attacker's side. Blood exploded across the wooden floor and the man's crumpled body sailed into the wall as if he'd been struck by a car.

The muffled whirr of a silenced machine gun sounded outside.

Drawing Ofniel, Felisa raced down the staircase. A sharp prickle warned her as she reached the bottom. Felisa ducked. An axe blade whooshed above and *thocked* into the door frame.

Ofniel before her, she lunged, driving the blade up beneath her attacker's ribs and out his back.

The man gasped and dropped the axe. His shoulder-length hair looked thin, stretched across his swollen head. Blue veins spider webbed across his face like cracked, old porcelain. The man's bulging eyes rolled toward her not in pain or fear, but amusement.

Tingles laced Felisa's throat. She bent away as his hands clawed for her neck, swiping empty air. Twisting her body, she wrenched the blade free. Clomping feet charged up the front steps. A second attacker ran between the open doors, a metal pole braced below his arm like a spear.

Muffled pops rattled behind her to the left. Bullets ripped through the man's chest, spraying blood. He staggered but didn't fall.

Ofniel's warning made her spring to the side as the first attacker lunged at her from behind. How was he still alive?

Across the room, the ruin of the one Luc had struck dragged its mangled body across the floor. Broken ribs jutted from its bleeding side like spines.

Felisa's attackers circled, trying to flank her. Keeping to

the balls of her feet she danced between them, waiting for an opening or Ofniel's signal to dodge.

"The head!" Luiza shouted over the radio.

Another burst of automatic fire. It was Yoder, his weapon tucked into his shoulder and eye fixed down the stubby scope. The attacker with the pole took two shots through the head. This time it fell, but immediately started to rise.

Seizing on Felisa's distraction, the other one lunged. Tingles warned her of the upcoming attack. Springing to the side, she pivoted and slashed the fallen creature as it tried to stand. The blade tip tore through the top of its skull and the creature fell. Redirecting her momentum, she looped the sword up and back around, slamming the blade down into her other enemy's head. One of its eyes popped from its socket with a jet of crimson. It fell limp, nearly wrenching the imbedded sword from Felisa's grip.

More shooting thundered outside.

"Bullets aren't working," Epple radioed.

"Brass does," Uwe replied.

Yoder fired a burst out the door. "You have *brass* bullets?"

"Of course."

Setting her boot on the dead thing's chest, Felisa pulled her sword from its head. The plates of its skull shifted and slid beneath the skin. The blue veins began fading. But it wasn't burning. She'd never seen a demon that didn't burn upon death.

Luc smashed the head of the mangled thing crawling across the floor. Its head exploded like an egg struck by a golf club. Gore and black chunks of brain matter splattered across the plastic-draped window. Like the two she had slain, it didn't burn with colored hellfire.

"We need to get outside," Felisa said.

The big man nodded and hurried toward her.

Across the room, Yoder fired again. He backpedaled, laying a stream of bullets. A flaming Molotov cocktail sailed through the church's open doors. A round struck it mid-air and it shattered, spraying flaming petrol across the floor. A fiery drop splashed his boot, but Yoder continued firing at the large-headed woman charging inside, an unlit bottle clutched in her hand. Her red-stained blouse and brassiere were only tatters. A golden choker glinted at her throat. The puckered bullet holes cinched closed as she ran. A concentrated burst chewed off her face, spraying matter out the back of her head. Nearly decapitated, the woman fell. The bottle rolled across the floor, but didn't break.

Yoder stomped his burning boot toe and dropped the spent magazine. "Go! Out the back!"

Black smoke billowed from the burning petrol, quickly filling the room. One of the plastic drapes melted as flames overtook it. Her eye stinging, she hurried toward the back exit. Luc's running footsteps pounded behind her.

"Wait!" Luc hurried through a curtained doorway, the one used as the Valducans' quarters.

She followed him in. Empty cots and strewn blankets littered the floor. Luc tossed one of the beds aside. "Take it." He thrust a cardboard box into her arms and she instantly understood. Luc lifted a second box, this one long enough for a sword, the one Luiza and he had brought, and tucked it under his arm. "Don't let it go."

Yoder stood outside the room, his SMG covering the burning chapel. The flames had already spread along the plastic-draped wall.

Taking the lead, she ran out the open rear door. Bodies littered the perimeter of the yard. To Felisa's right, Luiza and Matt stood side by side. Luiza slashed the long shadow of an attacker coming toward them and the creature's head came apart as if she had hit it instead of the shadow. Matt tracked the darkness, his bladed revolver before him. On the other side of the yard, Uwe knelt before Kofi, his spear before him. Bullets bounced off a rippling disk extending from the spear like an umbrella. Kofi hurled Salvatio. The twirling axe curved behind the ruined outbuildings where the shooter hid.

A sharp pang stabbed Felisa's side. She bent away from it as a bullet whistled past. Matt swung his revolver around toward where the shooter knelt behind the perimeter wall. Orange light boomed from Dämoren's barrel and the shooter crumpled, the round hitting him above a bulging eye.

Hunkering, Felisa ran the rest of the way down the plywood ramp to Epple crouching beside one of the cars. He clutched one of the Valducans' pistols as he searched the darkness.

"Where's Gast?" he asked over his shoulder.

"Dead. De la Fuente?"

A bullet punched thorough the car's window, showering them in glass cubes.

"Haven't seen him yet."

Damn it. Clenching her teeth, Felisa scanned the grounds for their real enemy. If he were to make his appearance now, while they were dealing with ... whatever these abominations were, they'd be cut down. Hiding between cars wouldn't help. Luc's mace Velnepo, while powerful, couldn't protect him from bullets. Ofniel, however ... "Sergeant Epple, you, Yoder, and Luc stay here with this." She set the box between them. "Protect it with your life."

Epple nodded. "Yes, Paladin."

Gripping Ofniel tight, Felisa sprang and raced toward the perimeter wall. Tingles shot through her chest. She whirled to the side the instant before a shotgun blasted from the high grass. Was that the one that killed Gast? She ducked the second shot, grabbed the top of the stone wall, and swung onto the opposite side.

A bubble-headed teen with an open double-barrel shotgun fumbled as he tried to reload. He swung the empty gun at her. Felisa effortlessly dodged it and rammed her sword up under the boy's chin. She tore the blade free, and continued searching for more abominations. The stink of burnt wood, tar, and plastic choked the air. Her eyes watered, making it even harder to see through the thick smoke rolling from the chapel.

She found two more, one with an unlit molotov cocktail and another in a policeman's uniform. The policeman fired two shots at her before she brought him down. The last of the attackers was the man with a deer rifle firing at Kofi and Uwe from behind the buildings. Kofi killed him with his flying axe.

Flames engulfed one half of the old church. Fire and smoke poured from the bell tower, igniting the roof. Searching by the fire's light, Felisa tried not to think of Gast's body being roasted atop the shaft. She circled the property once, unable to find any more attackers.

Matt and Uwe were racing in and out of the rear doorway, throwing out as many of the supplies as they could. Luc, and Luiza maintained watch as the others scrambled.

Kofi hurried toward her. "We must go before police come."

"Where's De la Fuente?" she snarled.

"No sign yet," Luiza said, scanning past her. The bottle in her off hand was no longer pink. Red beads pressed against the inner walls.

Luc knelt beside one of the dead things, now fully returned to human form—a woman, early thirties in a pair of cut-off shorts. The killing shot had hit her mouth, shattering the teeth.

"What are those?" Felisa asked. "Why don't they burn?"

Luc shook his head. "I mistook them for skin puppets at first."

Felisa wiped the grass burrs from her pant legs. "A what?"

Luc turned the dead woman's head and touched a choker of woven brass wire.

Felisa leaned closer, recognizing it. "What is that?"

"They're all wearing them," Luc said.

"Careful with that," Luiza said.

"Why?"

She held up the blood compass and moved it closer. All the beads but one shifted away, but that one pointed directly at the choker. "There's a demon inside it."

Luc's hand snapped away from it like it had shocked him. "How?"

"De la Fuente," Felisa growled.

"That's my guess."

"But how?" Kofi asked. "There have to be twenty of them."

"Twenty-five," Luiza said. "And I think I know where he's getting the demons to power them."

"The eel," Luc said.

"You need to explain this," Felisa said. "What eel?"

"We'll explain once we're out of here. First, we need to gather all of these necklaces. Can't let anyone find them."

A spike of anger flared in Felisa's chest. Whatever secret

these knights had been protecting had nearly gotten them all killed. Gast's dead face flashed in her mind and the anger seethed. She pressed her thumb against her wedding band until it hurt. "Fine."

She looked back at the church. Flames licked out from the open doorway. Anything still inside was lost. "Yoder, you and Epple help us get all of these necklaces. Get your gloves."

"Yes, Paladin." Yoder wiped soot from his sweating face and began digging in a duffle bag for gloves.

Luc rose to his feet. "I'll help."

Kofi's gaze remained on the outlying shadows. "Where are you, Hernando?"

De Sota's gold lust had been his undoing. Greed is a sin. His demand that I give him Redemptor was his final mistake. The foolish attempt to avenge him had been his men's. They are all part of me now.

CHAPTER 23

Atacama Region, Chile

Carefully, Hernando twisted the coiled wire into the intricate weave. The brass bent easily, though a lesser man, and they all were, would require tools. Repetition had made him proficient at the braided collars. Even with the rumbling of the Dodge 4x4 along winding, dirt roads, his hands remained steady.

He bent the last piece of wire into a spiraling curl and touched it to the crown atop his head. Gold and teal illuminated the dark vehicle and faded. The collar shifted beneath his fingers, writhed as it gained Redemptor's blessing. Metal fused, warped, and retextured into something far lovelier.

The creature in the driver's seat beside him didn't show the least trace of being impressed. Eyes on the road, it simply drove. Hernando didn't know its name, and he had no intention of naming it. The badge on its khaki uniform said "Guerrero," but that was only the policeman it had been.

The drive from Buenos Aries had been long—flat plains and farmlands extending to the horizon. He had only one blessed collar when he'd set off. A hitchhiker received that one. His newest child at the wheel left Hernando's hands free to craft more collars. More hitchhikers followed until he had to conscript a second vehicle and the driver inside. By the time the

Andes peeked on the horizon, Hernando led three vehicles of his army. Their bulbous heads aroused memories of the *maché cebezudo* masks from his childhood, when festival celebrants would don giant-headed costumes and frighten children.

Following the songs of the distant weapons, Hernando avoided the main highway for a mountain pass. It had already closed for the imminent winter, but ice and snow did not frighten him. His children were strong and if the cold affected them, they didn't complain. Two Chilean officers patrolled the border where the paved Argentinean highway gave way to dirt and gravel. Guerrero had been one of them, and now Hernando enjoyed the comforts of their police truck.

He set the blessed collar with the four others on the console beside him. He checked the green dashboard clock. 23:35. His children that he'd dispatched to Colonia had begun their assault five minutes ago. Surely, they wouldn't kill all of the heretics. The demonic weapons made them strong, and now, with the memories of the great serpent whose name he couldn't know, Hernando knew who these hunters were.

Valducans. He'd heard the name before—in the memories of the Paladins he'd killed before his imprisonment. Like himself, they'd turned from the Church, but not for the right reasons. Their sin was the same as the Paladins' and they would suffer the same fate.

Hernando closed his eyes. The silver knife, his maddening companion since Brazil, sang its infernal song from the tail vehicle. It had become white noise, a lingering irritation that could almost but never fully be forgotten. But above its incessant *tre-le-la-le-le-la*, more weapons called out across the desert. Five of them, summoning him across a continent. They were close now. The orphans.

The nameless serpent knew that the Valducans always stationed one of their knights to guard them. One or two would be no challenge. Once he had the demon blades, he'd take them and the two he'd already secured back to Atik's pyramid. The power he could harvest would make him even stronger, more powerful than he'd ever thought possible. The Paladins and Valducans would fall before him.

He opened his eyes. Red lights glowed in the distance ahead, following the weaving road between barren hills. Hernando smiled. He'd thought that in such remote surroundings that they wouldn't find any other travelers. How many might be in that vehicle? Five, perhaps?

He pointed to the tail lights as they vanished behind a rise, their ghostly glow lingering in the swirling dust. The driver flipped a switch on the dash. Red and white pulsed across the rocky landscape. Sirens blared and Hernando pressed into the seat with the rush of acceleration.

Dressed in only his underwear, Max paced beside his bed, phone pressed to his ear. "Call me the moment you arrive in Buenos Aires."

"We will," Luiza said.

"We'll need to arrange a better location than the airport. This creature doesn't fear being exposed."

"The paladins are working on that now."

Max sighed. Placing themselves under the Church's protection only put the Order at their mercy. It was becoming habit. Once De le Fuente was taken care of, how strong was their alliance, really? What would happen next? But there wasn't much choice at the moment. "Very well. What of these chokers you seized?"

"Uwe wants to melt them down with a blowtorch."

"I agree."

"Me too. I'll have him start the moment we arrive, before anyone has a chance to stop him."

"Do you think they will?" Max asked.

"Probably not, but why risk it?"

"Take care of yourselves. I'll notify the other Masters what happened."

"We will," Luiza said. *"Talk to you soon."*

Ending the call, Max checked the clock. Just after midnight. That made it 5 a.m. in Belgium. 8:30 in India. He sighed, mourning the death of what he'd hoped would have been actual sleep. Now it looked to be another late night in a series of late nights. "Better make some coffee."

He pulled his trousers and shirt from the laundry. No need to dirty more clothes. Their day's use hadn't ended yet. From his dresser, he removed several rattling cases and set them on the night stand. Max unholstered the .357 Magnum revolver at his belt and dumped the six shells into his palm: silver, copper, nickel, brass, bronze, and gold. He returned the brass and gold ones to their chambers, but put the rest in their respective cases. Luiza had said brass hurt De la Fuente's minions. If De le Fuente was powered by a rakshasa, maybe gold would kill him. *As if I'd ever have the opportunity.* He loaded four more brass shells from the box and slid the gun back into its holster.

Stifling a yawn, Max headed toward the kitchen.

The music grew stronger as the caravan raced along the desert road. Hernando gazed out across the barren, rocky hills. In the distance, red lights blazed atop great white windmills, a field of clockwork flowers. Their spinning blades caused the lights to flicker with each lazy pass.

The police vehicle crested a low hill. A tall chain link fence, crowned with barbed wire, ran along the right side of the road. Reflective warning signs hung along it at regular intervals. They followed it a full kilometer before Hernando pointed to a gated drive. "There."

The bulbous-headed driver slowed as he turned, then gunned the engine. Gravel clattered along the Dodge's underside as they sped toward the gate. Across it, the words "El Sable" shone in the closing headlights.

Mei jumped, fighting with her sheets as alarms startled her awake. The shrill, electronic pulse blared in the hall outside her door. The blue numbers of her bedside clock read 12:53.

Heart pounding, she threw off the remaining covers, grabbed a pair of jeans off the floor, and wriggled them on. What was this? A fire? Had something happened to a turbine? Strapping Lukrasus on, she stumbled out into the hall.

"We're under attack!" Max shouted, running toward her. A small white light strobed on the wall behind him, out of time with the alarm's pulse.

"What?"

"Get your gear. Take Ester and Gabi to the library now."

Ester shuffled out of her room, wrapped in a sea foam green robe. She hurried across the hall into Gabi's room.

"Who?" Mei asked.

"Get to the bunker now!" A cold rage blazed behind the old man's eyes, a look she'd never seen. "Lock the door. Call Luiza. Call the Masters."

"What about you?"

"I'll hold them back." He hurried past her. "Go! There isn't much time."

"No," she said, adrenaline fueling her tone. "I'm Base Knight."

Max wheeled. "And your job is to protect the orphans, the archives. Go! Keep them safe." He continued toward the exit. "Brass bullets. Load brass."

Ester came back out into the hall, Gabi in her arms. The little girl was crying, clutching her grandmother. The blinking alarm lights glistened in the old woman's terrified eyes.

Their pleading looks snapped Mei out of her confused anger. *I have to protect them.* "Get to the library." She ran back into her room. Through the reinforced windows she saw a snake of headlights racing up the winding dirt road. Five vehicles. Crimson police lights flashed in the lead. *Shit!* She had two minutes max.

Mei threw open her closet door and grabbed the nylon straps of her go bag. Palms sweating and fingers numb with fear, she nearly dropped it. She threw it over her shoulder and ran toward the stairs, the big bag jostling her with each step.

The siren's deafening wail filled the stairway like a physical force. Clutching Lukrasus' handle with one hand, Mei jumped the steel rail and dropped the three stories to the basement. Gabi's eyes widened as she flew past them in a blur of speed. There was no landing on the first floor. The lowest level could only be accessed by the second. Mei flipped gravity as she neared the bottom. Her stomach lurched. The bag on her arm pulled upward. Her foot touched the inlaid floor that now felt like a ceiling, and she flipped gravity again.

Mei stumbled as the bag's shifting weight almost yanked her over. She punched her code into the keypad and opened the steel door.

"Wait," Ester cried, starting down the final steps.

Mei held the door and then ran down the concrete hall. The passage was wide enough to drive a car. Still holding the sword's handle, she flipped gravity to the side and fell up the square tunnel. Doors flew past her: the shooting range, Matt's workshop where they held their reloading parties, and several store rooms that she'd never entered. Echoes from the alarm bounced and dopplered around her. Bracing the bag, she flipped it again to slow and landed against the sturdy vault-like door of the library.

Stepping onto the floor, she keyed in her number. Bolts thudded. Interior lights flipped on as she swung it open. Steel and glass shelves. Paintings of dead knights and their weapons. The snarling obsidian ghoul face mounted above the safe. Mei heaved the black bag onto a table. A red light pulsed atop a white keypad near the door. Her numb fingers missed the code. *Damn it.* She got it on the second try. The alarm silenced.

The caravan raced along one of the wall monitors in black and white night vision. Three vehicles headed toward the lot. Another two continued on the main drive, circling around. Who was this? Some militia? Had the Chilean government figured out what they were doing?

She remembered Max's words. Brass. Brass bullets meant either ifrit or skin puppets. Luiza's team had just learned that. Was this an army of skin puppets?

Ester's slippered feet pounded up the hall outside. Panting, she ran into the room, set Gabi onto the edge of the table, and doubled over. Sweat streaked the old woman's face and neck.

Mei swung the library door closed. The bolts clicked. She twisted a stainless-steel wheel and a pair of heavy bars slid into place. Not even a pass code would open it now.

She pushed the rolling chair away from the wall station and picked up the phone. On the screen before her, the cars pulled into the lot. They were here.

A new song plays in this distance, growing stronger as I move westward. It is different than the other.

CHAPTER 24

Buenos Aires, Argentina

Matt had harbored a suspicion, or hope, that even though he disliked airplanes, flying in a helicopter would be fine. They didn't go as high or as fast and he liked the idea of hovering. More than once he'd entertained the fantasy of reaching out the open door of a low-flying chopper and picking off fleeing werewolves with Dämoren. *Boom-boom.*

He'd mentioned it to Luiza once, but she just shook her head. So, when the Paladins had offered to fly everyone from Colonia, across the bay to BA, he'd been excited. Luiza had given him a little smile as they took off. It wasn't too bad at first. He didn't suffer the itchy skin or palm sweating that the others laughed at him for, but when they banked and Matt saw the ground outside his window he spent the rest of the short flight staring at his knees.

Back at the hangar he almost wanted to apologize to Helen. There was far worse than travelling in the turboprop. Hopefully he'd remember that sentiment the next time he got on board. Luc and Yoder were busy setting up, trying to inventory and organize the gear. Uwe and Kofi had set up near the door, dropping brass chokers into a cast-iron pan and hitting each one with the blowtorch until a blood compass gave it the all-clear.

Matt had been given the most important job: making coffee. Their regular maker had been burned up in the church fire, but he found one tucked in the back of a cabinet in the hangar's kitchen. It made four cups, had no filters, and was crusted in about a decade's worth of dust. Thankfully they had coffee, and paper towels to make filters.

"How you holding up?" Luiza asked as she stepped inside.

Matt grunted, watching the thin brown stream dribble into the pot. "Tired."

Luiza slipped her arms around him. Her hair stank of smoke, but he probably smelled a whole lot worse.

Matt held her, kissed her head. "How 'bout you?"

"Shh," she whispered, squeezing him tighter.

They stood there in silence, the coffeepot gurgling and muted voices coming through the door.

Luiza's phone went off, ruining the short moment. "Ugh, I forgot to call Schmidt."

"No rest for the wicked," Mat said, releasing her.

Luiza pulled phone from her pocket. "Yes. I was just about—"

Matt could hear a woman's voice shouting on the other side. Mei?

Luiza's eyes went wide, white above the brown pupils. "What? How?"

Matt straightened. Had something happened to Gabi?

Luiza balled her fist. "Yes. Yes, we're on our way!" She clicked the phone. "We have to go!"

"What happened?" Matt asked, chasing her out of the kitchen.

"Uwe, Luc, load the plane. We're leaving!"

"What's going on?" Matt asked.

Luiza grabbed one of the plastic tubs loaded with gear. "It was Mei. They're under attack!"

"What?" Matt and Luc said in unison.

"Mei. She called. Her, Mom, and Gabi are locked in the library. A caravan of attackers just stormed the gates."

Matt's chest tightened. His veins felt like ice. "The orphans."

"What is happening?" Kofi asked.

Luiza was already heading toward the airplane.

"De la Fuente," Matt said. "He's in Chile. We keep orphaned weapons there."

Kofi swallowed. "How many knights?"

"One," Luc said. "And she's inexperienced."

"We need to go," Matt said. Christ, the flight took over five hours. It might be an hour before they could even get off the ground.

Felisa hurried in from the other room, her short hair wet and slicked back. "What's happening?"

"We're going to Chile," Kofi said.

"Excuse me?" Matt asked. The Masters would positively flip their shit if the Vatican visited their base.

"We're coming with you." He turned to Epple, who looked like he'd just woken up. His ginger hair was smooshed on one side. "Sergeant, pack your gear."

Uwe was already dumping water on the pot of melted brass, sending up a wall of steam.

Luc gave Matt an uneasy look.

This was no time for playing safe. His daughter needed him. "Fine," Matt said to Kofi. "Load up."

I discovered the music's source outside a jungle city no Christian had ever seen. Not a monster, but a weapon. Atik had known it as Phintiq, a strange mace with star-shaped heads on either end. The gold one creates fire. The silver one, ice. I slew its wielder and was about to destroy the abomination, but Redemptor stayed my hand.

CHAPTER 25

Atacama Region, Chile

The alarms blared out across the open desert as Max ran from the main building to the gym. He punched his code into the pad and glanced back to the headlights bouncing up the road. Maybe they didn't see him yet.

The automatic lights came on as he pushed open the steel door. Max slipped inside, closing it behind him, and raced past the array of workout machines. The alarms silenced as he reached the tower door.

Grabbing the handrail, he hurried up the steps as fast as he could. The metallic *thap-thap-thap* of his house slippers echoed up the stairwell. His body ached. He hadn't run like this in years. The last time was when Anya had attacked the Paris Chateau and he and Alex had fled for the armory. The still smoldering anger from that day flared, fueling his tired muscles faster. *Not much time.*

Max reached the third floor. The machine gun rested atop its pedestal facing the shuttered windows. While the other knights had questioned Max's insistence for it, he felt no gratification that its time had arrived. He'd prayed that it really was the paranoia of an old man.

He activated the monitors set high onto the wall. His attackers had reached the parking lot. Three cars. He couldn't see the other two but there was no time to consider it. Originally his plan would be to strike them on the road leading in. One thousand meters of open ground—perfect for holding back a small army with a capable gun crew, but that window had passed.

Max heaved one of the green ammo cans from the stack and in one sidestepping pendulum swing, set it beside the gun. A full belt was already loaded in the side cradle, but he had no doubts that he'd need more.

Taking position behind the weapon, Max swung it in the direction of the lot, and cocked the charging handle. He unhooked a corded control switch from the ceiling and killed the gun nest's lights. The pale glow from the tiny wall screens lit the room. He pressed another button, turning the screens off and plunging the room into blackness. The next button activated an electric whirr and the steel shutters along the wall slid upward.

Cold air blew inside, chilling his sweaty face and hands. The crimson lights of a green and white police truck flashed across the lot below. Two civilian vehicles were close behind it.

Max thumbed the safety and peered down the iron sights, tracking just ahead of the lead vehicle. His other hand still clutched the hanging switch, his thumb resting on the smooth bubble of the next button. Only a few more seconds.

The police vehicle stopped less than sixty meters from him. It was too dark to make out anything inside but vague shapes. The driver's silhouette looked like he was wearing a motorcycle helmet. Armor? No matter.

A dusty pickup truck pulled up beside it, nearly blocking Max's line of sight.

Max hit the button. Floodlights mounted above the windows clicked on, bathing the yard in brilliant white.

Shave and a haircut, the gun roared. Orange flames spewed from the muzzle.

Bullets tore through the police car. The driver's head, which he now saw, wasn't a helmet but swollen huge like a pumpkin. It exploded in the spray of blood, brains, and glass.

"Two bits." Max swung the gun to the pickup. The pumpkin-headed things were scrambling to get out. He wasn't going to let them. No one was getting into his home or hurting his family ever again. Mei might be Lukrasus' new protector, but Max was still hers.

Shave and a haircut. The gun tore through two of the things, blasting apart one's head and ripping a terrible path across the other's chest. The wounded one fell, its arm nothing more than a pulped stump. One round had hit it above the ear, but the hole was closing. Crawling with its good arm, it clumsily dragged limp legs through the pooling blood.

"Two bits," Max whispered, zeroing the sights on the wounded monster's head.

Red gore exploded across the black top and Max was already pivoting the gun toward one racing across the lot.

Shave and a haircut.

More were breaking from the cover of the cars.

Shave and a haircut.

"Two bits."

Shave and a haircut.

Orange flashed far to the left. One of those giant heads peeked from behind a hedge, a pistol in her hand. Max couldn't hear the shots. He could barely hear anything but a muted hum. The machine gun returned fire, shredding leaves and meat alike.

Seizing the opening, three of the intruders broke from the cover of the vehicles.

"No, you don't," Max hollered, swinging the barrel toward them. Weaving as they ran, one slowed long enough to get off a shot with a revolver before the stream of bullets found his melon-like skull. Max caught another, not killing it but sending it sprawling. The third runner made it to the edge of the compound and around a corner.

Max looked back in time to see a blur sprinting from behind the cars, faster than any human or any of these things could even dream. It was him! "You bastard!" Max fired, chasing and attempting to lead the demon paladin, but De la Fuente made it around the edge of the windows where Max was blind. "Damn it!"

Bullets pounded along the gun slit's edge, slinging up chips of broken concrete. The shots were coming from different directions. Too many had escaped the kill-zone and now he was boxed in.

Hunkering behind the gun, Max laid several more *shave and a haircuts*. Six more attackers fell before the gun went dry.

His enemies were getting smarter. Shots were now coming at the floodlights. One burst and went out as Max hit the remote switch dropping the shutters. He reactivated the monitors, giving him eyes on the rear of the building, most importantly the front door. Large-headed shapes closed in.

Eyes watering from the thick gun smoke, Max kicked aside the carpeting of hot brass and opened the spare ammo can. With practiced memory, he loaded the belt and snapped the receiver shut.

Less than fifteen seconds after he'd closed them, Max hit the switch again and the shutters slid upward. Bullets pelted the windows, bouncing off the concrete lip, and a few even made it inside. Max spotted one brave dumb fuck standing out in the open with a shotgun, so close the spider webs of veins framing his bulging eyes were clearly visible.

Shave and a haircut and it was gone. This ammo belt was different than the last, each tenth round a tracer. Ruby comets zipped down from the gun nest, the ricochets zinging off into the black desert night.

He fired at two others crouching at the edge of the building, but missed both. The shooters were getting better. A round whizzed past his ear. Max answered with a burst, firing into the darkness where he'd seen the flash.

Crouching, he checked the monitors. Three were at the building's door trying to batter it down. He snorted. They'd need a bomb to breech that thing and none of these monsters were sporting anything military. Most didn't even have guns. The ones that did were firing at where they knew he was.

Time to change that.

Max unclipped the machine gun from the pedestal mount and pulled it free. Gritting his teeth from the weight, he shuffled to the side, sweeping his feet to knock the brass out of the way. He peeked over the gun slit's edge, spied one of the pumpkin heads twenty meters away, and opened fire.

The stream of 7.62 chewed its head off above the mouth.

One of the shooters hiding behind the building leaned out and took a shot. It went wide.

Max heaved the gun toward it. "Two bits."

As he squeezed the trigger, an attacker he hadn't seen rose from behind the ruin of destroyed vehicles and fired twice. Max's left arm went out from under the machine gun. The huge weight pulled the barrel downward. His finger still on the trigger, bullets sprayed downward, striking the gun slit lip and wall. Trying to catch himself, he fell, banging his knees on the hard floor.

Hot blood ran down his arms. A sudden pain in his left biceps screamed. Max clutched the wound. The sticky wetness ran between his fingers. The bullet had gone through and through. He couldn't tell if it had hit bone, but didn't believe so.

Max checked his side, making sure the bullet hadn't struck him again after it passed. He knew all too well how easy it was to miss a bullet hole in you. Nothing else, but the arm was bleeding everywhere. His goddamn heart medication was making it flow like an open tap.

He needed to take care of this. Get back in the fight. Keep the attention off Mei. He had to protect her. Had to protect Lukrasus and the other weapons.

Cocking his arm hard against his side, Max let go of the wound and crawled across the floor. Scalding brass burned his palm but he didn't flinch. He didn't slow. Tears from pain and the choking gun smoke ran down his cheeks. The shutter remote hung from its cord beside the empty gun pedestal, swinging in lazy circles.

Max rose onto his knees, reached up, and hit the button that closed the shutters. His vision warbled, sliding in and out of focus. Pushing through the dizziness, he clicked on the lights and started toward the red trauma kit on the shelf beside the ammo cans.

A quick bandage, that's all he needed. Just wrap it up and jump back into the fray.

He wrenched the plastic case from its niche. Bloody fingers flipped the twin plastic latches.

A terrible crash sounded downstairs. *What the hell?* He glanced back at the monitor. The screen showing the back door was black. They must have broken the camera.

A second crash thundered, this one downstairs. They were inside the building!

Forgetting the trauma kit, Max drew his revolver. Awkwardly he opened the cylinder and spun it so that the gold bullet would be first.

Something slammed the door beside him. It hit again and again. The frame buckled and the door blew open.

A lean man stood in the doorway. Even if he hadn't seen the Vatican's sketch, Max knew the man's face—the knife-blade nose, the long, pointed goatee, the jagged bronze crown. A distant gleam shone in the dark eyes—zealotry or madness. They looked the same. Hernando de la Fuente gripped a black, tapered sword, the handle encased beneath a twisting ribbon of gold.

The corners of Hernando's wide lips curled upward. Not menacing, but impressed. Max knew this man, the creature he had become. He'd read its journal and could hear the smug words forming in its mind. "You have been a most worthy opponent, etcetera, etcetera."

Max wasn't going to give the bastard the chance to voice them. He snapped the cylinder shut and raised the revolver.

Lighting quick, De la Fuente closed the distance. The sword lifted, the fluorescent lights glinting along the polished edge like sparks.

Max pulled the trigger as Redemptor speared downward.

Lima has changed in my absence. The city weeps for Pizarro. I only regret Redemptor had not delivered the fatal blow and made us one.

CHAPTER 26

Mei loaded magazines as she watched the screens with growing dread. Seven of them had winked out, probably destroyed by the big-headed things running around out there. She'd seen Max cut through their ranks with the machine gun, but he'd stopped. Was he okay? There were radios in the gun nest, but Max had never turned them on. *Probably too busy.* He'd started firing the instant the cars had stopped.

There was no question that De la Fuente was behind this. Mei had seen him on the feed, as Max chased his ass with machine gun fire. She'd never seen anything move like that. She saw the sword, too.

Redemptor had come for the orphans. It had come for Lukrasus. Mei couldn't let that happen.

She'd called Luiza and then Master Turgen, telling them what was going on. Luiza and the others were on their way, but it was going to be forever before they could make it. Max was out there and she was locked inside a concrete room. They had a sink, so water wasn't a problem, but it wasn't like they had a bathroom in here. The Order had thought of everything in case of a siege, but somehow a bathroom had skipped their minds. At least Gabi had stopped crying.

Ester was telling her a story, trying to get the toddler to sleep, but Gabi could sense the terror in the room. Mouth curled into a frown, she shifted and refused to stop looking at the wall monitors until Ester had physically placed herself in the way.

Mei finished one magazine of brass and loaded it into her sidearm. Her go bag held an assortment of various nine millimeter bullets, preparing her for just about anything. Only fifteen of which were brass jacketed. She'd dug through the rest, finding a dozen others of various metals that had a brass nose cap. Twenty-eight bullets.

Each magazine could hold fifteen. With one full mag, plus one in the pipe, that left only twelve for the backup. She loaded her five gold-capped rounds in a separate mag. Five bullets. Max had fired a hundred at him and hit nothing but air. *Better make 'em count.*

She slid the last magazine in her underarm pouch. The shoulder rig felt weird with the bulletproof vest. Not as snug. She'd worn them together before, but those were training exercises with Matt. This was real and everything felt so big all of a sudden. She didn't feel like the badass she'd felt like then. She felt like the Michelin Man. She was sweating like crazy under all this shit, despite the seventy-four degrees on the thermostat.

"Are they gone?" Ester asked, peering over her shoulder at the screens.

Mei searched the remaining video feed, seeing only bodies. She'd seen large-headed shadows moving across the first-floor windows earlier. The building's security system said there was a broken one, but none of the cameras or motion sensors had detected anyone inside. "I don't see anything," she said after several seconds.

"Where's Max?"

"I don't know."

"Maybe he's hurt."

"What do you want me to do?" Mei snapped. She sucked two deep breaths to steady her voice. "He told us to stay here. I have to guard the weapons."

"But he could—"

"No. We are to stay here." Mei's eyes burned from the tears she was holding back. *Knights don't cry.* She held her breath until the sensation passed. "Max is fine."

The old woman must have seen Mei's worry. She simply

nodded and returned her attention to Gabi.

"Don't like it here," Gabi whined.

"It's all right," Ester said in her grandmotherly voice. "We're playing a game."

"I want to go!" Gabi yelled, the temper tantrum looming.

Ester hugged the child close. "Not much longer."

Mei clenched her jaw and searched the monitors. *Where are you, Max?*

Nothing.

She tugged at the vest's stiff collar and checked the thermostat again. Crap, it was stuffy in here. Mei glanced over at a steel-framed square in the concrete wall. When the French base had been attacked, Max and Master Turgen had been trapped with no means of escape. So Max had installed one in here. Opening only from the inside, and protected by a massive concrete block that might take a nuke to dislodge, the door led to a tunnel that let out near the turbines. If Ester closed it behind her, Mei might be able to get out, see what was going on, and lend Max some support. With Lukrasus, she could zip down that passage in no time.

If Max didn't need support, then he didn't have to know she'd even left. Even if the intruders somehow made it in here, and the ghoul mask didn't send them running, there was still the orphan safe. It was intentionally too big to fit through the doors, and opening it required two combinations. The idea was that no one person could access it. Max, Luiza, and Uwe knew one. Luc, Matt, and her knew the other. The orphans would be safe, at least until she got back.

But this is your job, she reminded herself. *This is your first mission. It's a crap job, but this is it.*

Still … she was the only knight here. She couldn't just sit here while their enemies destroyed everything the Order had built. Mei ran her thumb along Lukrasus' steel pommel and eyed the escape door.

An electric ping interrupted her debate. One of the doors had opened. Relief, like a cool weightlessness, swept down her body as Max appeared on one of the monitors. "He's inside," she called back to Ester.

The old woman hurried up beside her. "Where?"

"There." Mei pointed to a quadrant in the upper left screen. He'd used his entry code to access one of the doors along the western side, away from where the intruders had been. He nervously glanced through the glass door behind him, and began limping up the hallway.

Mei's relief vanished as he neared the camera. Blood smeared his cheek and chest. He cradled his left arm in a sling made from his missing shirt. It and his pants were also soaked, clinging tightly to his lean frame. He carried something long and wrapped in cloth in the hand clutching his wounded arm.

Ester's hand went to her mouth. "He's hurt!" She clutched Mei's biceps, the grip uncomfortably tight.

"Get the trauma kit." Mei gestured to one of the cabinets. "Under there."

The old woman released her death grip on her arm and hurried to the cabinets.

Mei could only watch as Max ambled up the stairs to the second floor. He leaned against a wall for several seconds, catching his breath. It was then that she saw the twisted metal hilt peeking from the bloodstained bundle. Redemptor! He had Redemptor! Was De la Fuente dead? He had to have been. Probably afraid to touch it, Max had wrapped it in cloth.

Max drew two deep breaths, then headed to the basement stairwell.

Ester heaved the red canvas bag and plastic case out from under the counter.

Mei's hands began to sweat as Max worked closer. The old man looked like he might collapse. Her first aid training was suddenly forgotten. There was a medical ward on this floor. Maybe if—

Lights flared on one of the screens. Mei looked up in time to see headlights and a closing bumper hurtling toward the north entrance. It slammed into the glass, shattering it, but the window held. The door frame buckled and the bottom part of the laminate popped free.

Looking up as the intrusion alarm began cycling its shrill wail, Max quickened his shuffling pace. Gabi began crying, her hands clamped against her ears, as the alarm reverberated through the concrete bunker. Mei tapped the code, killing the terrible noise.

The truck backed up and rammed again. The window held fast, but the door itself pinwheeled inward and crashed off to one side. Two of the large-headed monsters stormed inside as the truck backed from the hole. One held a short sporting rifle, the other clutched a revolver. Weapons raised, they hurried down the hall.

Max had reached the basement. He was running now, hunkered over the injured arm. The intruders wouldn't catch him. Even if they knew the way down, there were two steel doors blocking the way and they couldn't get a truck in there to batter them down.

Mei clicked the intercom button, activating the speaker outside the library's door. "They're inside."

He hurried the rest of the way and banged on the door. The sound barely made it through. Using his elbow, he pressed the call button below the camera. *"Open the door!"*

Ester rushed to the door and grabbed the wheel to open the locks.

Mei threw out her hand. "Not yet!" Something was wrong. How could he have crossed the grounds without a weapon? Max was never without a gun. "Is that Redemptor?" she asked into the mic. Stupid question. What else would it be?

"Yes. I shot him. But I'm really hurt."

Ester was looking at Mei, her brow creased in an expression of puzzlement and anger.

Mei licked her lips. "Sh... show me your hands."

Max grinned weakly. The *"I trained you well"* look. Leaning the sword against the door he held his right hand up, and then carefully opened the slung left one. There were no rings.

A horrible fear erupted in Mei's stomach. It clutched her lungs, making it hard to breath. There were *no* rings. He wasn't wearing the gold pinky ring with the green gemstone—the ring of the Valducan Masters. She'd never seen him without it. It wasn't him. Mei's head swam. She squeezed Lukrasus' handle.

Max was dead. She eyed Redemptor still leaning against the

wall beside the creature with her mentor's face. It had killed him. Eaten his soul.

The Max-thing looked back at the door expectantly.

Mei forced herself to speak. "All right. We're opening it now." She waved her hand at Ester and hissed. "It's not him. Don't open it."

"What?" Ester asked.

"It's not ... it's not him. Don't open it."

The old woman gave her a look. "But—"

"Max is dead!" she hissed. The words seemed strange, as if somehow it was now real.

"No," Ester said, eyes fixed on the imposter on the screen, the monster wearing Max's face.

Mei shook he head. "It's not him." Tears welled in the corners of her eyes.

"*Mei, open the door!*" the Max-thing pleaded through the intercom.

She didn't reply.

"*Mei, please.*"

She shook her head, wishing she was wrong, but she knew. He'd be pale if he'd lost that much blood. No, his skin was pink and healthy.

The Max-thing looked directly at the camera. The face of the man she loved seemed to transform, harden. He reached up toward it and the screen went blank.

Grief and terror gave way to rage. Mei turned away.

Ester was still staring wide-eyed at the blackened screen. "No," she mumbled, voice weak, shoulders slumping. "No. No."

Mei hugged her and the old woman held her close, still muttering "No, no, no." Ester flinched as the door banged hard, like a sledgehammer wailing on it.

Boom. Boom.

"He can't get inside," Mei said. "Not through that."

Ester shook her head as if desperately trying to evict a nightmare. "What do we do?"

"The others are on their way. We just have to hold tight."

"That'll be hours."

"Yes, but they can't get through." She pointed to the ghoul mask. "That can protect us."

Ester shook her head, evidently not believing it either.

The door continued thunking.

Boom. Boom. Boom.

Gabi screamed.

"Grab those tables," Meis ordered. "We'll barricade the door." Both women began sliding the sturdy tables across the tiled floor, bracing them against the door. Mei figured if De la Fuente could make it through that, a couple tables wouldn't do squat, but it was something to do.

The booming had ceased as they laid a heavy-duty desk onto its side, pens and supplies tumbling around inside its metal drawers. Using her hip, Mei pushed against the stainless door. Ester rolled a few chairs from the back, laying them on their backs.

Wiping sweat from her brow, Mei searched the room for anything else to use. Like the safe, the steel and glass book-shelves were bolted to the floor. God, it was hot. Not just beneath the stifling armor, but her cheeks, her hands, every-where. She began pulling the cords out from the back of the computers. There were six. Maybe she could stack them.

Arms loaded with bric-a-brac from under the counters, Ester dumped them before the growing pile. She stopped, held her hand toward the door. "Mei," she said, voice rising.

Mei lugged one of the metal computer cases over. "What is it?" The wall of heat hit her as she neared. The *ting* of hot metal scented the air. Dropping the computer onto one of the chairs, Mei opened her palm toward the vault door. It was like moving her hand above a hotplate.

The stink of melting nylon yanked her attention to a trickle of smoke curling from the debris pile. "Oh shit!"

Frantically they began pulling the pile away from the hot door. The edge of a black-cushioned chair sizzled where it touched the steel. Mei yanked it away before it might catch fire.

She wiped the sweat sheeting off her face. It was like being in a giant oven. The thermostat LCD read 102.

Now 103. No telling how hot that door was. It wasn't red hot, but it didn't need to be.

"What do we do?" Ester tugged at her sweat-clinging night gown. "We'll be cooked alive."

"Water," Mei said, running to the sink. "We'll cool it off." There weren't any pitchers, only a small collection of glasses and a stack of bright plastic cups Gabi hadn't claimed. She filled two of those from the tap and ran back to the door. She slung them empty and water sizzled and steamed, boiling away as it ran down the door. She passed Ester with her own sloshing cups as she raced back to refill them.

Two more cups hissed as they met the stainless steel. Then two more. The thermostat's LCD continued to climb.

109.

110.

It wasn't enough. They needed a hose. The floor was getting slick from splashed water. Mei's foot slipped. She caught herself but not before adding half a cup more to the wet floor. Steam curled in the air, giving everything a dreamy haze.

After several rounds, the water could make it to the bottom before bubbling away. "It's working!"

She refilled and the next two cups didn't boil at all.

108.

107.

"It's working!" A growing puddle spread along the base of the door. They needed to corral that somehow.

The door groaned, a high ugly noise. Mei slung two more cups, and frost crystals spread across the metal.

What the hell? Most of the water ran off the surface, but some froze in little rivulets or tiny, icicle buds. She held her hand toward the door. Instead of feeling like reaching into a stove, it was like an icebox. The steamy air frosted against it, thicker at the middle, where earlier it had felt the hottest.

"Phintiq," Mei muttered, remembering the Incan holy weapon De la Fuente had turned into a gold and silver necklace. Fire and ice. Surely that wouldn't be enough to take down the door. Would it?

The air was chilling faster, her sweaty face growing cold.

Mist rose from the ice-crusted door. Mei backed away. The library's temperature read 67 and falling quickly.

The door groaned again.

"If we don't cook, we'll freeze," Ester said, clutching her gown.

"The room's too big. He can't freeze or heat that much air. It'll be uncomfortable, but we'll be fine." *Fine as long as no one plugs the vents.*

60.

59.

Mei started as the door boomed. Frost rained off the vault door as hammer-like blows slammed it from the opposite side.

Gabi was sobbing in the corner, her head tucked between her knees. A solid, maddening minute of *boom, boom boom,* and then the blows silenced.

Mei's heart was racing. Squeezing Lukrasus' grip hard, she fought to slow her gulping breaths, each one pluming in the cold air.

The remaining door frost began melting. The door gave a sick, painful groan. *He's heating it up again.* "We're not going to last six hours."

"What do we do?" Ester asked.

Mei looked at the safe. There was no way she could open it. The orphans would be safe from her, but if De la Fuente could make it in here, the safe would be a breeze. If he found and killed her, then he'd know both combinations. She couldn't fight him alone. Everything Max had taught her, De la Fuente knew. He'd be ready for it.

"We escape." Mei nodded to the door. "It's the only way."

Ester barked a humorless laugh. "With those things out there?"

"We don't have a choice. He's going to get in here. We can get out, hide somewhere."

The old woman shook a soggy slipper. "You think I can run with these, across rock?"

Mei shook her head. Even barefoot, the old woman couldn't outrun the things outside.

Melted frost hissed along the door.

"Then you can hide in here."

"Here?"

"Yeah, De la Fuente can sense the weapons. He'll know where I am, but he doesn't care about you. Only the weapons. Once I open the hatch it won't be as bad in here. We can hide you in one of the cabinets."

"What about Gabi?" Ester asked.

"I'll take her with me. She's light enough, I can carry her. With Lukrasus we'll fly right out of here."

"But—"

"No." Mei picked her go bag off the floor and began removing the nylon strap. "We're out of options. Help me."

She peeled off the holster and ballistic vest. Weight and Gabi were now priority. It took some trial and error of straps before they fashioned the vest into a sort of harness.

"Come here, *anjinha*," Ester said, Gabi's nickname of "little angel." She cinched the vest onto the little girl and began tightening straps so she couldn't fall out.

The air thickened with humidity. Condensation beaded along the glass cases, running down in weeping droplets. The green LCD showed 114.

Mei disabled the mask's dedicated alarm, and with Lukrasus, climbed up the wall and removed the sneering obsidian face. No need to give De la Fuente one more demon spirit to his arsenal. She wrapped the mask in an extra shirt from her bag and tucked it into some of the straps.

"How's this?" Ester held the holster straps that were affixed to the vest.

"Perfect." Mei slid her arms in so that Gabi was positioned at her chest, a sort of home-grown tactical baby carrier. "Buckle it in the back."

The door sounded its mournful sigh as the temperature began plummeting again, but the room was still sweltering.

"How's that?" Ester asked.

"Good," Mei said twisting and moving her arms. It wasn't comfortable, but it wasn't too restrictive or feel like it might slip. "Very good. Now let's get you hidden."

The old woman kissed them both, telling Gabi she loved her

and assuring she'd be okay. Crying, she crawled into the back corner of the deepest cabinet, drawing her knees to her chin. Mei piled some of the spilled debris—stacks of printer paper, a cardboard box of folders, and some other odds and ends—to hide her. Bending was difficult with the little girl strapped to her stomach, her head down at the crook of Mei's neck. Mei scattered the rest of the items to complete the illusion of a rifled but empty cabinet.

Furious pounding came from the now frosted door. Something cracked.

Mei drew Lukrasus and kissed the top of Gabi's head. "You ready for a ride?"

"No," Gabi whimpered.

"Then close your eyes."

The little girl pressed her face into Mei's chest. Mei gave one final look at the pounding door, and then entered her code in the escape hatch's number pad. A light blinked from the security console but there was no alarm. Probably ruin the point of a secret escape if it blared when it was in use.

Steel ground against concrete, setting Mei's teeth on edge. Then the eight-foot block slid smoothly aside. Mei peered down the square tunnel, not more than four feet to either side. Only a pair of small lights glowed along its length, no more than nightlights, chasing away the shadows. A third light, far in the distance, marked the second door.

Grabbing the metal frame with her free hand, Mei swung herself inside, flipped gravity, and fell down the tunnel. It was harder than she'd thought. Lukrasus' gift only affected her, so Gabi's weight slammed her down into the floor as they slid. Gritting her teeth, Mei changed gravity's pull, angling it up. She jolted up toward the ceiling. She managed to catch herself with her forearm, painfully grinding it, without striking her face against the concrete.

The first light whipped past as Mei changed gravity's direction again, trying to keep them somehow in the middle. It wasn't pretty, not the smooth plummet she'd envisioned, but more like hops or a high-speed wave.

The second light flew past. Mei could barely see the final

door down between her shoes. She reversed gravity again to slow their fall. Gabi's weight jarred her down, slapping her ass against the floor. One of the buckles along her back ground on concrete. Mei slowed, and flipped it again before they began falling the other way. Her feet touched down against the second door.

"See?" she asked. "That wasn't so bad."

Gabi only whimpered.

Now for the real test. Max had known where the exit was, and even if they couldn't get through it, his troops would be out there waiting for it to open. She'd have to be fast.

Mei punched her code in the keypad. The tunnel lights flipped off, plunging them into darkness. The concrete block began to shift. Cold night air rushed in through the opening gap. Shadows moved outside. Standing sideways against the door, Mei dropped through the gap the moment it was wide enough and they plunged out into the night air.

She bounced off the side once and then shifted gravity's pull sharply up and out into the sky.

Gunfire sounded behind her. Mei shifted gravity again, turning as fast as her momentum allowed. Wind whipped in her ears. She shifted again, aiming herself toward the great white turbine towers.

Smoke tinged the night air. One of the cars Max had shot up was engulfed in flames. A few tracer rounds zipped past her, the bullets so close they buzzed.

Her attackers opened up the machine gun, not bursts, but a full stream. Mei changed the pull again and again, switching directions and fighting Gabi's earthly pull. Everything moved so fast and she had to keep sight of the turbine lights just to remember which way was up. Gabi retched hot vomit onto Mei's chest.

The wind pulled her to the side, making it even harder to steer. She'd never flown this high or this fast. Mei's eyes watered in the cold wind. She'd have given anything for some goggles.

Mei veered far to the side, then cut right, the little red comets chasing her like Max's remote-control plane. The turbines were just ahead but Mei realized she was coming in too fast.

She flipped gravity again to slow down but her inertia was too strong. She banked up. The spinning blades on Turbine 4 roared below her. She thought of the eagles smashed and killed against them, every bone shattered in an instant.

Tracers chased her up but were too far to the side. Mei slowed and experienced a weightless moment before she and Gabi plunged back toward the earth below. She pulled to the side, using the turbine for cover. Bullets stitched along Tower 6 and they flew past it.

Their momentum slowed, Mei flew toward Turbine 10 and landed in a crouch against the side. She couldn't hear anything past the deafening blades, but didn't see any more shots.

Panting, her chest and neck covered in chilling puke, she climbed like a spider up onto the top and caught her breath.

"Is it over?" Gabi sobbed.

"The worst is," Mai said. The hatch atop the turbine only opened from the inside. No one ever expected a pair of girls to get up here the hard way.

Mei peeked over the edge. Figures moved in the distance, coming their way, but not direct. They didn't know where she was, but De la Fuente would. He was probably too busy with the safe, but he would come for her. Two streams of smoke bled from the side of Turbine 6. The bullets must have fucked it up bad because the twin ribbons were growing visibly thicker.

Mei looked back down at her pursuers. There were four of them, spread out. She could try to take them one at a time, swoop down like a raptor, slash them and fly back up, or she could flee.

Not with Gabi. If one of those things tagged her with a lucky shot, then Gabi was dead, too. She couldn't risk it. *"Never forget the stakes,"* Max had warned her.

Mei decided that they were too high. Outnumbered and outgunned, she waited until she'd caught her breath, and then shot off into the night.

Stories tell of a paladin, obviously my former master's successor. Three months before my arrival, he traveled north to San Francisco de Quito. The memories from the priest he met tell me his name is Fedele LiPari, a Sicilian. I shall meet this holy warrior and pledge my services to Rome.

CHAPTER 27

Matt stared out the open window, watching dawn's orange light play across the snowy peaks. The Andes formed not only a geological seam between nations, but time. Dawn on one side, night on the other. Only once the rising sun had scaled the mountaintops would morning break in Chile. Nestled in the shadows of the western slopes, a single light burned far in the distance, the only sign of life anywhere. Matt wondered who exactly lived this far out in the middle of nothing and if they noticed the low-flying airplane sneaking across the border.

God, please tell me Gabi is safe.

Scrunching his eyes, Matt turned forward in his leather seat. Uwe reclined in the opposite chair, head lolled back on the headrest giving Matt a perfect view up the snoring German's nose. Matt envied him and the rest. Aside from Luiza piloting Helen, Kofi was the only one still awake. The slender paladin sat reading in his chair, the tablet's screen lighting his face, the deep shadows of sharp cheekbones reminiscent of the mountains outside.

Matt was too tired to read and while the plane's drone lulled everyone else to sleep, it only increased his anxiety. He was riding on three hours sleep. Whatever those bobble-headed things were, they didn't burn when Dämoren killed them. Normally, a demon kill meant a nice recharge. One touch of demon blood and everything was fine. But not these bastards. All the work but without the payoff.

The only thing keeping him going was Gabi. De la Fuente had attacked his home and every time Matt closed his eyes the images of what he might find shivered him to wakefulness. While he feared for Ester, Max, Mei, and all the holy weapons he'd sworn to protect, the only thought consuming his world was Gabi.

In his time as a demon hunter, he'd been shot, stabbed, beaten, hit by a car, and set on fire. He'd broken more bones than he could count, and even lost two fingers once. He'd endured more pain than most people could imagine and if De la Fuente hurt even a single hair on Gabi's head, Matt would inflict every bit and more on him. Not that he'd get much of a chance if Luiza got to De la Fuente first.

The plane shuddered, a sudden jolt of turbulence and the momentary weightlessness of free fall. Matt clenched the armrest until he was sure it had passed.

"ETA twenty minutes," Luiza called from the cockpit.

Matt's mounting dread flared, a thousand hot needles burrowing into his gut. In only a few minutes, he would know if his fears were true.

Uwe blinked awake, gave Matt a nod, and unbuckled his seat belt.

The others stirred as well, pulling on gear and checking their weapons. Matt shuffled up to the front where Luiza and Epple sat. The Swiss Guard wasn't versed on flying this particular plane, but a half-trained copilot was better than none.

"You need anything?" Matt asked, peeking his head through the half-open curtain.

Luiza craned her neck. Dark circles sagged below her eyes. The light sheened off her waxy skin. A faint black soot scuff along her hairline remained from her wiping her face after the church fire. Matt knew that he didn't look any better.

"Nothing now," she said, her tone somehow distant from the looming task. "Epple was about to take the stick so I can gear up."

Epple looked back and nodded. His eyes were a little red, but looked like he'd gotten an hour or two of shuteye. "Best get started. I have this."

Luiza thanked him and slipped out of the pilot seat. Matt led her to where everyone was awkwardly trying to put their vests and holsters on without bumping into anyone else in the five-foot-wide cabin.

Matt helped Luiza into her vest. "No word?" he whispered.

She shook her head. "Nothing since the first call."

"It doesn't mean anything. Communication's out. That's all."

Luiza smiled weakly. "That's what I keep telling myself."

He kissed her and pulled her close. "It'll be fine."

She broke the embrace first. "Better get ready." She kissed him and wove her way back to the cockpit. Felisa watched them with an almost analytical sympathy, like she wanted to say something, but was running calculations for what that could be. Everyone else was performing a fine job of pretending as if they weren't watching.

Matt smiled at the small paladin, an unspoken thanks for an unspoken statement, and he began suiting up. He opened Dämoren's loading gate and rolled the cylinder, checking that all seven chambers were loaded. He'd known they were, having checked them once already, but the final inspection was ceremony. The remaining twenty-three rounds were already on the belt, he having cleaned and reloaded them all with an engraved hand press shortly after takeoff. Satisfied, he holstered the big revolver. In the galley, which was really just a micro-fridge nestled beside the head, he removed two small water bottles and with the aid of a medical lancet began making blood compasses.

"It's coming up ahead," Luiza announced from the cockpit.

Everyone craned their necks at the window, hoping to steal the first glimpses of the wind farm. Matt could see only desert mountains out his side, but across the aisle, beyond Kofi's bald head, he eventually got his first glimpse at the white turbines lazily spinning.

"Look at Six," Luc rumbled.

"Not good," Uwe said. The German was out of his seat and

hunched behind the big man, blocking Matt's view. "Someone might have seen the fire, called SEC to report it."

Matt's breath caught as Turbine Six slid into view. A black scar engulfed one half of the generator housing. Streaks of soot ran from the shaft neck and around the sides like racing stripes. Its top hatch was gone, only a blackened hole where wind-fed fire had evidently melted it away. At night, the blaze would have visible for miles, a distress beacon to summon the Energy Superintendence to make sure there would be no outages along the grid. But how had it even started? Had the attackers set fire to it to draw them out?

They circled the grounds once. Smoke drifted from a tangle of burned out cars in the lot. A semicircle of bodies littered the grounds around Schmidt's gun nest. Several windows were broken in the main building and Luc said the north door was completely gone, but Matt had already stopped looking.

Years before, when Mal had raced them across France to find the chateau attacked, Matt hadn't felt it. That hadn't been *his* home. He hadn't built it and made memories there. It was only a place and he a visitor. This was entirely different. His daughter was down there and Matt's guts roiled with each terrible sight.

Again, he replayed that moment in the streets of Montevideo—De la Fuente atop the car and Matt's hesitation. Had he taken the shot, probably delivering him to a South American jail cell, how many lives would he have saved? His rational brain repeated that he'd made the only choice he had at the time, but right now it was losing that fight. If Gabi, or Ester, Schmidt, or Mei were hurt, it was his fault. He could have taken that shot, and every time he replayed it, he remembered just a bit more clearly how he could have stopped this.

The plane circled wide. Landing gear hummed below his feet, emerging from their hidden shells. Matt drew a breath and held it, his hands gripping the padded armrests. From the corner of his eyes he saw the mountains rising above the level of the windows. Matt stared intently at his knees and the plane leaned back. He imagined the wheels suddenly tearing free, the rushing ground shearing off the tail section, his chair tumbling out the back with him still strapped inside.

A light thump and the plane touched down. Wind buffeted off the wing flaps. Matt clenched his teeth and the plane slowed.

He released his breath. Uwe watched him from the facing seat, unhidden amusement tugging at his lips. *Dick.*

Matt opened his mouth to say that, but glass and plastic exploded into the cabin as bullets tore through the airplane's side.

"Down!" Yoder screamed.

Shards of debris and puffs of insulation filled the air. Matt fought with his seat belt as another strafe of machine gun fire stitched toward him. He fumbled the buckle open and rolled to the floor beside Kofi, who was trying his best to crawl under his seat.

Specks of blood dotted the light gray carpeting. A bullet struck the chair anchor beside Matt's hand. Yoder was crawling atop Felisa to act as a human shield.

The plane veered left, leaning sharply. Tires squealed. Bullets hammered the rear hold. Matt lifted his head, knocking shards of acrylic glass from his hair.

Uwe was across from him, struggling to get Tuerie's head between himself and the wall, but the spear's shaft was caught on everything now littering the floor. Blood ran from a ragged gash across the German's thigh. Matt scrambled over the debris-mulched floor and helped position the spear.

Tuerie's scabbard peeled off as the force field opened with a shimmering ripple.

"You're hit," Matt said.

Uwe nodded. "Graze." Blood was seeping everywhere.

"I'm the one that's supposed to get shot, remember?" Matt looked around for something to tie it off with.

"You made it look fun," Uwe rasped, his voice pained.

"Well, that'll show you," Mat said, still looking for something to bind it without lifting his head. The slowing plane jolted like it had been kicked. Matt came off the floor and slammed back down. The plane stopped abruptly. Something toppled and crashed in the hold. Matt's knee knocked painfully into one of the spilled ammo bags. The right side of the plane was angled higher, giving everything a skewed, fun-house feel.

Half buried beneath Yoder, Felisa tore off her black head scarf and held it out. "Here!"

Matt took it and began binding Uwe's leg.

"Shit!" Uwe hissed as Matt cinched the wrapping.

"I don't whine like that when I get shot."

"Not funny." Uwe yelped as Matt tied the scarf off.

"Then stop getting shot." Matt looked around. "Everyone okay?"

Everyone spoke up, saying they were. Luiza had killed the engine and now everything was eerily quiet, save for the wind whistling through the thousand bullet holes. Acrid smoke trickled from Yoder's punctured seat. Tracer round. Thankfully the stuffing was fire retardant.

Matt met Luc's gaze. Luc motioned his head to the door beside him. Matt nodded and began crawling toward it. The gunner had been on the starboard side. The door was on the port, so maybe they could get out without being cut in half.

Carefully, he rose and stole a peek out a window. "Looks clear."

"Sir." Yoder crawled toward him, rifle in hand. "Let me go first."

"No time for protocol." He motioned to the blood compass still resting in his chair's cup holder. The other one was nowhere to be seen. "But if you could toss me that, I'd be grateful."

Yoder scrambled to Matt's pulped seat, covered in stuffing, bits of wall, and polished veneer. He grabbed the bottle and gave it a good underhand toss toward the front.

Matt caught it. "Thanks." He checked the compass. Two beads. Far side. "Let's do it."

Luc grabbed the big metal handle and yanked. With a kick, the stair door swung down with a pneumatic hiss. Not hesitating, the knights were both out, their weight bringing the door down the rest of the way.

Matt drew Dämoren from her holster and crouched to see under the plane, using the landing gear for cover. Bullets had taken out the port tire. Cocking the revolver's hammer, he searched the far side of the airstrip for any signs of the attacker. Everything was still. Silent. Gray, stinking tire smoke drifted across the empty runway.

Feet rumbled down the gangway behind him and then Felisa was there. Luiza came next, followed by Kofi.

"I don't see anything," Luc said, leaning out from behind the front wheel.

Squeezing Dämoren's ivory handle, Matt crept forward. One of the sheds stood open. It looked like where the shooters would have been, but nothing moved inside it. The pair of blood compass beads pointed directly at it.

Matt raised two fingers and pointed. He motioned to Luiza, telling her to go around.

Yoder moved up beside him, rifle in hand. He sighted in on the shed. Epple crawled to the rear of the plane and did the same.

"I see them," Epple said. "Two gunners. They appear dead."

"What?" Felisa asked. "How?"

"I don't know. Guns on the ground. Lot of blood. One of them is missing an arm."

"Do you see collars?" she asked.

"Can't tell."

Matt glanced at the others. Luc's attention was on the main building. Luiza and Kofi were circling around, using an earthen lip along the runway for cover. He really wished Uwe was okay to walk, they could just let him lead with his spear out front but that wasn't an option right now.

"I'm going forward," Felisa said.

"Bullshit," Matt said.

"They can't hit me."

"Can you dodge a machine gun?"

"Epple, keep them covered." Felisa moved out from behind the plane, her sword ready.

Son of a bitch. Matt followed her out, Dämoren up at the ready. He saw the two dead things now, their giant heads deflating. The compass didn't show anything more.

"What are you doing?" Felisa hissed.

"You're not going alone."

"Stay here," she said.

"We can stand and argue or we can get to cover."

Felisa shot a wry smile and started across the runway. Movement flickered to the right—Luiza and Kofi crouch-running across to the hangar. Not wanting to draw attention, Matt kept his eyes forward on the shed. Arcs of crimson splatter stained the sheet metal wall, running down in long dribbles.

"There!" Luc shouted behind him.

Matt spun. To the left, toward the main building, a figure walked toward them. Dust coated her clothes and tangled, shoulder-length hair.

Mei?

She held a broadsword in her hand, the bloodied blade out to the side. Some kind of harness covered her torso, like a backward backpack, but then Matt noticed the round dome of black hair sticking out of the top.

"Gabi!"

The little girl twisted and squealed, "Daddy!"

Matt started toward them but stopped. A single red bead pressed against the blood compass' wall, pointing directly at them. *No!*

Mei was walking toward them. She looked half-dead and the little girl's kicking looked like it might pull her over.

No.

"Gabi!" Luiza shouted behind him.

Matt threw out his hand and leveled the gun at Mei. Felisa's sword came up in unison beside him. "Stay back!" he shouted.

Mei froze, her eyes locked on the bladed revolver.

"Matt, what are you doing?" Luiza asked, voice rising.

Keeping his eyes on Mei, he lifted the compass. His mind reeled. One bead, two girls. He seriously doubted De la Fuente could impersonate Gabi, which meant it had to be Mei. It explained the chest harness well enough. Human shield. But why kill the gunners?

"What are you?" he demanded.

"I ... I'm Mei," she said.

"Bullshit." Goddamn shape-changers. It was one thing to kill his friends, but wearing their faces ... "Drop the sword. On your knees. Now!"

Tears ran down Mei's cheeks. "Why are you doing this?"

"Drop it." Could he shoot if she ran with his daughter strapped to her chest? "Hands where I can see them."

Slowly, Mei knelt and gently dropped Lukrasus onto the runway.

Luiza and Kofi ran up beside him. Luiza took a few steps past him, but stopped.

"I thought they were gone," Mei sobbed. "We saw the plane so we came back, but then I saw them shooting, so I ... killed them."

Keeping clear of Epple and Yoder's lines of sight, Matt moved around to the side. The blood bead rolled along the compass' wall, but he still couldn't tell which was demon-corrupted.

"Daddy!" Gabi shouted as he came into view.

"Hey, baby girl, you stay very still, okay?"

Mei was looking at him, her wet eyes a combination of fear and disbelief.

"Where's Schmidt and Ester?"

"Max is dead," she said. "I don't know about Ester. She hid in the library when we escaped."

Her words hit like a drunken slap. Schmidt? He'd thought of the old bastard as invincible, a monument, giving Matt hell until they both died of old age.

"Put me down," Gabi protested, fighting the ballistic vest harness.

"Did you ..." Luiza asked. "Did you take anything off the men you killed, a choker?"

Mei shook her head.

"Then what's this?" Matt asked, gesturing with the compass. She only looked at it. "I ... don't know. I'm human. I promise I'm human."

Matt glanced around, searching the rocky landscape and building's dark windows, but seeing nothing. If Gabi was possessed, what would he do? He couldn't kill her. He'd die first. What would he do to anyone who tried to? First, he needed to know which one was corrupted. Maybe he could lock them up, wait for Mal to get here with whatever voodoo shit he did and fix it. "All right, this is what we're going to do. You're going to slowly take off that harness and step away from Gabi."

"Wait!" Mei said.

Matt's grip tightened on the gun.

"The mask, the ghoul mask, would that set your compass off?"

"Yeah," his hold loosening a tiny, hopeful fraction.

"I have it. I took it from the library so De la Fuente couldn't get it. I'd wedged it between me and Gabi."

"Show me," he said, "Slowly."

Tears slicing down her dusty face, Mei unclicked and untied the vest. Gabi squirmed free and scrambled to Luiza. The red bead didn't follow her, releasing Matt from the impossible weight of fear. Luiza wrapped her arms around her daughter, clutching her tight.

The blood compass didn't point at Mei, either. It pointed at the bundle tied to her stomach, a white t-shirt. Mei pulled it from the straps and the bead tracked the movement as she set it on the ground.

Matt lowered the hammer. "I'm sorry. I had to be sure."

Mei sobbed, dropping to her hands and the tears pouring. Jesus, what had she been through? Max dead, an army of monsters hunting her, and he'd thanked her with a loaded gun. *I'm a fucking monster.* "Hey." He holstered Dämoren and knelt beside her. "Hey, it's all right. We're here."

Mei threw her arms around him and cried, trembling.

He held her. "It's all right. It's all right. Are you hurt?"

She shook her head.

"You did good. Tell me what happened."

Matt hadn't been entirely sure what to expect after Mei's account of the attack. He knew it would be bad, but the archive room's shattered door was beyond what he'd expected. Deep fissures stretched across the remaining steel. Jagged chunks of it littered the floor, peeled and broken away as if it had met a bomb blast that hadn't touched anything else.

The intense heat had activated the sprinklers, flooding the hall and several of the adjoining rooms in about an inch of water. Steam had sent it everywhere, and fat, dripping beads of condensation coated the ceiling and ran down the walls. Thankfully, none of the water had made it over the lip and into the library.

Matt checked his compass.

Still pink.

Dämoren out front, he stepped inside and found the archive strangely intact. He scanned the corners, making sure they were clear. The bookshelves were untouched, thank God, but the safe stood wide open, empty, the sapphire blue of its felt interior a beacon of color against the bland concrete wall. The weapons were gone. Matt sighed, the micron of hope withering to dust.

"Basement clear," he said into his radio.

"*Weapons?*" Luc radioed back.

"Gone."

"*No sign of De la Fuente up here. Save for the two that shot at us, none of the dead have brass chokers.*"

"Looks like Mei was right," Luiza said, stepping through the door behind Matt. "He fled before we could arrive." She eyed the open safe. "How did he open it?"

Matt shook his head. He'd expected a horror show like the archive door, but the alternating heat and cold would have destroyed the weapons. "Either Max knew both combinations or knew where to find them." He glanced down the long tunnel that Mei had used for her escape. Dusty footprints ran along the floor, the leavings from the invaders who had rushed in probably moments after her exit and opened the door for their master.

He shivered, imagining Schmidt, twisted and evil, stepping through the battered door like a conquering emperor. Had Matt just pulled the trigger … *Stop*, he scolded. This wasn't his fault.

"Mama," Luiza said approaching the cabinets beneath the counter. She knelt and peered through the half-open door. "Mama, are you in there?"

Something shifted in the back. A stack of paper towels topples over.

Luiza opened the door the rest of the way and slid a box aside. "Mama?"

"Luiza?" a weak voice replied.

"Yes, Mama, it's me. We're here."

"Gabi?"

"She's fine, Mama. Mei kept her safe. Come on out. It's okay now."

The old woman crawled out from the cabinets. Bloodshot eyes scanned around from sunken sockets. The stink of urine came with her. Ester had wet herself hiding in the dark from the monsters. She wrapped her arms around her daughter and Matt stepped in, holding them as they wept.

"Are you sure you want to do this?" Matt asked as they reached the top of the tower steps, a folding stretcher beneath his arm.

"I have to," Mei said, her stony expression unreadable.

Matt nodded. "I understand."

He stepped through the broken door frame. Brass casings and belt links carpeted the floor. The shutter control dangled beside the empty pintle mount, a dried and bloody handprint on its button pad. A pickup slid across the monitors above, Luc at the wheel beside Epple with Uwe propped in the back looking none too happy.

Maximilian Schmidt, Master Knight of the Valducan Order, lay naked in the corner like a discarded garment. The brown and red streaks of half-dried blood shone in sharp contrast against his ghostly pale skin. A web-work of scars traced along the old warrior's body. A single stab wound pierced the center of his chest, the white hairs around it caked in blood.

He seemed so small now, nothing like the titan of will he'd been in life. Schmidt's eyes were, thankfully, closed. Matt wasn't sure if he could handle the dead knight's stare. He'd been Clay's best friend and had shared many stories of their glories and adventures. Now, those memories were lost.

No. Not lost.

Stolen.

"I'm sorry," he said, his voice a hoarse whisper.

"They just threw him in the corner," Mei said. "No ... dignity."

"Yeah," he said, cursing himself as the single word left his mouth. Christ, he needed to say something comforting, something for the girl who had just lost her mentor, but his brain was at a loss. "He went down fighting."

"He died protecting me."

Matt unfolded and laid the stretcher out beside Max's body. "He held them back as long as anyone could have."

She unfurled the blue plastic tarp from under her arm and laid it across him, covering his nudity. "I should have been here, not hiding away."

"Hey." Matt put his hand on her shoulder. "You did exactly what you had to do. You saved my daughter. You did everything you could, so don't blame yourself. Please." His voice caught in his throat. "This isn't your fault."

Mei nodded, scrunching her eyes to fight back the tears. They wrapped Schmidt in the tarp and moved him onto the stretcher. Matt strapped him down.

"If Redemptor killed him," Mei said. "then his soul is gone? So that's it? He's just ... nothing?" Her brown eyes pleaded for him to disagree.

"I ... uh ... I don't entirely know," he said, wishing to God he could sound half as wise as she seemed to think he was, "but I don't think so."

Her head cocked. "How? You shared your mind with Dämoren. I've read your account. You said you *tasted* souls of the demons you killed."

"Yeah, but that was different. It's not like it was an entire soul. Simply ... a taste. I think destroying a soul is a bit harder than that."

"So demons killed by the holy weapons aren't dead?"

His throat clicked as he swallowed. "Not entirely, I suppose. We know Tiamat has been killed twice, but I don't think they can come back on their own."

Her gaze fell to the wrapped body. "So Max might not be dead. At least his soul?"

"I don't know for certain, but I don't think it took a taste and let him go. I think Redemptor trapped him, so it's still ... absorbing him."

"You're not very good at comforting a girl, are you?"

Matt shook his head, more to himself than in answer. "Think about it this way, if we destroy Redemptor, we can still save his soul."

LiPari's death was neither my intention nor avoidable. His sword, what we had believed to be the spirit of a holy angel, was impure. Rome is mistaken. They are not angels we serve, but monsters. The Devil has deceived us again, and Redemptor has revealed the truth to me. Praise be to God.

CHAPTER 28

Armed with a pair of slender tongs holding a fold of gauze, Felisa dabbed Uwe's leg as Kofi worked a tiny suture needle along the ragged cut. The sight of blood had never bothered her, and she'd seen more than her fair share. There wasn't much bleeding now, anyway. Time and a few CCs of epinephrine had seen to that.

Once the grounds had been checked as clear, they'd carried the injured knight into a first-floor conference room. The infirmary downstairs was flooded, and she'd helped fetch the necessary supplies, soaking her boots in the process. She couldn't help but marvel at the Valducan's setup, this desert fortress guised as a corporate wind farm. They'd known the Order had substantial finances, but this was beyond any expectations.

Uwe propped himself up on his elbows and peered past Kofi's gloved hands. He glared at the bullet graze, his lips curled and chin crinkled into a scowl as if it were some faulty piece of equipment and not his own body. "Nice work."

"Lie back down, please," Kofi said, pulling the slender thread tight.

"You tended bullet wounds before?"

"Many times." He pushed the tiny needle in again, hooking it through. "Lie back down, please."

Uwe lowered his stance, but didn't lie down. He turned his attention to Felisa. "He ever sewn you up?"

"No," she said.

"You don't trust him?"

"Of course I do," her voice rising with a defensive edge. "With my life."

"Paladin Gaspari has never been injured in my presence," Kofi said. "She finds it easier to avoid bullets and claws."

Uwe nodded. "Uwe approves of this idea. Getting shot sucks." He lay his head back on the conference table. "So how did you learn to stitch bullet wounds?"

"Mali," he said. "Somalia, after that."

Uwe grunted. "Was this before you became a paladin?"

"Yes and no. My time as Paladin has sent me to many regions in need."

"Bad business," Uwe said to no one in particular. "So, you've never been hurt?" he asked Felisa.

"Hunting?" She shrugged. "I twisted my ankle on my second assignment."

"And that's Ofniel? I saw you dodging bullets."

She nodded.

"Uwe thought he only worked on cameras. Always looking directly at them like they owed you something."

She smiled. "That's only a small part of it. Ofniel warns me of danger. He's old and not entirely used to the idea of photography."

"We called you Sister Gaze."

"Really?"

Uwe nodded. "We called him Scarecrow."

"I've been called worse," Kofi said, tying a new suture.

But Felisa had stopped listening. Sister Gaze. She liked the sound of it. Her life as a paladin had always been secrecy, a constant battle to avoid detection or notice. Most, even in Vatican City, had no idea who she was—another nameless face in a habit. But not to the Valducans. To them, she'd been a mystery, a face and an evocative name. She touched her wedding ring, hidden beneath her latex gloves, and pressed it not with self-admonition but pride, thanking her glorious husband for this surprising, albeit secret, notoriety.

Felisa rode that high until after Kofi had finished his work, telling Uwe to keep off his leg as much as possible. Armed with crutches, they escorted him to the elevator. Luc had disabled certain keypads, allowing them limited access, which she appreciated.

Sister Gaze.

She liked the sound of it. Scarecrow, not so much, but Kofi wouldn't have cared either way. He was her opposite, and being noticed was nothing he'd ever had to desire if he were so inclined. Once Uwe was safely in his room with promises to go to sleep, they found Luiza and Luc in the large dining room. A grayish-green walkie-talkie stood upright on the polished mahogany table between trays of sandwiches, fruit, and steaming eggs speckled with peppers and meat. Felisa's stomach tightened at the smell, saliva flooding her mouth. Aside from a small bag of granola on the plane, she hadn't eaten in hours.

Luc stood barefoot before a stainless tower pouring coffee into a cobalt blue thermos mug.

"I understand," Luiza said, phone pressed to her ear. A short crack and smudge marred the large window behind her, an errant bullet strike, Felisa guessed. Outside, Yoder and Gast inspected the bodies—twenty-one including the pair that Mei had killed, and only those two still wore the brass demon chokers.

Taking a chair beside the door, Felisa pulled off her wet boots and deposited them on a towel beside Luc and Luiza's. Few of the chairs in the house had arms, and none of the ones she'd encountered had arms on the left side, making it easy to sit with a belted sword. In Vatican City, her own home, Ofniel was resigned to his case, hidden from curious eyes. Here the Valducans wore their weapons with pride, even modifying their furniture to accommodate.

"No. Plane's shot." Luiza pressed her temples, working circles with thumb and middle finger. "We have some cars, so we'll pick you up in Copiapó when you land. Just let us know.

Yes. I know. No … she's fine, just shaken. Talk to you soon."
She clicked off her phone and blew out a tired breath. "Mal's
stranded in Houston. Plane trouble."

The muscles in Luc's jaw tightened. "How long?"

"Overnight. Says there's a flight out tomorrow afternoon to
Santiago, then back up. About seventeen hours."

"This is the American knight you're waiting on?" Kofi
asked, filling his plate.

Luiza nodded.

Kofi rubbed his stubbled chin. "We should be able to help.
I'll make the calls. Try to secure a direct flight to Copiapó."

"The Church can fly him down direct?" Luc asked.

Kofi nodded. "Of course."

The big man grinned, sharing an amused look with Luiza,
her lips pursing into a faint smile.

"It's really no problem," Kofi said.

"Oh no," Luiza said waiving off his concern. "We'd appreciate it. That's extremely generous."

Luc concealed his mouth beneath a hand, his cheeks still
raised from a broadening smile.

"What is so funny?" Felisa asked, approaching the giant coffee pot. None of the empty cups matched. Most appeared gaudy,
or touristy—one shaped like a shark's open mouth, another like
a Mexican sugar skull with flower eyes the color of pistachios.

"I'm imagining Malcolm strolling into the basilica, guitar
case in hand, and asking for a ride."

She selected a plain cup of thick, white porcelain. "They'd
leave from the airport."

His smile broadened, filling his face. "Then you might want
to warn them before they meet. Malcolm is very … not Catholic."

Kofi shook his head. "If he is wed to an angel, then he is a
holy warrior."

"You should still warn them."

Kofi's brow crinkled, a puzzled question on his lips.

"Don't worry," Luiza said, moving toward the coffee pot.
"Thank you. Really."

"We should check with the others," Felisa said, moving
aside after filling her cup. "Find out what supplies they might

need." Customs was rarely a concern for the Church's private planes, especially in Catholic nations. She poured milk into her cup and stirred. "How is your daughter?"

"She's fine," Luiza said. "Exhausted. We got her to bed for now."

"You should get some sleep, too."

Luiza smiled wanly. "Too much to do."

Felisa gave an understanding smile, choosing a new approach. Hunters didn't respond well to being told what to do. "There is, but after flying all night, I'm sure you're exhausted, too."

The Brazilian only nodded.

"And your mother ... Ester? How is she?"

"Shaken. She's who made all this." Luiza nodded toward the food. "She'll be fine."

"Is she in the kitchen?"

"No," Luiza said, absently. "I think she went to check on Gabi."

"Might I have a word with her?"

Luiza stopped. "What for?"

"I would like to talk with her, see how she is." Felisa licked her lips unconsciously.

"She's fine." Uncertainty lingered in Luiza's tired, brown eyes.

Kofi and Luc silently watched from their seats.

"I understand. But, you had told me that she still practices the faith and I supposed that maybe speaking with me might help. If that's all right with you, of course."

"No, I mean, yes. Yes, she might appreciate that." Luiza gave an approving nod. "Thank you."

"It'll be my pleasure."

Once finished with breakfast, Felisa left Kofi on the phone making arrangements and made her way toward the living quarters. She found Ester in her room, the door open. The gray-haired woman sat on the edge of her bed, staring out the window, a white plastic basket of folded laundry beside her.

Felisa knocked on the door frame. "Missus Moreira?"

The old woman jumped. Her hand shot beside her, gripping

a blued revolver that Felisa hadn't noticed. A sense of recognition dawned in her eyes, overcoming the panic. "You? You're with the Church."

"Yes, ma'am. Felisa Gaspari." She smiled, maintaining eye contact and pointedly not looking at the gun. "I wanted to check on you. Make sure everything was all right."

"Yes." Her hand relaxed, but the fingers remained on the rubber grip. "Call me Ester."

"Ester. Thank you for breakfast. It was very good."

Ester gave a distracted nod, the same one that most who experienced horrors gave, somehow hardwired into the human consciousness.

"May I come in?"

"Of course." Seeming to forget the gun, the old woman stood and offered a chair.

"Thank you," Felisa said, taking the seat. Framed pictures blanketed the wall and the simple night stand beside her. A yellowed wedding photograph in a silver frame stood prominently among them, the smiling bride a near duplicate of Luiza. The groom and most of the guests wore gleaming breastplates with sapphire blue half-capes. More pictures of the same people, aging between photos, the passage of decades in one scan of the eye. Some of the faces vanished as time passed. Photos of a young Ester with her husband holding a blanketed baby, first steps, baptism, holidays, and vacations. Luiza grown up, her father now absent from the pictures. Ester's black hair dulled to steely gray as she poses at her daughter's wedding, only a handful of the original wedding guests, gray-haired themselves, stand beside the smiling couple. Then pictures upon pictures of baby Gabi. This was a woman who loved her family, lived for them, and had seen many die.

Felisa ran her thumb across her wedding band, finding the strength for her next words. "I'm extremely sorry for what happened last night. I can't imagine how terrible that was."

Ester swallowed. Her gaze averted toward her knees.

"I know you must be very tired," Felisa continued, "but your daughter enlightened me of a terrible burden, and I wanted to address that as soon as possible."

The old woman straightened, apprehension creasing her eyes. "Burden?"

"Many years ago, a misunderstanding led to a grievous mistake, a mistake that for our part had been forgotten. I have brought this error to the attention of His Holiness and he agrees and begs your forgiveness for the pain that his predecessors have caused you and your family."

"His Holiness, begs *my* forgiveness?"

"He does." Felisa reached a tentative hand and placed it on Ester's. "Your husband was married to an angel."

The old woman tensed at the mention of her husband, but Felisa continued, pushing onward before any protest might begin.

"His soul was pure and strong. His Holiness assures me that no holy warrior could ever suffer *vitandus*."

Ester's hands began trembling. She blinked, the tears welling.

"His Holiness has rescinded the declaration. He will issue a papal decree acknowledging this terrible injustice. Your husband, and his father, and all those before them are in Paradise. And before ..." Felisa's voice cracked. "... before you go to sleep, and mourn the souls of those you loved, I needed to set this right with you and to beg your forgiveness."

Ester was crying now, tears running down her cheeks.

"Can you forgive us?" Felisa pleaded, her own tears falling.

Nodding, the old woman tried to speak but only gave a squeaking cry. She opened her arms and Felisa reached forward and held her tight as Ester wept. It wasn't a lie, Felisa knew. His Holiness would rescind the decree once she had a chance to tell him. She had no doubt of it. Somewhere in the recesses of her mind, Ofniel assured her that her words and intentions were true. The wrong would be righted, but Ester needed it now. Felisa would call His Holiness today.

"Thank you," Ester managed.

Felisa held her close, allowing the decades of pain and grief to wash through her arms. Finally, once the storm of tears had passed, she released the embrace and met Ester's red eyes. "Will you pray with me?"

"Yes."

Matt pinched the corners of his eyes between thumb and fore-
finger, pressing lightly on his lids and rolling out the grit of
sleep. He sat on one of the thick, leather seats of the conference
room and listened while Master Alex Turgen spoke on the giant
wall monitor.

The rest of the knights sat in the room with him. Kofi and
Yoder were out keeping watch while Felisa and Epple rested up
for the next shift.

"We must consider this Priority One," Turgen said. "One
Master dead, another knight out of action, four weapons stolen,
a possible two more at risk. The Chilean base has been com-
promised and electric production is down by two percent. Any
more will result is investigation by the SEC. Everything Max
knew is now in the hands of our enemy, so none of us are safe."

"I've already contacted the Takaira Clan," Master Sonu said.
Daiyu, a Chinese knight with short, boyish hair, and Dawood,
a Pakistani knight with a neatly trimmed beard, sat on either
side of the old hunter. "Susomu sends his deepest condolences,
but will stay in Japan until he has found a jorogumo terrorizing
Kyoto."

Matt gave an understanding nod. He didn't blame the
samurai for not jumping at the opportunity to help the Order.
The last time had ended with two stab wounds, a ghetto blood
transfusion, and two weeks in a hospital bed. Given the choice
he'd have chased a demon-spider, too.

"The airplane is completely out of service," Luiza said. She
sat beside him, nursing what Matt guessed was her five hun-
dredth cup of coffee. She'd been going for thirty-six hours now.
The battle at the church that morning felt like a week ago.

"Can our new friends help us with that?" Allan asked, seated
beside Master Turgen. Matt was pleased to see that his best
friend, the youngest of the Valducan Masters, hadn't adopted
the formal suits that seemed required for the rank, choosing
instead, a tight gray T-shirt and blue jeans.

Victoria, Allan's unofficial fiancée, sat to his right. Her
blonde hair had grown out some, now tucked behind her ears.
Her bronze khopesh, Allan's old sword Ibenus, peeked from

her hip between them. The rest of the European team was off somewhere, training their newest recruit.

"Probably," Luiza answered. "They've already offered to secure us a suitable plane, but it will be a few days."

Matt grunted. They'd originally offered a helicopter, which sounded to him like the worst idea in the world.

Turgen shifted in his seat. "I'm not entirely comfortable with our newest associates."

"Nor am I," Master Sonu said, "but they have been helpful."

"They've been very eager to work with us," Luiza said.

"Of course they have." Turgen squeezed his knee. "You have a common enemy. They need us as we need them. Simple fact. My concern is how that amicability will hold up once that enemy is gone. We have spent centuries hiding our activities from them and they now know more about us than ever before."

"Times have changed," Matt said.

Luc and Uwe nodded in agreement.

"Perhaps," Sonu said. "But I agree with Alex, we must be careful with how much we share or come to rely on them."

Matt wasn't exactly sure how that was supposed to work, the Exorcists living with them and all and Mal currently on a Cardinal's private jet.

"We'll be cautious," Luiza assured. "But right now, De la Fuente is still out there and we need them as much as they need us."

Sonu gave a resigned nod. "He's probably rebuilding his army."

"Perhaps set up a wide perimeter," Allan suggested. "You're pretty isolated out there. Easy to spot a caravan heading your way. Ambush them."

"Maybe." Matt sipped his lukewarm coffee. "But remember he can sense our weapons. Anyone setting an ambush can't have weapons on them or it ruins the surprise."

Allan frowned. "Maybe the Swiss Guard, then."

"Maybe, but if they try to take him out alone they'll die."

"We can't assume he'll charge up here again," Luc said. "He might come out of the mountains from behind."

"He could already be back there," Uwe said, cracking open his second energy drink.

Matt unconsciously glanced to the giant window beside him, as if expecting bullets to suddenly begin hammering the bulletproof glass.

"He's not," Mei said, breaking her silence. Except for her debriefing, sharing the story of De la Fuente's attack, Schmidt's death, and hours spent dodging searchers with Gabi strapped to her chest, Mei had spent the videoconference near the back of the room, staring at a laptop beside her.

"Why do you say that, Lady Tseng?" Turgen asked.

"Because he left. He could have stuck around for everyone to show up and bring him the weapons. He knew they were coming. But he didn't. He took the rest of those things, two cars, and left a good hour before they arrived."

"And why do you believe he did that?"

"He has four, maybe six weapons. He knows facing all the knights at once would kill him. I think he left to harvest the ones he has, turn them into weapons to use against us. Why else would he have driven all the way from Argentina to here, when he could have just attacked everyone at that church?"

"Shit," Matt said. "She's got a point."

"So you think he's breaking them right now?" Allan asked.

"Probably not yet," Mei said.

"Why not?"

She swallowed, her confidence softening. "Ah … I, uh, don't think he can just do it anywhere. Fashion the weapons into jewelry, I mean. I think he has to go to the pyramid to do that."

Allan straightened. He looked at Turgen, and then Victoria.

"Why do you say that?" Master Sonu asked.

"Well, his journal shows that he captured Eremiel, and the next entry, weeks later, says he'd returned from the mount and talked about the steel cuff. I went through the journal to figure out which mountain he was referring to, but the only one he ever really talks about is the pyramid where he made Redemptor."

Several of the knights had already pulled up their tablets or opened laptops, searching for what Mei described.

"But why would he need to return?" Sonu asked, apparently unfazed by Mei's discovery.

"I don't know," she said. "But there is a gap of over a month before he writes about the cuff."

"Makes sense," Matt said. "Malcolm told me that harnessing the spirit in a holy weapon was seriously hard. He said *he* couldn't even do it. Maybe the pyramid helps contain it long enough to trap it in a different item."

Sonu nodded, slow and deliberate. "So De la Fuente is going to the pyramid to break and re-bind the weapons into armor or jewelry." It wasn't a question. "He has a day's head start."

"Do we know where this pyramid is?" Luc asked.

Vacant stares and shrugs answered him.

"Maybe the Exorcists do," Uwe offered. "We've had this journal only a few days. They've had centuries."

"Then ask them," Turgen said. "If they don't, we need to figure out where it is."

"I've already started." Mei turned her laptop around toward the camera, showing a crude map. "I've been going over his entries of the expedition, using maps and satellite pictures. There isn't any description of a pyramid like that anywhere, so it's probably still in the jungle somewhere, and pictures of those areas are low-res at best."

"Very good," Luiza said. "Brilliant."

"Mei," Turgen asked, his voice deathly serious. "Did you tell Max any of this?"

She shook her head. "No. We didn't really get a chance to talk about it and I wanted something to show before I brought it up."

"Good. Very good."

"Well, if he's heading there, we need to find out where it is and get there fast," Matt said.

"Agreed," Turgen said. "But we can't say for certain if that's his intent. This is only a theory."

"And I believe it."

"As do I."

"So, what is the plan?" Luc asked.

All eyes turned to the giant knight.

"First," Matt said, "we ask if the Exorcists know where the pyramid is. If they don't, we find it. Then once Mal lands we head on up, maybe beat De la Fuente there."

"Probably need helicopters," Luiza said. "No runways in a jungle."

Matt paused. "I'd guess so," he said, swallowing back a grimace.

"Uwe can't go," Luc said.

"Uwe can go," Uwe huffed. His seat creaked as he leaned forward, his leg still propped before him. "Just a little cut."

"Twenty stitches," Luc said.

"Just a cut," Uwe repeated.

"Someone has to stay," Luiza said. "We need a Base Knight, and you're the least fit to fight. Schmidt is dead and its Mei's right to avenge him. That leaves one of *us* to stay."

"The orphans can come with us," Uwe said. "Dividing our—"

"No," Luiza said, cutting him off with that sharp, "don't argue with me" tone that Matt knew so well. "We're not taking Ozkareen or Fuertod with us, not to *him*. There's also the archives and someone has to maintain and get repairs started."

The German snorted. "Oh sure, Uwe can't fight but Uwe can fix a hundred-ton turbine by himself."

"No, but Uwe can pump water out of the basement."

"And dispose of three burned cars, one of them a police SUV someone's looking for by now, get rid of twenty-one bodies, fix the gate, fix the doors, tow the plane ..." Uwe counted them off on his fingers. "What else is Uwe forgetting?"

"Sir Uwe does bring up a point," Turgen said. "We cannot abandon our responsibilities at the wind farm. And its current state may draw attention, especially with any missing persons reports or the National Energy Commission."

"We can't stay until that's all fixed," Luiza said. "It could take weeks."

"Maybe the Exorcists could help," Luc said. "They could send people."

"I'm not inclined to give the Catholic Church more intimate knowledge of our facility than they already have," Turgen said.

"Then what do *you* suggest?" Luiza said. "We're running out of time."

The old man opened his hands in surrender, but it looked more like a magician about to do a trick. "I don't know."

Matt strummed his fingers along his armrest, an idea forming. "I might have someone that can help."

"Who?" Luiza asked.

"Old friend. Owes me a big favor."

"It'll take more than one person."

"Yeah," he said, the idea still crystallizing. "But he's not alone."

"Can we trust them?" she asked.

"Absolutely." Matt stood. "Tell you what, give me a few minutes to check and see if it's even possible. If it is, we'll discuss it. But I don't want to waste breath until we even know if we can do it."

His wife gave a questioning, but consenting nod. "All right."

Matt politely nodded to the wall camera and stepped out into the hall. He tapped his pockets, verifying where his phone was, and drew it out. He stared at the screen, summoning to memory a number that had never been saved in any phone he'd ever owned, a number he hadn't called in three years.

Discovering it, dusty but still in his mental Rolodex, he tapped it out and held the phone to his ear, making a silent prayer that the number was still good.

It picked up on the second ring. The windy hum from the inside of a moving vehicle.

"*Nivam Transport.*"

"Cesar, this is Matt Hollis."

"*Ho! Holy shit, Matt! I don't believe it. Long time.*"

"That it has."

"*Canada, right? Shit,*" Cesar blew a laugh. "*What's been going on? How ya doin'?*"

"Life's been good, man. Got married."

"*No shit?*"

"No shit. Got a daughter, too."

"*Well, look at you. You still ... doin' that thing?*"

"Oh yeah," Matt said. "Wife, too. There's a lot of us that do it."

Cesar gave a little grunt. *"Huh."*

"Look, man. I got a problem. I think it's time to call that favor and I mean big-time."

"You know I'll do it," Cesar said, the joviality replaced with the cold sincerity he'd had when they'd first met.

"Where you at?" Matt asked

"Ah ... Kentucky right now. Headed to Knoxville, but I'll dump this load and head your way. Where am I goin'?"

"Chile. Atacama Desert."

"Oh ..." Cesar said. *"Well that's a little different. It's going to be a little hard, you know."*

"That's all right, man," Matt said, pacing up the hall. "How's the family? They still kickin' it in Putumayo?"

"Of course."

"Look, it's a nasty drive, but I got a big job and I need a lot of warm bodies. Construction and some other details. It'll pay good."

"What other details?" Cesar asked.

"Remember that thing we had to do that time after that shit happened? This is about three times bigger."

"Shit. Matt, you know they're good for it. We owe you."

"Well, we'll pay them and still call it square. Like I said, it's a big job. We need someone who can handle heavy equipment and help if there's any ... further problems. We got the hardware, just need the manpower, and we need it fast."

"Absolutely, my friend. I'll need to make some calls."

"I need to run this past my associates, but if the family can send me down ten, maybe a dozen, I'd be real grateful. I'll shoot you details once I have the green light."

"You got it, my friend," Cesar said.

"Thanks." Pleased, Matt hung up the phone and headed back to the conference room.

Master Sonu was on the screen, saying something about, "Around the clock," when Matt walked in. Everyone silenced.

"So?" Luiza asked.

Matt slid back into his chair. "About eight years ago I was in Colombia. Asanbosam. Real nasty fucker was terrorizing a village. Racked up a good body count before I got there. Anyway, the locals all know me. One family, the Prietos, sort of adopted me. Said they owed me a huge favor once it was all done. I used to work with one of them back in the states, guy named Cesar. I used him whenever I had to find or move something under the radar. I told him that I needed a dozen or so that can handle construction and body disposal, even some muscle. He said they're up for it."

"And you trust them?" Turgen asked.

"Hundred percent. If Cesar says they're good then they're good."

"So you want to trust a dozen armed Colombians to rebuild and protect our home?" Luiza asked.

Matt shrugged. "Anyone got a better idea? I know them and I know they can do what we need. And yes, I know your mom will hate it."

Luiza's brow arched pointedly, an unspoken, "You think?" On more than one occasion, Ester had let her opinion of Colombians be known, a holdover from being born and bred Brazilian.

"What is their trade?" Master Sonu asked.

"Coffee. But they had to protect their property and didn't shy from getting messy."

"How fast can they get there?"

"Three days. Two if they hurry."

The old knight's lips tightened, vanishing beneath his thick moustache. "I can agree to this."

After a few more questions, and some colorful protests from Uwe, it was decided.

"Very well," Turgen said. "We haven't much time. Let us now focus our attention on finding Mei's pyramid."

The Serpent of Temptation has burrowed deep in Rome. They cannot grasp that they serve Lucifer. I will best these arch demons, these spawns of Hell, and bend them to God's holy will. I am His Paladin. I am the savior for His ignorant flock. I am the shepherd and Redemptor my crook.

CHAPTER 29

Amazonas Region, Peru

Hernando enjoyed the moist air blowing through the truck's open windows as it rumbled up the winding mountain road. He'd missed the sweet smells of leaves and wet rot and flowers. This was life, not the barren wastelands where the demon-worshiping Valducans had erected their fortress temple. Great leafy trees, heavy with twisting vines, loomed above, the lowest branches brushing along the top of the vehicle. Birds and long-tailed monkeys hopped away as the convoy passed. The infernal sounds of the weapons droned in the back of his consciousness, ignorable but never forgotten. For now, he enjoyed the whoops and clicking songs of the sleepless jungle.

Without headlamps, the forest shone in hues of crimson and pale blue. The narrow gap in the canopy gave glimpses of the scintillant line of God's river high above. The last hill Hernando had crested had given him a view of a second thread, though he could not yet see the point of their meeting. But he was close now.

Rolling sweat tickled down his stubbled cheek and neck. He scratched at it absently, knowing it would do no good as only more would come. The face he wore was that of Chus Ojeda, Sergeant Second Class in the Peruvian National Police. He wished for his own face, and could change it at will, but he required this one for now.

Crossing a concrete culvert, the sinewy road wound its way up the adjoining slope. A white light flickered between the trees near the top of the rise.

They were here.

Choosing a bend out from the light's reach, Hernando stopped the police truck. In the mirror, brake lights ignited in succession as the four other vehicles halted in line.

"Go," he said, not looking at the swollen-headed servant seated beside him. "Prepare for my signal. Do not be seen."

The mute creature opened its door and climbed out.

Hernando watched through the mirror as others emerged from their vehicles and started up the jungle slope, vanishing between the trunks and underbrush. He waited several minutes, savoring the jungle smells and sounds before starting the engine, and turning on the headlights. The other vehicles waited behind as he drove.

A narrow guard shack stood at the top of the hill. A cloud of swirling insects orbited the light above the door. The reflectorized sign, emblazoned with the National Police coat of arms, read "Station A3-17." Beyond the lowered gate pole stood five squat buildings with corrugated metal roofs. A cluster of mud-spattered police vehicles sat off to one side. Hernando eyed his prize resting near the center of the clearing like a green and white idol atop an asphalt altar: a helicopter.

A uniformed man with a large mole at the corner of his lip stepped from the shack, his eyes blinking away the remnants of sleep.

"Good evening," Hernando said, cocking his elbow out the open window in the manner of Sergeant Chus Ojeda.

"Hello," the officer said, his tone betraying any attempt to conceal his surprise.

"Sorry, it's so late. Flat tire." Hernando motioned his head toward the back. "Bringing some new monitoring system." He extended his hand to the approaching officer.

The man looked at it as if debating shaking it, then seemed to notice the embossed steel cuff about Hernando's wrist.

Power surged down Hernando's arm and blasted the officer back. His head struck the edge of the cinderblock guard shack and the man crumpled facedown. Blood spread across the back of his olive cap.

The camp remained silent.

Drawing Redemptor, Hernando stepped out of the idling truck and thrust the sword into the unconscious man's back. The misty light of the dead man's spirit sprang from the wound and was sucked into Redemptor's blade.

He closed his eyes, scouring his newest memories for the information he required. The outpost served not only the tiny villages that lacked any real police presence, but to locate and combat illegal loggers, drug manufacturers, or terrorist cells that might be hiding in the lush valleys along the roots of the Andes. It housed twenty-four officers, but only two could pilot the Bell UH-1 helicopter, nicknamed Papa Pitufo. Hernando found their names and where they now slept.

He willed his likeness to that of Specialist First Class Mario Heredia, feeling the bulbous mole sprout below his mouth like a mushroom. The rank on the now loose uniform didn't match, but Hernando wasn't concerned. This would be over quickly, and Hernando would again wear his true face. First, Redemptor needed to taste the blood of Jose del Mar, and teach Hernando to fly. Julio Martin, the second pilot, would join the ranks of Hernando's subjects. There were more than ample collars for the rest in the camp.

Leaving the parked truck blocking the drive, Hernando stepped past the lowered gate bar and pointed to the barracks house. Shadows moved from the surrounding jungle as his soldiers closed in on all sides.

Golden light sparkled off the dew-wetted canopy as dawn peeked above the horizon. No clouds hindered its brilliance. Engine thrumming, Hernando peered out the cockpit window as they approached the point where the seams of power converged.

While he'd known the possibility, he couldn't help the surprise at finding the pyramid swallowed beneath the jungle canopy. Bright blue birds scattered as the helicopter neared. The blanket of vines and twisting branches dulled the pyramid's shape, but they could not entirely mask it. A giant four-sided hill, its slopes aligned with the cardinal points.

Even in this world of enormous edifices of concrete and steel, Hernando marveled at its size. Its architects had built more than a stone monument, they had constructed a bridge to God. Centuries of neglect had hidden it. No wonder God had abandoned this world during Hernando's imprisonment, but that would change.

There were no clearings suitable for landing. Hernando circled around until selecting a nearby gash in the canopy. He hovered lower. The downdraft buffeted trees, bending the gap wider and sending leaves out in every direction. The morning sun's light stretched the helicopter's elongated shadow across the canopy beside them.

With his free hand, Hernando shot a hard gesture, pointing downward. The side doors slid open. Roaring wind whipped through the cabin as Hernando's soldiers moved with rapid efficiency. Slender coils dropped from the shadow helicopter's belly and then the rappelling troops slid down.

The helicopter was far too small to carry all of Hernando's men. Unable to speak, there was no need to leave any behind on the Police Outpost's radio. It would take four trips to bring them all. By that time, they would have cleared enough space for the helicopter to land. Hernando would then send his men with the helicopter to collect the *chaska chiqui* hidden along the distant highway as he would begin the cleaning of God's pyramid for the work ahead.

If Rome serves demons, then are we not in Hell? We must purify this world before it can be worthy for God's return.

CHAPTER 30

Atacama Region, Chile

After the conference with the Masters, Mei had slept for twelve hours, deep and dreamless. She awoke to what she first thought was an empty house. Every muscle had tightened over the night, payback for the exertions she'd put them through. Rolling her neck, she shuffled down the silent hall toward the kitchen.

A mountain of dirty plates and cups filled the large, stainless sink, and spilled across the counter. Most of the food was also gone, but thankfully someone had at least spared a single yogurt in the fridge.

Spooning it, she wandered into the dining room, to find even more discarded dishes and a picked-over platter. The burned-out cars were still outside in the lot, though someone had thankfully removed the bodies. Far across, the plane still rested off the runway like one of Gabi's discarded toys, one wing angled high like a giant sundial.

Where was everyone?

Tossing her empty yogurt cup in the trash, she headed downstairs.

The hum of motors drifted up from the basement. The standing water was gone. Several fans had been set up for the monumental task of drying what the pump hadn't cleared.

A steady *chunka-chunka* thrummed through the workshop's open door.

She poked her head in to discover Matt, wearing candy-red headphones and seated at the reloading table with trays of loading parts spread out around him. One of those Swiss Guard guys, Yoder, she remembered his name as, operated a bullet press.

The workshop was twice as big as the Archive. Candid pictures and movie posters covered two walls. The rest were hidden beneath tool-laden pegboards. The couches where they watched movies for reloading parties had been shoved against one wall and draped in plastic, making room for a pair of heavy folding tables. An orange brass tumbler hummed away beside buckets of dirty shell casings and tangled belt links. Uwe sat off to one side, a scarred Plexiglas shield over his face as he worked at a saw.

Yoder noticed her first, giving a respectful nod.

Matt looked up at him, turned, and smiled. "How's it going?" he asked, pulling off the headphones.

"Fine." She almost had to shout with all the noise. "What's this?"

"Ammo factory." He nodded to a windowed room behind Uwe. Through the glass, the big, avocado-green bullet-making machine strummed loudly. Gleaming slugs tumbled down a ramp on one end and into a black tray. Chunka-chunka-chunka.

"Brass works on those big-headed bastards, so we're making all we can."

"Where's everyone else?" she asked, stepping inside.

"Luc and Epple are off to pick up Mal. Should be back in a couple hours. Everyone else is upstairs, scouring maps for your pyramid. The rest of the Order has joined in that hunt. Once they find it, we'll be moving out."

Mei checked the trays of finished rounds, plucking one out. Brass shells, brass jackets. They weren't even capping them, just round noses.

"You had breakfast?"

She nodded.

"I'm guessing you want to join the pyramid hunt, being as it's your idea and all." Matt shrugged. "Unless you want to hang in the dungeon with us."

"Hmm," Mei said with an exaggerated wince, "I think I'll join the hunt."

"Don't blame you one bit. Once Mal comes in we'll assign out details. We're putting Max to rest tonight, so we understand if you need to take it easy today."

"No." She dropped the brass round back into its tray slot. "I'm not resting until we find that bastard."

Matt nodded. "I figured you'd say that. Go on up. Find him before anyone beats you to it."

"There they are," Luiza said.

Mei looked up from her monitor where she'd been scrolling through miles and miles of low-resolution satellite images of rain forest, just an endless field of blurry greens. They'd narrowed down the most likely location for the pyramid to a 2,400-square-mile strip along the Peruvian-Ecuadorian border. After that, they'd divided it up into ten-by ten-square-mile plots and assigned them out. Kofi swiveled in his seat to the window behind him.

A bright yellow helicopter with a black-striped tail gently lowered onto the lot outside like a robotic wasp.

"Let's go greet your Uncle Malcolm." Luiza rose from her seat, extending her hand to Gabi, who was scratching crayons across white printer paper on the floor. It wasn't the big loopy curves that Gabi normally scrawled, but dense angular shapes in purple and red. The little girl hadn't said much after her mother had told her that Uncle Max wasn't coming back. No tears, just silence and sharp-edged drawings.

Still clutching her Crayolas, Gabi stumbled to her feet and accepted her mother's fingers.

Mei marked her place on her current grid square and followed them downstairs.

Cold air greeted them as they emerged from the compound. Dust spun through the air, kicked up by the helicopter's now slowing blades. Felisa, who'd been on guard detail, was already there. They stopped just outside the blades' perimeter as the doors swung open.

Luc unfolded himself from the rear door as a man with

caramel skin and a tight black ponytail stepped down from the front seat beside Sergeant Epple.

The man's dark eyes scanned the area once, then he gave a toothy smile and headed toward them, knees bent until he'd cleared the spinning prop.

"Hey, Mal," Luiza said.

"Hello, darlin'." He gave her a hug and then knelt before Gabi, peeking from behind her mother's leg. "Hey, Gabi."

"You remember your Uncle Malcolm?"

Gabi gave a noncommittal hug.

"And you must be Mei," Malcolm said, offering his hand. A stylized orange and blue eye was tattooed on his right palm. "My deepest condolences," he said after she accepted it. "Master Schmidt was a great man."

Mei swallowed as she smiled weakly. "Thank you."

He gave her hand an assuring squeeze before releasing it.

"Mal." Luiza extended her hand to the two paladins. "This is Paladins Kofi Aggrey and Felisa Gaspari. Paladins, this is Doctor Malcolm Romero."

Mal grinned. "Scarecrow and Sister Gaze," he purred. "It's a pleasure to meet you. Thank you very much for your help with my getting down here."

"It was no problem at all," Kofi said.

"So where are the others?" Mal asked.

Behind him, Luc and Epple were unloading gear from a hatch at the rear of the helicopter.

"Matt and Uwe are down in the workshop," Luiza said. "The rest of us are searching for De la Fuentes's pyramid. Tonight, we're putting Master Schmidt to rest."

Mei glanced down. Burning Max seemed wrong. She was expected to say something, but she wasn't ready. It seemed so … final. Would he have a turbine dedicated to him? A turbine that would always draw her eye and that she'd take extra care to maintain and visit when she needed to be alone or work through ideas?

Mal nodded. "Let me go down and give my helloes. Then let's get to work."

"So what do you think?" Uwe asked, his voice high with builder's pride and hope.

Matt bounced the homemade grenade over in his hand, enjoying the weight of it. It was cylindrical, about the size of a miniature soda can. The inside was packed with the diced remnants of brass demon chokers. It still smelled of the flat gray spray paint Uwe had coated it with.

"How's it work?" Matt asked, checking the knurled stainless knob at the top.

Uwe plucked the mockup from Matt's fingers. "Give it a good half-twist," he said, demonstrating.

Matt took an unconscious step back. The German had told him first thing that there was no powder, just sand. But a grenade was a grenade.

"Relax," Uwe said shooting him a flat stare.

"Yeah. Yeah. Go on."

"Half twist and the cap comes off." He pulled the metal knob away, revealing a coil of braided wire, about five inches long, connecting the cap to the grenade. "Then give it a good pull." He yanked the knob and there was a barely audible *tick*. "And throw."

"What's the fuse delay?"

Uwe gave a little side to side shake of the head. "Five … six seconds."

"You sound real confident there."

"Uwe's only had two days. The design is good. The Order made some of these years ago, but Uwe's working with what he has."

"So five seconds?"

"Just pretend it's three. Throw the moment you pull the cord, but don't get excited and forget to pull it first."

Matt grunted. "How many do we have?"

"Six. Uwe will have to work out a different detonator if we want to make more."

Matt pictured the little can bombs all bundled up in a clear plastic six-pack ring in a cooler. "We'll need to test one. Make sure they work and let the other see it."

Uwe straightened defensively. "They work."

"I'm sure they do, but we need to anyway."

"But you only have six."

"Then we'll only have five. Luiza's not going to like this and we need to show her before she lets us use them."

"But you're Arms Master," Uwe insisted.

"Uh huh, and Luiza is Team Lead."

"But if these work as advertised, talking her into it won't be too difficult. At least … that's what I'm hoping."

Three days. For three days Felisa had scanned endless blurry jungle, broken by only the shadows of mountain peaks and the occasional tiny village or stream. Combating the desire to skim, she had to force herself to look away every few minutes, look out the window, sip her coffee, or simply rub her eyes. Only meals, sleep, and guard shifts broke the monotony, but even those few reprieves were soiled by the knowledge that right now Hernando might be destroying God's weapons and perverting them into weapons of his own. His slaves.

She was scrolling north, the screen at its maximum clear zoom—three centimeters representing two hundred meters of jungle. That gave her a little over a kilometer's width across the screen. A narrow, muddy river, not much more than a creek, wove back and forth in curving arcs like a loosely folded ribbon. De la Fuente's journal had said they'd found the pyramid after fording a river. Felisa had initially been excited when she'd found her first river, scouring every pixel for telltale signs. Yet the Amazon's mountains held hundreds if not thousands of such streams and the intensity of her searching waned.

Blinking, Felisa looked away. Outside, a team of stocky men and one woman carefully towed the wounded airplane back onto the runway with a heavy-duty truck. The Colombians had arrived that afternoon, led by a man named Alfonso, who appeared quite happy to see Matt. They asked no questions and after introductions had been made, promptly disposed of the burnt-out police truck and cars by crushing and burying them with a backhoe far away in the desert along with the burnt remains of the dead.

The fluffy orange and white cat lounging by Luc's feet mewed and rolled onto its back. Experience told her that calling the cat over only encouraged it to ignore her more. Malcolm, the new American hunter, sat to Felisa's left. Multi-colored tattoos decorated his arms. He had been one of the Valducans they'd known the most about, a practicing voodoo witchdoctor of some repute. He and his bone-handled machete Hounacier had caused quite a stir in New Orleans some years ago. The Archdiocese paid him special attention, sending their reports to Rome without knowing why. Depending how this business played out, maybe she could arrange a formal meeting between the voodoo knight and her contact there.

Pondering how that meeting might go, she returned her attention to her computer and scrolled up. Felisa stopped. There had been something.

She clicked the down arrow until it came back. There was nothing there, just more green treetops. But yet ... something in the texture had caught her eye.

Felisa ran her tongue along the ridges of her molars, eyes intent. She was about to pass it off as imagined, the amusements of a tired brain, but then she saw it. A straight diagonal shadow. Not perfectly straight. It warbled with the shape of the trees, but it stuck to a distinct 45-degree angle from north to south.

Felisa zoomed in, losing clarity, and zoomed out again. A distinct vertical edge ran up the western side. It was difficult to tell for certain. The giant map she'd been studying was an amalgamation of various satellite images captured over an extended period and assembled by a computer. Sometimes the lighting of different days varied or the images didn't perfectly line up this far from civilization. But those inconsistencies were always square, running vertically or horizontally along the edges of individual frames. That might explain the western line but wouldn't account for the angle it joined.

She rotated it a few degrees to change perspective and determine if there was a southern line as well, forming a triangle of shadow.

"You find something?" Malcolm asked.

"I ... I'm not sure."

"Let me see." He rolled his chair over beside hers. "What are we looking at? Wait, no. Let me see if I find it."

Felisa scooted out of the way to let the knight have a closer view. She realized she was holding her breath. Kofi and the other knights had all looked up as well.

Malcolm stared at it for several long moments and ran his finger across the angled shadow. "That it?"

"Yes," Felisa said.

Malcolm didn't reply. He executed the same tests—zooming in, rotating the view. He zoomed out very far, the scale showing a kilometer for every three centimeters. He slid the position to the left and right. "Felisa might have found the pyramid."

"Where?" Luiza asked.

Mei rose from her seat and peered over Malcolm's shoulder.

Malcolm clicked the GPS coordinates and pasted them in an instant message window, blasting it out to everyone, even in other continents. All the computers gave a simultaneous electronic *bloop*. "It's overgrown, but the shadows betray its shape. I'm guessing two-fifty, maybe three-hundred feet wide. Stepped. No easy way to guess height."

Squinting, Luiza leaned her head to the side. "I don't see it."

"I do," Mei said.

More *bloops* started pouring in with questions and exclamations of joy.

"East of where the river bows wide," Malcolm said.

"There it is. How in the hell did you spot that?"

Felisa smiled shyly. "I nearly didn't."

"How can you tell that's not just a hill?" Luc asked.

"Placement," Malcolm said. "The closest slopes are southeast. This one is by itself. Also, it lines up too neatly with compass points. If the sun had been higher at the time the picture was made we wouldn't have seen it."

"This doesn't mean it's the right one," Luiza said.

"No, but there are no known Mesoamerican pyramids anywhere near that part of Peru. Most of those are west of the Andes. There could possibly be more than one in the Amazon region, but no one's heard of *any*. If anyone had found one it'd be a massive archeological discovery."

"Okay," Luiza said, diffusing Malcolm's mounting excitement. "So, we can safely guess that this is it."

"Most likely. We'll need to play with the contrast some, see if any more details emerge. But I don't believe it's a trick of the light."

"Fine." Luiza tapped on her keyboard. "That's in the Condorcanqui Province. Pretty remote. It's going to be a bitch to get to."

"We can worry about that," Kofi said.

Felisa nodded. "Epple is on patrol. I'll see what he thinks about getting there."

"Very good. Let's start getting ready. Once we're sure this is the place, we need to hustle."

The next several hours moved in a blur—meetings, video conferences, phone calls, and packing. Matt outfitted everyone with ballistic vests and radios. They all received the shiny brass ammunition he'd made. Felisa shared Luiza's concern about the grenades, but no one vetoed them. Desperate times, as they said, and De la Fuente commanded an army of the damned.

Shortly after midnight, the band of the Milky Way stretching across the heavens above, Felisa hurried beneath the helicopter's whirling rotors, crouched, her face lowered to shield her from the loud, battering down-blast. The prop wind snapped at her pants legs. She climbed up into a cushioned seat beside Mei, across from Kofi, and shut the helicopter's door. Her heart hammered with the excitement and welling trepidation.

"Fasten your seatbelts," Epple said from the pilot's chair.

The small craft couldn't carry all of them with their gear and it would require two flights to shuttle them all to Copiapó where they'd load up into a private airplane and a twenty-six-hundred-kilometer flight to Peru. There, once it was ready, they'd take a larger helicopter north, deep into the Amazon for Atik's pyramid.

Surprise wasn't an option. Their enemy would hear their approach. He knew all their secrets, their strengths and weaknesses, and either choose to fight or to flee. Felisa closed her eyes as the helicopter launched into the air and prayed that De la Fuente had not yet destroyed God's weapons.

Today I slew a thief with my dagger and drank his lifeblood. His soul entered my body, and I felt a refreshment that only those at Christ's final supper could have beheld when they consumed our Lord.

CHAPTER 31

A haze of thick smoke drifted across the lush valley as Hernando's soldiers piled more and more of the felled trees and vines onto the blazing fires. The clatter of chopping axes, crashing trees, chisels, and shovels along stone echoed on all sides. Once again in his true face, Hernando stood atop the great pyramid, surveying its reemergence. The centuries of neglect and swelling roots had damaged it far less than he'd expected. The tight seams between the great stones had allowed very little room for purchase. Trees had grown inside his forge, shattering it, but Hernando wasn't concerned. With his necklace that had been Phintiq, he could heat his materials faster and hotter than any hearth.

Two mute slaves swept the black soil and peeled tangled roots from the deep circular channel along the pyramid's flat top. More were currently grinding the sacred white powder for the coming ceremony. He would require much powder, as there were many demon weapons to harvest.

Far away, he could hear his enemies drawing close. An airplane, judging by their speed. They'd divided their forces, three weapons remaining in Chile while seven raced his direction. He recognized those songs, knew which demons they were and who carried them.

Hernando lifted his gaze to the great intersection high above. Could God see him through those cracks? Yes. He knew it to be true.

He would not flee this confrontation. Under God's eyes, at God's great temple, Hernando would harvest God's enemies, conscript them into the Holy War, and then battle these worshipers of the devil.

It was time to begin.

A moist breeze blew steadily off the mountains, pushing clouds across the dark skies. Torches blazed atop the ruined walls in the courtyards below and at each corner of the pyramid's four platforms. The buzz of insects and cries of monkeys were the only sounds as Hernando ascended the wide steps toward the top.

The first time, centuries before, Atik had beaten a drum for this. But Hernando knew that it wasn't necessary. He had no pagan gods to appease, and his god, the true god, required no such homage.

He wore but a loincloth and his sacred jewelry. Redemptor hung from his waist, swinging side to side with each step, her gold hilt gleaming in the torch lights. In one hand he carried a wide, lidded bowl. A lesser man would have required both hands to handle its weight, but not him.

He reached the pyramid's top. A solid stone block stood at the center, its engravings worn and one corner long broken. His tools and offering were already laid out atop it.

Hernando stepped over the now clean trench running a ten-meter-wide circle around the stone altar. Kneeling onto the cool stone, he lifted the lid from the bowl. A mound of chalky white powder filled the vessel, some of it trailing away on the breeze. With his free hand, he scooped handful after handful, carefully pouring it into the eight-inch-deep ring, deep enough that wind could not disturb it. Sweat rolled down his bare back, tickling down his spine as he worked, but Hernando took his time, making sure the white circle was unbroken.

Once finished, he set the empty bowl aside and placed

the lid back atop it. Rising, he approached the altar where the weapon awaited.

Hernando had hoped the first would be the *chaska chiqui* he'd recovered in Colombia. The Incan weapon had escaped his notice five centuries before and he intended to correct that error. But after his men had fetched it, and he had time to hold it with Redemptor to divine its secrets, Hernando realized that he hadn't the proper materials for binding. A sapphire of the appropriate size and quality would be easy to procure once he returned to civilization, but there was no time for that now. The copper mace would have to wait.

He lifted the curved, silver-hilted knife from the altar and raised it above his head, displaying it to God. It would be first. He'd had ample time with the weapon to know its demon's weakness and he had gathered enough palladium for the task. Casting the bracelet would be no difficulty. Aside from his own experience, Hernando possessed the memories of many artists in the craft, and he'd made an expert mold worthy of their talents.

Hernando mouthed the sacred words that Atik had taught him. He did not know their meaning. God's Tongue, Atik had called it, and it surely was the language of righteousness and of angels. Voice rising as he repeated the chant, Hernando lowered the blade before his lips.

He blew. Frost crackled across the metal. Hernando continued the chant, pausing between each loudening repetition to blow again, freezing the steel colder and colder. Steam wisped off it in the humid air. A phantom breeze whirled around him, ruffling his hair and loincloth, but touching nothing else.

By the tenth repetition, the once whispered words were now shouts reverberating across the valley. He blew a final icy breath and drove the blade down into the stone altar. The metal snapped, cleaving clean in two places.

A flash of violet light that only Hernando's eyes could see blasted from the broken blade. It surged like fire caught in the tempest of the unfelt wind. The light spun and cycloned around him, unable to break free of the powdered ring. The purple light reflected off nothing, not the ground, nor his sweat-slicked skin.

Enraged at its imprisonment, the phantasmal demon buffeted him, again and again, trying to make Hernando break his chant. Once, this might have worked, but Redemptor had made Hernando strong and the demon's assaults carried no more effect than the slaps of a weary child.

Still chanting, he moved to the readied mold, its halves tightly bound with bailing wire. Beside it, a black crucible held a handful of silvery white pellets. Pausing between chants, he blew into the vessel. This time, instead of cold, heat surged from his pursed lips.

The panicked demon thrashed against him, battering his sides with ineffective blows, but Hernando continued his mantra, blowing heat until the pellets had melted. In the back of his mind, he could hear the Valducans coming. They were closing in, flying low, but they were too late.

Once the molten palladium was ready, he lifted the crucible with a pair of iron tongs and slowly poured it into the mold. Steam issued from the sprue holes as the hot gasses escaped. Gently, he tapped the mold's flat sides, knocking free any latent air bubbles.

He waited. Still chanting, Hernando lifted his chin skyward. High above, through the eye of this glowing storm, the beautiful lines seemed to swell. God was watching him.

Hernando blew cool air onto the mold, not enough to shatter the hot metal, only enough to expedite its completion. Once he was sure enough time had passed, he popped the wire binding free. The panels peeled open and he dug the warm bracelet from the heat-blackened sand. The mold could be used only once, but that was all he required. Hernando wiped the rough surface clean and inspected it. It appeared as a swirling pattern of water or smoke. The vague form of faces hid in the design. The casting was good.

Sensing its fate, the demon escalated its assault, slamming into him and tearing at his arms, but Hernando continued his chant. It could not hurt him.

He cut the fingers of excess metal free and with a round file, cleaned and polished it to a lustrous shine. Once, such work might have taken hours, but with the speed Redemptor had bestowed on him it took mere minutes, his hands working in a blur. Friction made the metal hot, but not enough to harm it.

His enemies were close now, mere minutes. They'd stopped just beyond the rise.

Welts and scratches from the demon's attacks covered Hernando's exposed skin. Blood seeped from half a dozen deeper cuts, but they meant nothing. He inspected every minute section of the white metal bracelet, filing any remaining flash and imperfections. Satisfied, he set it atop the altar and drew Redemptor.

Screaming the chant, Hernando thrust God's sword into the swirling storm of purple light. The mist shuddered and surged around the blade. He twisted Redemptor, snaring more of the demon's essence along the blade and pulled it down.

It stretched like tar, peeling from the storm's wall. Hernando touched the blade to the palladium bracelet. A howl erupted on all sides, a sound unheard but felt. The fiery light surged down into the sword, along the blade and into the bracelet.

The white metal writhed. Details emerged as if worked by invisible hands. The palladium clouds wound and curled, weaving tighter. The faces they formed grew more distinct, their expressions twisting into mixtures of joy and terror, ecstasy and agony. New faces sprang from the tangle, so many that one could spend years searching for them all.

The phantom cyclone slowed and stilled. The last of the purple light fled into the bracelet.

His body aching, Hernando kissed Redemptor's blade. "Thank you."

The approaching songs of the Valducans' weapons were circling around. Now that the demonic storm had ceased, he could hear the helicopter's thumping approach. Hernando strode to the pyramid's edge. His silent army waited below, watching him.

Hernando pointed in the direction of the coming aircraft. "It is time!" he called.

They hurried into position, weapons ready. There was no fear, no hesitation. Smiling, Hernando slipped his hand through the sacred bracelet. Power coursed up his arm, spreading through him. Tonight, under God's eyes, he would defeat these heretics with his newest sacred gift.

I am the last of Christ's true disciples.

CHAPTER 32

Sticky air roared in through the helicopter's open side, rattling the cluster of carabiners fixed above the door. The dark jungle spread out in all directions, as far as Mei could see, various shades of black on this overcast night. Treetops buffeted a dozen feet below them as Epple hovered.

Yoder checked the lines dangling from the clips.

"Are you ready for this?" Luiza shouted. An array of lenses and tubes jutted from the goggles masking her eyes. With the black helmet and body armor, the only hint of the knight's identity was her cupid lips.

Mei nodded. "You can trust me."

"I wouldn't do this if I didn't." Luiza tossed a canvas bag out the door, the attached rope spooling out as it fell.

Yoder leaned out the helicopter's open door to watch it. He nodded, flashing a thumbs-up. Luiza slid to the door's edge and swung out, pivoting around, and she stood on the landing skids, facing the inside of the helicopter.

"Go!" Yoder ordered.

Luiza gave Matt a nod and then she was gone, zipping down the line and through the opening in the black tree canopy.

"*Clear,*" she said through the radio.

Matt was next, a monocular night scope covering one eye like a cyborg pirate. "You'll do great," he shouted into Mei's ear. "Don't be late." He threw his own deployment bag out, and once Yoder gave the order, he was gone.

Preparations had been short and the plan wasn't without

its rough spots. In fact, it was mostly rough spots. For one, only four knights had rappelling experience. Yoder served as Rappel Master since he was the only one who'd done it from a helicopter before. The other hitch was Mei's part. Her first actual hunt and she was the lynchpin. Everything was riding on her.

"*Clear.*"

Malcolm crawled up and tossed his bag outside. Unlike the other hunters, he wasn't wearing a low-light scope at all. One of his many tattoos blessed him with supernaturally good night vision. Bandoleers of shotgun shells crossed his chest like a Hollywood bandito. He'd insisted on carrying the folding SPAS instead of a rifle.

"Go," Yoder said.

Mal gave a little grin and slid down after the others. "*Clear.*"

Felisa moved out next. The slung assault rifle looked huge on her.

"*Belay on,*" Luiza radioed from below, meaning that she had hold of Felisa's line in case she slipped.

The small paladin gave Mei a respectful nod and jumped.

"*Clear.*"

Despite his inexperience, Kofi moved through the steps like he'd done them his entire life. Graceful and confident, he swung out onto the bar hanging below the door.

"*Belay on,*" Matt radioed.

"God is with you," Kofi said and then he was gone.

Luc scooted up last, the huge machine gun strapped to him like it belonged there. He gave Mei a gloved fist bump and dropped his own bag out into the night.

"Go," Yoder said, and he did.

"*Clear,*" Luc's voice growled in the ear bud.

Yoder quickly unhooked the ropes and tossed them out so they wouldn't get hung up on the landing skid. "Lines away."

Epple immediately started up and to the right. The whole deployment had taken under a minute. Mei's own safety harness rattled from its ceiling anchor, giving her enough room to move around the small helicopter, but that was it. Lukrasus across her lap, she held on as they banked to the side, giving an impressive view of the trees below.

The ancient helicopter that had begun its life in the Peruvian Army before moving to a life of firefighting, had eventually been sold to Catholic Hospital which hadn't the funds to refurbish it. While significantly larger, the relic wasn't anywhere near as comfortable as the one they'd taken from the Chilean headquarters. Mei's seat was nothing more than a folding metal square with patched canvas stretched across it like a drum head. The back of her boots pressed into the nylon bag fixed beneath her. Its own safety harness stretched up to the ring above her.

Wind whipped across her exposed mouth and whooshed up under her helmet as she leaned as far out as she could to see ahead of them. She wore wide, curved goggles instead of the night scopes. They looked like something you might rent at a low-end snowboarding shop. Matt had explained that while handy for most things, night vision messed with your depth perception too much for sword play. And she needed as much depth perception as she could get for her big debut.

Passing a low rise, a golden-yellow glow emerged before them, emanating from a giant hole in the jungle canopy, like peeking into the caldera of a volcano. Nimbuses of firelight flickered from the smoke-filled clearing, forming a broken gridwork of roads and half-walls. Dark shapes scurried through the haze. At the heart of it all, fifty yards from each deforested side, a giant stepped pyramid stood towering above the jungle. Torches decorated the corners of each level. A trio of figures moved atop it. Two with bulbous heads like motorcycle helmets, the other appeared normal.

"It's him," Mei said.

No sooner had the words left her mouth than star-shaped muzzle flashes pulsed from behind the crumbled walls and along the tree line. The helicopter banked hard. Mei grabbed hold of her harness line before she might tumble out of her seat.

The helicopter rose and dipped, falling behind the cover of tree tops, but didn't circle around.

Yoder shouldered his rifle. The night scope's green glow casting along his neck and cheek emphasized the Swiss Guard's stubble.

The helicopter lifted up, just enough to see the ziggurat.

More shapes ran up the long stairs. De la Fuente stood at the middle before a stone block the size of a Buick, his feet apart. He held Redemptor up at his side, challenging. Yoder brought the rifle up and fired.

Nothing.

He worked the bolt and fired again, but De la Fuente was walking toward the pyramid's edge leisurely—unhurried, not the speed from which he'd fled Max's gun. The two big-heads were returning fire.

A plume, like mist, erupted from De la Fuente's back on the third shot, but he didn't react.

"Damn it," Mei growled. She hit her radio. "The gold slug did nothing."

"It went right through him," Yoder added. "He's fuzzy, as if he were smoke."

Three bullets punched through the side of the helicopter, each one a distinct pop. Epple sped, banking into a dive.

"*Just keep them busy,*" Luiza replied her voice breathy like she was running.

Hovering above the trees, Epple waited for Yoder to change to a Sig rifle loaded with thirty rounds of brass.

"Ready," Yoder said, shouldering it.

The helicopter climbed up. The shooters started again, their muzzles flashing. Epple continued higher, bringing the clearing into view for only a moment, before dipping back down. The helicopter moved side to side, rising and dropped below the clearing's field of view.

More big-heads were racing up the temple steps.

Epple stopped the helicopter, hovering it thirty feet above the trees. In the five seconds before he moved again, Yoder brought his rifle up and fired a burst. Bone and brains blasted out from one of the shooter's heads and it crumpled.

"*We're almost there,*" Luiza said. "*Five minutes.*"

Five minutes was a long time to get shot at, but this was the plan.

Epple circled a quarter of the way around the clearing, careful not to move so far that their attackers might turn around. The helicopter lifted straight up. The pyramid slid into view. One of the shooters stood atop the stone block on the top. Another hunkered behind it, gun flashing.

Yoder missed the standing one's head, hitting low. The creature tumbled back, arms flailing. He fired a burst at the other one, missing. A second burst and its head exploded. Two more reached the top, their giant heads rising into view. Yoder fired.

De la Fuente stood at the center of the bloodbath, unmoving like a defiant statue.

They circled back the other way and hopped up, drawing more fire. The clearing pulsed with muzzle flashes. Yoder returned fire, emptying his mag. Mei tucked her head, waiting for that one lucky shot to find her. If the helicopter was taken down, would she be able to unstrap and fly out the open door before it crashed?

Two more passes. Yoder killed another atop the ziggurat, but Mei couldn't tell if he'd gotten any more.

"*We're in position*," Luiza said. "*Watch your fire. Mei, you're up.*"

A fresh surge of adrenaline hit, electric and cold, not fear, but a strange calm. This was it. She unclasped and pulled the heavy bag out from under her seat. The copper end of Akumanokira's grip protruded from the end. The holy weapons were secured firmly inside, not rattling as she heaved it up onto her shoulders. She clicked the pack's waist and chest straps, cinching them tight.

De la Fuente knew the weapons were in the helicopter. That was the idea. To outsmart him, they'd have to outsmart Max. They had to do something the old knight or any of the knights De la Fuente had killed would never do: leave their holy weapons behind.

Mei removed the safety line connecting her to the helicopter, and drew Lukrasus. "Ready."

The helicopter launched straight up, high and fast. Shots erupted across the wide clearing. De la Fuente still stood atop the pyramid, ten of his big-heads around him, all firing. His arrogant pose softened. He cocked his head, seeming confused. Maybe he sensed that the weapons were bundled and not spread out across the helicopter on knights' belts. Maybe deep inside him, Max recognized one of Matt's crazy-ass plans when he saw it. De la Fuente turned toward the shadowy tree line behind them, the tree line that all their exposed backs faced.

Too late.

Automatic fire erupted from the jungle, cutting across the line of hunkered monsters. Red tracers streamed from Luc's big machine gun.

Shave and a haircut. Shave and a haircut.

Two explosions detonated within a cluster of enemies still wheeling around. Uwe's grenades shredded the unarmored minions. The double *Boom-Boom* sounded a moment later.

Yoder lay on his stomach, firing out the door at the demon-bound on the opposite side of the pyramid.

The knights moved into the clearing, a V-shaped wedge firing on all sides.

Another grenade exploded, sending up a cloud of dust and smoke.

"*Mei!*" Luiza shouted.

Stepping behind Yoder, Mei pulled open the door on the opposite side of the helicopter. Roaring air blasted through the craft, coming in from both sides. She squeezed Lukrasus' cord-wrapped handle and launched out into the night.

The rotor wind hurled her downward. Mei flipped in the air and changed gravity's pull to the side. De la Fuente screamed. Several of his minions turned their rifles toward her.

Mei shot upward and then down, bullets buzzing past her. A fourth grenade detonated below. Keeping her eyes on the knight's location, made easier by the streams of crimson comets spewing from Luc's gun, Mei banked hard toward it, her momentum dragging her far to the side.

Wind buffeted her clothes. The bag was an uncomfortable weight, but it was secure and changed gravity with her, making it infinitely easier than Gabi had been. The knights were close now, fifty yards at most. Zigzagging to avoid shots, she flew upward and crested down.

A bullet cracked against her helmet, knocking Mei's head to the side. Yelping more in shock than pain, she nearly lost her grip on Lukrasus. Even then, her broken concentration sent her hurtling toward the earth. Head ringing, she caught herself, bending gravity up and to the left. She gulped air, her heart pounding.

You're not dead. You're not dead.

The fear was back, cold and terrible, each second dragging for an eternity. Unseen bullets zipped past her but she couldn't stop. She couldn't hide in cover to collect herself. Mei had to make it to the knights. They were depending on her.

Twisting her body, she angled herself to the right as if about to head that way, but feinted, hurling herself down, falling sideways. She flipped again and shot straight to where Kofi and Malcolm were dodging between mounds of crumbled wall. Reversing gravity's pull, she slowed but not enough. Her boot heel collided with the stump of a freshly cut tree and she popped up with a jolt of pain. She switched gravity again, softening the blow and hit the ground fifteen feet from cover.

Bullets pelted around her, showered Mei with dirt, and chipped rock.

"Mei!" Kofi shouted, starting toward her, but a barrage of fire forced him back down.

She changed gravity again and fell along the jungle floor, sliding across tangled upturned roots and coming to a stop just beside Kofi.

He seized her by the pack and dragged Mei to safety. "Are you hurt?"

Panting, Mei blinked. Her aching skull throbbed with each pounding heartbeat and her stomach was still doing somersaults. "F ... Fine." She unbuckled the pack and he helped pull it off her.

Malcolm fired two blasts with his shotgun and knelt. "That was spectacular." He drew several red plastic shells from his bandoleer and loaded them into the shotgun.

Kofi opened the bag and raised his palm. Salvatio flew out and into his hand. He heaved the bag toward Malcolm.

Wetness trickled down the side of Mei's neck. She couldn't tell if it was sweat or blood. She ran a gloved finger across her helmet, feeling a hole. The icy terror returned. She'd been shot! She was bleeding!

Mei tore the helmet free and flipped it over in her hands. The black paint had shattered off in a rough circle the size of a Coke can lid, revealing the yellow beneath. The small dent at its heart was deep, stretching the woven Kevlar, but didn't go all the way through. Mei released her breath.

Malcolm was looking at her. He held Hounacier in his hand. "Shit. Little too close there. You sure you're good? You look shaken."

Mei swallowed. "Yeah."

"Take a moment. I'll get this to the others," he said, nodding to the bag.

"No." She pulled the helmet back on and snapped it secure. "This is my job." Mei grabbed the bag with one hand, clutched Lukrasus, and hurled herself down the line to where Luc was firing.

When Matt was thirteen, Clay had taken him out to an Alabama field with a dozen watermelons they'd picked up from a roadside vendor and taught him how to use the Ingram. That afternoon spent vaporizing them in sprays of juicy red was one of his more cherished memories.

"Now you got it!" Clay's voice echoed in his mind as Matt squeezed the Ingram's trigger, pulverizing one of the bigheaded goons with a spectacular gush of skull and brains. In the green night vision, their heads even looked like melons.

More of the creatures were charging around the side of the massive ziggurat. The imposing structure itself was a hundred yards wide, as big as a football field, and towering sixty high. Weird, irregular blocks formed the ancient structure. Some were no bigger than basketballs. Others were as large as tractor trucks. The end of its long stair ramp began only twenty yards ahead of them, past a nest of dead melon-heads. Their plan has worked, directing most of their enemies on the wrong side of the assault. Matt fired two more bursts, taking one of the creatures down. The gun clicked empty.

"Out!"

Only problem with the Ingram was how ridiculously fast it chewed through a thirty-round mag.

Ten feet ahead of him, Luiza opened fire with her rifle, flames licking from the muzzle. She dropped one more.

How many of these things were there? Fifty? Sixty? They'd killed half that, Uwe's home-grown grenades taking the lion's share. He'd be happy to hear that. Blood compasses were about useless. Too many beads to count and without them dissolving after death, it was impossible to tell which were still alive unless they moved.

Matt hunkered down behind a mound of rocks woven together with tree roots and jammed in his last Ingram magazine. This one was gold and meant for De la Fuente until he got Dämoren. Matt pulled his own slung rifle around and stole a glance to the other knights. Mei had flown across to a crude foxhole and was issuing Luc and Felisa their weapons.

"Target is heading your way," Yoder called over the radio.

Matt peeked up to see De la Fuente marching down the pyramid's steps, wearing nothing but a breechcloth. The cursed jewelry decorated his chest and arms. A golden-brown crown sat atop his head. Bullets pelted the stairs around him as Felisa and Luc opened fire. His body rippled as round after round tore through him to no effect. Trails of what looked like smoke streamed out his back with each hit and then drew back into him.

"Bullets aren't working," Malcolm said.

"Gold?"

"Double-ought didn't do jack."

Shit. There went that idea.

Kofi hurled his axe, it spun through the air toward him. The weapon curved and flew back before it could reach him. He must have been too high for its range, but De la Fuente stopped just the same.

He's afraid of holy weapons. Matt just needed Dämoren. There weren't any bystanders or witnesses to save the demon paladin this time.

"Luiza. Matt," Mei shouted, not even using her radio.

Matt hunkered back behind cover as Mei shot like a missile across the open span and landed feet-first against a gnarled stump between him and Luiza.

Luiza was the first to descend on the bag. She pulled Akumanokira out from the top. Flipping her night vision goggles up out of the way, she shouted, "Epple! Spotlight!" into the radio.

On cue, a brilliant light silhouetted the pyramid, rising like sunrise. The helicopter lifted above the far side, the searchlight beneath its cockpit illuminating the entire clearing. Matt's night vision washed out. He flipped the monocular up out of the way.

De la Fuente turned toward the helicopter. Light shone through his translucent body, casting a faint shadow down the steps toward Luiza.

Matt scrambled for Mei's bag. Dämoren rested inside, the last weapon. He drew her out. The spotlight gleamed from the tiny red stones along her gilded barrel and the edge of her ten-inch blade. Matt cocked the hammer and brought her up as De la Fuente streaked up the stairs with inhuman speed. The demon-man wove side to side as he ran, denying any shot and then he was gone, up and over they ziggurat's top.

Damn it.

The other knights were busy firing, not at De la Fuente, but at the melon-heads shooting at their helicopter.

"Come on," Luiza shouted. "He's getting away. Luc, Mal, you keep them off us."

Matt pulled the coiled police belt from the bag, Dämoren's twenty-three spare rounds filling the bullet loops. With no time to put it on, Matt threw it over his shoulder and charged after Luiza.

Shadows moved around them, lengthening and turning as the helicopter circled above, weaving to avoid the incoming fire.

Matt hopped a low berm near the base of the stairs. The mangled bodies of melon-heads hit with one of Uwe's grenades littered the recess. One of them, a shredded ruin missing one leg was feebly clawing at the side. Bones jutted from its tattered hand. A pellet of brass shrapnel had struck its temple. The large, irregular hole looked like it had been eaten by acid. Black froth sizzled along the edges. Its brain like a mass of bloody, gray worms writhed and wiggled, foam bubbling between them.

Curling his lips in disgust, Matt shot it once, point blank, splattering himself with goo. The creature stilled and Matt continued on. The steps up the pyramid's ramp were steep with little purchase. Dämoren in hand, Matt climbed up, his rifle and Ingram bouncing against him.

Luc's machine gun roared, cutting through a mob of creatures surging around one side of the pyramid. Their final grenade boomed on the opposite side, punctuated by Malcolm's twelve gauge. Kofi hurled his axe up at monsters coming down from the top. A pair of melon-heads came around the corner of the second tiers as Matt drew closer.

Shots buzzed around him. Matt spun to face them, nearly losing his footing on the narrow step. Dämoren boomed, taking one in the eye. Swinging the gun to the next one, he cocked the hammer as the creature fired its rifle.

Plastic exploded at Matt's chest as the first round shattered his slung rifle's stock. The second round hit his stomach and a third bullet struck his hip. Bone crunched, a horrible noise he felt in his teeth. Then Matt was falling, sliding and rolling down the unforgiving steps.

His elbow slammed into stone but he'd stopped rolling. Grunting in pain, Matt clawed with his free hand as he slid. A boot heel managed to catch the lip of a crooked step and he stopped. His right hand ached from smashing into the steps, but he hadn't dropped Dämoren.

"Matt," Luiza called.

Gasping, he craned his neck. He'd rolled about thirty-five feet, about the level of the first platform. Sharp pain flared with each breath. His left leg felt like burning jelly. Dämoren's spare ammo belt rested about ten feet above him. Matt rolled, trying to rise to his knee. Bone crunched and Matt slipped down two more steps, banging his knee.

Warm wetness seeped down the front of his shirt beneath his vest. It crept down below his waistband and into his underwear.

He checked his armor. The round had penetrated the vest on the left side just below his ribs. Blood dribbled from his pants leg, sprinkling the ground. He couldn't tell if it had broken his femur, his pelvis, or both.

"Baby?" Luiza said, hurrying down toward him. "Matt?"

Felisa and Kofi were still charging up. Mei was nowhere to be seen.

"Go," Matt wheezed, clutching his bleeding hip.

Luiza crouched above him, her chocolate eyes wide in terror. "Baby?"

"Go. No time," he said, forcing the words. "Kill the fucker."

"We'll get you out of here. Get you to a hospital."

"Then go." Matt lifted Dämoren and aimed at a melon-head charging Mal's position. "I'll cover you."

Dämoren boomed and the creature fell dead.

Felisa's thighs ached as she raced up the steps. Kofi was faster, but he'd slowed to match her pace. Side by side they ran up the ancient ruin to meet the Paladin-killer. She'd seen Matt fall, but there was no time to help him now. Their survival, their very souls, hinged on beating De la Fuente here and now.

They passed the third tier. Only one left to go. The smoke of torches, gunfire, and grenades blanketed the valley. A figure moved along the edge high above.

Felisa peered down her rifle's holographic sight as one of De la Fuente's minions came into view. She lined its grotesque head into the reticle and squeezed. Its face disintegrated in a wet spray and she continued up, Kofi at her side.

"Let me first," she said as they neared the top. De la Fuente would surely try something once their heads were in view, but he couldn't hit her. Nothing could hit her.

Kofi knew it, because he slowed. Once whatever surprise was unleashed, he'd charge in. Their system had never failed them.

Felisa crouched as she grew closer, ready to spring. She let go of the rifle. Its sling pulled taut and she drew Ofniel from his scabbard.

De la Fuente had fled Luiza's shadow katana. His men had singled Matt out, eliminating his holy gun. Bullets didn't hurt the demon man, but he feared the sacred weapons.

She surged up the final steps. Sharp tingles blossomed up her chest and she dove to the side as one of the minions opened fire with a sidearm.

The pyramid's top was a twenty-meter square high above the jungle. De la Fuente stood before a stone altar, Redemptor in hand. His smoky form solidified as his other hand raised toward her, ringed fingers splayed.

Ofniel's warnings screamed across Felisa's entire body and she sprang to the side. A blast of wind shot from De la Fuente's hand, sending dust into the air with enough power to have launched her off the pyramid's top.

More piercing tingles. She rolled as the minion continued firing. The shooting ceased as Kofi's axe split the creature's skull.

In the full second before Salvatio returned to Kofi's hand, De le Fuente charged. Felisa lunged in to meet him, her sword raised before her, his tip aimed at his open back.

Sensing the attack, De la Fuente spun. Redemptor moved in a blur, the sword so fast the warning tingles came all at once from every side. Unable to parry such speed, she leapt back, but De la Fuente advanced, madness blazing his wide eyes.

He drove her further back, toward the platform's edge. It took everything in her to dodge Ofniel's flood of warnings. Her choices grew thinner: lose her soul from the sword or fall a dozen meters to the platform below.

De la Fuente suddenly whirled around, striking Salvatio out of the air. Seizing the opening, Felisa lunged, but De la Fuente shot away with a blurring sidestep and Felisa stabbed only empty air.

"Almost there," Luiza huffed through the radio.

Hacking her sword, Felisa twisted around the face her enemy. De la Fuente moved around the far side of the altar, his form again translucent. Bullets from Yoder's rifle pelted through him, leaving wispy streamers in their wakes.

The shooting ceased as Felisa and Kofi closed in.

Lifting Redemptor, De la Fuente solidified and stepped toward Kofi. A sudden shock pierced Felisa's eye straight through to the back of her skull. She dropped to a kneel and thrust up and out as De la Fuente completed his feint and stabbed above her head. Ofniel nicked the demon-man's side, only a scratch, but first blood nonetheless.

Snarling, De la Fuente sprang away, drops of crimson

arcing the air. Kofi moved in, hacking his axe in a succession of downward blows, each ringing against Redemptor's blade. De la Fuente leaped to the left, raising Redemptor as Mei landed beside him, their swords ringing. Screaming in fury, Mei hacked and thrust, forcing the demon man back with the barrage of blows from both her and Kofi.

Felisa lunged, trying to flank De la Fuente while he was on the defensive.

Sensing the closing weapons, De la Fuente leaped upward, curling his legs five meters above their reach as he flew up and behind them, landing atop the altar. His hand shot out and air whooshed from his open palm.

Kofi let out a surprised grunt and flew backward, his heels coming out from under him and Salvatio sailing out into the night. His body slid across the uneven stones and stopped only centimeters from the edge. Mei launched toward him, sword raised. A second blast of air sent the flying girl hurtling end over end into the night.

De la Fuente charged toward Kofi.

"No!" Felisa dove between the demon man and her stunned partner.

Redemptor's blows struck with more strength and speed than she could possibly handle. But De la Fuente wasn't interested in her, he wanted Kofi. The polished metals of his cursed jewelry gleamed in the glare of the helicopter's light as if this were some grand, stone stage for this performance.

Groaning, the paladin rose to hands and knees.

"Go!" Felisa barked as De la Fuente drove her back.

Kofi scrambled, but De la Fuente followed, Felisa all that stood between them. An electric tingle lanced through Felisa's chest and De la Fuente lunged. If she moved, Redemptor would surely skewer Kofi behind her.

No. Refusing to move, Felisa swung Ofniel. She struck the spearing blade, parrying it off its deadly course, but not enough.

Redemptor plunged through her vest, the Kevlar parting and an icy cold blossomed in Felisa's breast.

Gasping, Felisa looked down at the blade buried into her. Through the corner of her vision, she saw Kofi's escape. She'd saved him. Perhaps he could call Salvatio while she had De la Fuente's attention. Desperately, she struggled to lift Ofniel, plunge it into him, but her fingers held no strength.

Her knees buckled and her weight came down hard on the impaling blade. Numbness swept up from her fingers and toes, up her body and toward Redemptor. Darkness swam at the edge of her vision. She felt herself being sucked away, oblivion imminent.

Someone shouted in her ear bud, but she couldn't tell who or what they were saying.

The side of De la Fuente's head exploded. Blood and meaty chunks splattered Felisa's face and neck.

The bronze crown spun into the air, catching the light and revealing the bullet hole that had entered from the top left. Yoder's shot had taken half of De le Fuente's face with it. One eye was gone, the other bulged stupidly out from its socket.

De la Fuente staggered back, seeming stunned but still not dead. Felisa screamed as Redemptor tore free of her, pulling her over with the force. The sensation of numbing emptiness fled, replaced by terrible pain.

A second shot blasted through De la Fuente's chest and out his back. He pitched backward and fell over the pyramid's side fifteen meters and then a loud thump.

The cherry red blood staining the stone and Felisa's face evaporated into copper-scented mist.

"They're making a break for it," Malcolm said over the radio.

Rolling onto her side, Felisa looked down over the edge to see the last of De la Fuente's minions fleeing into the jungle, Malcolm and Luc's shots chasing them. The crown's destruction had shattered their loyalty. Her gaze lowered to the platform below and a terrible weight fell inside her stomach.

De la Fuente staggered to his feet, crimson mist swirled around his open skull, solidifying into bone and hair.

She coughed the words. "He's not dead."

Wind ruffled in Mei's ears as she flew, a cruise missile headed straight for Max's killer. Her hatred raged. Matt and Felisa might be dying and this motherfucker was still going.

Redemptor lay ten feet from him. Stumbling, he scrambled toward it, but wheeled around as she drew closer. His open hand stretched toward her, readying to strike her with another punch of air, like the fist of God.

Mei bent her gravity, but was coming in too fast to escape it. Gritting her teeth, she braced for the punch.

An axe sailed down from above and buried into De la Fuente's shoulder.

With no time to correct her new course to hit him, Mei bent her gravity toward a new target and sped faster, Lukrasus raised.

De la Fuente cried out as he realized her intent, but it was too late.

She swung Lukrasus down and batted Redemptor with the flat of her blade, just like Max's rubber ball. Metal clanged and the demon sword sailed off and away from the pyramid, twirling as it fell.

"No!" De la Fuente screamed. He charged toward the edge, but Salvatio wrenched from his shoulder and flew back toward Kofi's open hand. Jolted off balance, De la Fuente sprawled onto the stone, still screaming Redemptor's name.

Mei looped around, momentum carrying her far across the jungle clearing. Bodies littered the ground below her. Luc was charging for the fallen sword, his empty machine gun forgotten.

Blood pumping from the wound in his back, De la Fuente crawled toward the edge, leaving a glistening red smear. He peered over the lip and shrieked, his eyes wide with terror as Luc drew Velnepo from his belt, readying to smash the demon blade.

Speeding through the air, Mei braced Lukrasus tight. De la Fuente's head lifted and turned toward her.

His shriek cut off as the blade cleaved through De la Fuente's open mouth, separating his head from his body.

Mei curved gravity to the side and flipped it around, coming to a stop against the pyramid's wall.

A loud whoop of cheers sounded in her radio as Luc crushed Redemptor with his mace. But Mei didn't see it. She didn't care to. Her eyes instead focused on the blood smearing Lukrasus' polished blade.

Hernando de la Fuente was dead.

Atik showed me the lines stretching through the sky and earth. Lines of power, the intersecting points are where man and God are the closest. Holy temples are erected at those junctions. But I now realize that those are not rivers, but seams in the very fabric separating our world from another. And like all seams, they are the easiest point to tear.

CHAPTER 33

Atacama Region, Chile

From its prominent throne atop the kitchen counter, the espresso maker hissed and belched scented steam. Matt opened the cabinet and found his Easter Island mug staring at him from behind Luc's blue one, its eyes peeking around the edge like a nosey neighbor. The mug was more than just a fun memento. Shortly after their arrival in South America, he'd taken Luiza there. Not a hunt, but an actual vacation. He'd spent his whole life traveling, but had never taken one. There was no one to take one with until Luiza.

Reaching up, he removed it, but paused as he discovered the towering white mug behind it. It was as big at Matt's, but plain. Its rounded bottom gave it the appearance of an elongated eggshell with the top sawn off. Schmidt's cup.

They'd cleaned up most of the old man's effects, giving most of it to Mei and Master Turgen. A painting had been commissioned from some of his old photographs, and plans were in motion to dedicate a turbine to him, his cremation urn to be buried at its base. No one had even considered Schmidt's signature cup.

It'd be wrong to throw it away or box it up. So now it would sit like a sentinel in the cabinet, used only when dishes were too dirty or on the rare occasion of guests. There were many unused cups at the Valducans' other bases, and now the Chilean home had its first silent memorial of one who had passed. Neither paintings nor monuments could carry the impact of an unused cup, a reminder that the honored dead were no different than anyone else. Clay's had been a dented, aluminum double-wall, perfect for their car's cup holder. Matt had no idea when he'd lost it and the guilt needled down his throat.

The espresso machine beeped, breaking the line of thought.

Giant cup in one hand, cane in the other, Matt shuffled to the machine and poured a steaming cup. Armed with his morning dose of caffeine, he made his way down the hall. Stairs were still a problem for his hip, so he'd commandeered the second-floor conference room as his current office.

Mewing, Celeste padded toward him and tried to rub against his legs. The cat had never given one shit about him, but now with the very real possibility of tripping him, she loved nothing more than weaving around his cane.

"Shoo," he scolded, waggling a foot at it. "Fuck off."

The cat sat on her haunches, green eyes staring innocently up. She mewed again, but didn't follow as Matt shuffled on. He'd expected the abdominal shot to have been the worst. The bullet had torn him up pretty badly before embedding in his liver. Recovery was slow but nothing compared to the torn tendons and cracked ilium. Had it been any other knight, the injury might have retired them. But not Matt.

The last few weeks had been a desperate search for any signs of a demon he could shoot and use to heal up. Just one drop of demon blood and he'd be good as new. Preferably he'd find something that lived on a first floor.

A baby gate stretched across the office door. A Technicolor minefield of bright Legos littered the carpet beyond.

"Daddy." Gabi looked up from a chaotic construction merging a mermaid's castle and the Ewok tree village.

"Whatcha got there?" he asked, trying not to spill his coffee while wrestling the gate.

She shrugged. "Play with me."

"I will in a bit, sweetie. Let daddy have his coffee first, okay?" Maneuvering past the spilled toys, Matt eased himself down into his chair with a grunt.

Through the window, a crane was lowering the new gearbox and brake assembly into Turbine 6. Fixing the plane had been far outside Alfonso's know-how, but he and the rest of Matt's adopted family had plenty more to do. The foundation had already been poured for the second gun turret that Schmidt had wanted, and Luc was working out the details for installing pop-up bollards on the road leading to the compound.

Matt checked the time at the corner of the laptop monitor. Three minutes until Allan's video call. Good.

Sipping his coffee, Matt finished reading the latest article concerning the tragedy and discovery of the lost, megalithic pyramid. Current estimates believed it to be pre-Incan, with cyclopean polygonal masonry similar, yet vastly different than anything found at Saksaywaman or Tiwanaku. Many archeologists had already declared it the Discovery of the Century, eclipsing even the finding of Heracleion in Egypt.

Investigators believed that the site was first discovered by a team of illegal treasure hunters, ranging from as far south as Argentina. Local police became aware of the unlawful dig, and the resulting confrontation claimed the lives of forty-three people. It was unknown how many may have escaped, but three officers were still missing. Holes in the narrative, such as none of the known perpetrators having any experience in archeology, had led to a few colorful Internet conspiracies, one being that the police had kidnapped and forced them to work the site. A prisoner revolt had caused the deaths. Neither story held much water, but people subscribed to the theory that suited them best.

Matt wondered if certain details, such as brass bullets, would ever be reported. So far no one had mentioned any sightings of giant-headed freaks terrorizing the area.

After they'd helicoptered him and Felisa to a hospital, Luc, Malcolm, and Mei had stuck around, using blood compasses to collect the brass demon chokers from the dead. They'd also recovered the stolen holy weapons, including the Incan mace taken from the Colombian museum. Matt and Luc had wondered what would happen to their little truce with the Paladins with De la Fuente gone and the newly discovered holy weapons up for grabs. But Luiza surprised them all when she freely offered the mace to the Exorcists as a sign of good will. The Masters hadn't cleared that decision, but it was too late to back out. Besides, they were the ones about to receive the rewards for Luiza's generosity.

A green pop-up appeared in the corner of Matt's screen with a loud *bloop*. A round, three-year-old picture of Allan smiled from the pop-up's middle, revealing the caller's identity.

Right on time. Matt clicked "Accept," and Allan's face filled the screen, hair a little shorter than the icon's, but still smiling that toothy grin. "Hey, man."

"Hi, Matt. How are you this fine morning?" Allan's normally casual clothes had been traded in for a dark suit with an emerald-green tie done with a Windsor knot. The wall behind him appeared to be standard hotel bland, the color of vanilla ice cream.

"Hangin' in there. Luiza's spending time with her mom, so Gabi and I are holding the fort."

"How's the leg?"

"Eh." Mat shrugged. "Sucks."

"Well, serves you right for getting shot again."

"I get enough of this from Luiza and Uwe." Mat sipped his coffee.

"I'm sure you do. We got a pool going on how long it'll be before you let it happen again. I say you've learned your lesson. Uwe gives it your second mission before you take another."

"What about Luiza?" Matt asked, refusing to believe that if there were such a pool she'd join it.

Allan grinned. "She says you'll go three hunts before you forget and try something stupid."

Shit. That actually did sound like something she'd say. "Well," Matt said, with a sarcastically big smile, "I'm glad to know I'm loved."

"Just remember, I'm the one sayin' your days of getting shot are over."

"Noted. So how about you? How's Rome? You ready for your big meeting with the Pope?"

"Fine. We'll be heading up in about an hour. We met with the Paladins last night. They had some good things to say about you."

"Felisa's doing okay?"

"She seemed well enough. There was this Father Soldati with them. He did most of the talking. Sort of a middle-manager, I gather. Sonu and I weren't all that impressed, but Turgen charmed him."

"That's his gift."

"That it is. Regardless, the Vatican is very enthusiastic in working with us, so we'll see how that plays out. Turgen intends to propose a joint effort to salvage the Flor de Oro, the ship the real Redemptor was lost on."

"You looking for sunken treasure?"

"In a way. There wasn't any gold on it, so no one's really bothered to look. But if we can recover Redemptor ..."

"She's probably rusted to nothing," Matt said.

"Not the gold. And if she is too far gone, the Vatican can display her remains. Nothing else, it'll help heal any bad blood between us. If Redemptor really is gone, then maybe they can reforge her for real."

"Are you kidding? That's what started this whole mess to begin with."

"No. Redemptor was still alive when De la Fuente tried it. She was sitting at the bottom of the ocean. The problem was De la Fuente didn't know what he was doing and tried to use a demon mask. But if Redemptor is truly gone now, the Vatican can properly reconstruct her. They have records of how she was first made."

Matt saw his frown in the lower corner of the screen. "I'm not real sure how I feel about that, man."

"Why? You're the one who said that each holy weapon was a unique spirit and that's why no one could repeat the method for creating them. But if the weapon is gone, and the spirit free, we can just follow the recipe."

"Yeah, but that's not what I was suggesting."

"Uh huh. And how many times has Dämoren been remade?"

"That's … different."

Allan cocked an eyebrow. "Look, mate, we have records on how several holy weapons were forged. Any that we can confirm are gone, we should try to bring them back. Obligated. We can use Redemptor as the trial run. If it works …" He opened his hands, a gesture somewhere between a surrender and a ta-da, "… we can do a lot of good."

"I don't know, Allan. It just seems … I don't know."

"Bit surprised to hear that from you."

"Maybe before Redemptor I might have agreed."

"The other Masters are in support of it. Bringing back lost weapons is a big deal."

Matt nodded. "No. I agree. I just think it might be a little harder or more dangerous than you expect."

"That's why we want to let the Catholics try it first." Allan winked.

"Hopefully it'll go better than last time."

Allan chuckled. "Hence, why we need to confirm Redemptor's condition. Let Mal give it a look and make sure. After that," his lips curled into that hesitant smile Matt knew so well, "we'll talk to Luiza."

Matt blinked. "What about Luiza?"

"Well, Redemptor, the original one, sorta had a brother. Little younger, but also a Tuscan blade. Same family made it. Nephew, I believe."

"No," Matt said, his voice strong enough to make Gabi cringe from her playing and turn toward him.

"If we can reforge Redemptor, then we can reforge Feinluna."

"No," Matt repeated. He straightened in his chair, the movement eliciting a wince of pain. "I can't believe you're even suggesting it."

"Think of Luiza."

"I am. Allan, losing Feinluna tore her apart. She's moved on. She has Akumanokira now. Can you imagine what it would do to her if Feinluna came back? It's not like those feelings just go away. It'd …" He shook his head. "No."

"Maybe we should ask her."

"I don't want to put her through that decision. It's like her dead husband coming back to life after she's remarried. It's cruel."

"What do you think she'd say if we asked her?"

"Yes, of course. Who wouldn't? But if it works, and she has to see Feinluna in the hands of another, it'd tear her apart."

"I know the feeling, but I'd rather see Ibenus in Victoria's hands than be dead."

"It's not the same. Please, man, we have other weapons that could be rebuilt. Just think about that."

Allan sighed. "Well, we'll have to discuss it later. We're still a long ways away and there's much to do first."

Matt swallowed, his temper cooling. "All right. Look, man, you have fun meeting the Pope. I expect pictures."

"I hope to." Allan grinned, any sign of their disagreement vanishing. "Felisa alluded that we'll be receiving an official redaction on our excommunication. Nice, but I'm hoping we can get a peek into their archives."

"Knowledge before damnation, huh?"

"Damn right."

"Good luck, Allan."

"Thanks. You take care."

Matt clicked the icon ending the call. He shook his head, amazed at how quickly everything had changed. The Order was about to make a powerful ally from a former enemy. He wondered just how much it would change things and prayed it would be for the better.

"So," he said closing the laptop and swiveling his chair toward Gabi. "What do we want to build today?"

ABOUT THE AUTHOR

Raised in the swamps and pine forests of East Texas, Seth Skorkowsky gravitated to the darker sides of fantasy, preferring horror and pulp heroes over knights in shining armor.

His debut novel, *Dämoren*, was published in 2014 as book #1 in the Valducan series; it was followed by *Hounacier* in 2015, and Ibenus in 2016. Seth has also released two sword-and-sorcery rogue collections with his Tales of the Black Raven series.

When not writing, Seth enjoys cheesy movies, tabletop role-playing games, and traveling the world with his wife.

Visit Seth's website: http://skorkowsky.com/

Curious about other Crossroad Press books?
Stop by our site:
http://store.crossroadpress.com
We offer quality writing
in digital, audio, and print formats.

Enter the code FIRSTBOOK
to get 20% off your first order from our store!
Stop by today!